FRIENDS IN HIGH PLACES

A NOVEL BY

PHILLIP DUNN

PUBLISHED BY FIDELI PUBLISHING, INC.

PRINTED IN THE UNITED STATES OF AMERICA

This book is dedicated to the warfighter...
and those of us fighting our own personal battles
every day.

PROLOGUE

The sleek haired mass of muscle, bone and try that made up the big sorrel gelding exploded past the timing line like a shot from a black powder cannon. The little girl along for the ride had her rein hand out over his neck giving him full permission to do what he was born and bred to do — run that cloverleaf pattern of the barrel race. She was kicking and whooping, mainly to make herself feel like she was a part of the race, but in her heart she knew she was a passenger and the horse could win this race without her.

It was over in seconds. She eased her horse to a stop in the alleyway of the arena and waited to hear her time. Her horse, Chasing Midnight, was still amped up from the run but let out a big blow of air and calmed down. He was a professional, for him it was just another job finished.

The rodeo announcer yelled into the brassy sounding microphone, *"Folks let's have a big round of applause for Phoebe 'The Flash' Hansen. That was the fastest time this arena has ever seen and it just won her a ticket to the Intercollegiate Finals in Casper Wyoming! It looks like this girl is unstoppable!"*

Phoebe rode Chasing Midnight around the grounds for a while to cool him down before she loaded him into the trailer. They had another rodeo to get to tomorrow afternoon. She knew there would be no congratulations from the other competitors. It was lonely at the top, and that was her stomping ground.

The team of girl and horse consistently won every rodeo they entered and the other barrel racers hated them for it. Phoebe had no friends on the college rodeo circuit other than the steady stream of cowboys wanting to be the boyfriend of the champion with the pretty face and long blonde hair — reverse buckle bunnies.

She had no use for those that had only one use for her. She was all business when it came to barrel racing. Her peer group saw her as stuck-up but she was just focused on success. This was the way her daddy raised her: to win at all costs. Just win.

Her father, Willis Hansen, had a failed rodeo career back in college. Failed mainly due to his slight stature and inability to stay on any animal in the rodeo. If an easy chair was covered with hair and had a head for the foot rest, he'd fall off it.

He was like many parents of good athletes — living vicariously through his child. His victory in life was his livelihood, which was the law. He'd built a career as a high priced lawyer who made it big by going after the deep pocketbooks of big corporations. His nickname was "The Falcon" because he was small and vicious.

Money was no problem for the Hansen family, other than the covert problems that too much money brought with it. Willis Hansen's job was to make the money and his wife Victoria Hansen's job was showing the world they had money.

In her younger days, Victoria was to be crowned Miss Texas, a lofty title back then. The award was pulled away from her due to her connection to a competitor's wardrobe sabotage. According to her, it was a conspiracy against her. She claimed she couldn't draw a penis on a piece of paper, much less one on the front of the evening gown of her competitor.

Unbeknownst to Phoebe, the Hansen family had a chip on its shoulder. Mom and Dad kept the blinders on her and the only thing in their field of view was a gold buckle. All Phoebe knew was she had to win. When she didn't place well in any event, all hell would break loose at home. She had to win at all costs, just for self-preservation.

On that night, the pressure to win weighed as heavy as a bag of horse feed on Phoebe's shoulders as she sat on Chasing Midnight, waiting to make the final run of her college rodeo career. In her preprogrammed mind. Her life hinged on the outcome of this barrel race pattern.

Victoria stood beside her, looking like she'd stepped off a page in a western wear catalog. "You have to win this run Phoebe, we have a big celebration party planned for later and all my friends will be there," she told her daughter. "We have to win."

It was the last night of the Intercollegiate Finals, and Phoebe was glad. She was wired tight and strung out from the endless highway miles and pressure it took to get here. Her father already had plans for her professional career. He was having a new trailer built and a new truck outfitted by 2L Custom Trucks in Poolville, Texas. He also had sponsors lined up like chickens around a pile of hen scratch — everybody wanted a bite of her success.

She was up next, and as the pair of champions moved into the alleyway, Chasing Midnight knew it was game on. He was tensed and ready. Phoebe gave him the cue and hung on as he released the coiled spring that was his body and exploded into the arena.

As fast as her horse was running, her mind was spinning faster. Spinning like a Wichita Falls windmill during tornado season, then a blade came off. Something in her mind snapped and she had a fleeting moment of clarity regarding her life thus far.

It was a flawless run, just like all the other times. Three turns and take it on home. Except this time, she didn't rein in her horse in the alleyway. She never even slowed down. Behind her, she could hear the crowd roar as the announcer said, *"Phoebe 'The Flash' did it again!"*

Phoebe kept riding past all the trucks and trailers on the rodeo grounds, and on past the entrance gate. She just kept going.

Later, Chasing Midnight was located at a stable on the edge of town. Phoebe Hansen had not been heard from since.

BURDEN OF RESPONSIBILITY

"Why don't you come with me?" Mack asked as he rolled out of bed and switched on the light in the bedroom of his old ranch house on The Dead Dog Ranch.

The sudden illumination had all the subtle nuances of a flash bang grenade in a séance. His girlfriend Samantha grabbed at the covers, pulling the Indian blanket over her head to shield her eyes from the insulting glare. Her bare feet were exposed at the foot of the bed and he seized the opportunity to jump back on the bed, grab her sensitive feet and begin tickling.

Mack had been with Sam a long time but evidently not long enough to know she hated having her feet tickled. After the years they'd been together, he should've known this currently important fact. She screamed like a drive belt on a bound-up threshing machine. If they were in town, the police would've been called at that point.

He was saying, "Come with me, come on." Her right foot got loose from the grip of tickling torture and planted itself on the left side of Mack's head. The kick had enough force to light up his brain with a spark of light as bright as a bolt of lightning in a west Texas thunderstorm and send him flipping to the floor.

When she caught her breath, she looked up for him at the foot of the bed then crawled over to the edge to see him sprawled on the floor looking at the ceiling. There was a look of wide-eyed shock on his face. With a female mix of anger and concern in her voice she asked, "You okay?"

"Uh-huh." His gaze shifted to her as he asked, "Why did you have to do that?"

"Don't ever, *ever* tickle my feet. Ever. I didn't mean to kick you. It just happened. I'm sorry, but don't *ever* do that again. Okay?"

He sat up, leaning against the wall and rubbing his head. "You got it. I'm probably not even going to look at your feet when I tell a joke." Mack shook the stars out of his vision and asked again, a little less emphatically, "So, why don't you come with me?"

"Do the math, Mack. Twelve hours in a pickup truck looking at country I've seen a thousand times or riding in a private Gulf Stream jet to New Mexico. How many times will I ever get a chance to ride in a private jet?"

Still rubbing the rising knot on his head, he said, "Yeah, I see what you mean. I just figured if you'd ride out there with me, we could spend some time together. Last night was the first time in a month and a half that we've even gone out together. We're getting too busy." What he wanted to say was you're getting too busy.

In a calmer voice she invited, "Turn out that damn light and get back up here." She threw the covers back so he could get into bed next to her. Mack stood on uncertain legs and took his time hitting the light switch. She was picture perfect, lying on his bed with her shiny black hair splayed out over broad shoulders and ample breasts. Her smooth olive skin, a gift from her Native American heritage, covered her athletic muscled body. She continued, "I'm sorry, babe, but things are just blowing up at the ranch. To be invited to this training clinic in New Mexico is a big deal. I'll be presenting with all of the big name trainers whose books I read growing up. To be included in that is a miracle, but to be flown out there on a private jet is a dream. I just can't pass that up."

"Yeah, I agree. I guess you have to do it. Heck, I sure would. How long are you going to be out there?"

"I'm supposed to do my class the first two days, after that I'll just be hanging out talking to folks. Jay Clayson has the jet and he wants to stay all week. He's my ride, so I guess I'll come back with him. Hanging out there with all the greats will be a blast. I doubt it'll get boring. I'll be on a ranch in Springer, just a couple of hours south of Cimarron. Why don't you come by? It sure wouldn't hurt your business to meet some of these horsemen. How about you come by before you drop off those saddles and they can see what you do."

Brightening at the prospect of breaking up his trip by spending some needed time with Sam, he said, "Yeah, that's a great idea. I'd like to see you work your magic on those horses and you're right, sure won't hurt to get my foot in the door with those boys. I'll tell my customer in Cimarron I might be a day later."

Samantha snuggled in closer under the covers. She wanted to send a silent message that she missed their time together, too. She played with the hair on his chest, stoked his flat belly and kissed the knot on his head. "Good, we can have some time away from here. This place used to be so easy and sort of peaceful but now it's gotten busier than a catfight. I'm still trying to figure out how to run this show. There's just not enough time in the day. But anyway I'll be through with what I have to do up there so we can fit in some time together. Do you think you and the saddles will be ready to go by Monday?"

"They will be if that's the schedule, even if I have to burn the midnight oil. I'll work hard at it if there's a chance to kick it out of gear for a while. Is that when you're supposed to leave, on Monday?"

"Clayson said to meet him at Meacham Airport at seven o'clock on Monday morning. If you have your stuff ready to go, could you just run me by there? That way I won't have to leave my truck there."

"Yeah, I can do that." Mack paused then asked, "Who *is* this Clayson guy? I'd like to meet him." A mustard seed of suspicion took root. "I don't think I've heard of him. Seems like a guy with a jet would be loud, proud and well known."

"You probably don't know him because he doesn't ride your saddles. He's actually pretty quiet. He inherited his family's oil company so he has some money to get in the cutting horse game with. He's about my age and he sure works hard at anything he does. He placed pretty well in the non-pro last year at the futurity. I know you've seen him around. I've been working on a few horses for him. He was going to this clinic up in Springer and when he found out I was giving a class he offered to fly me up there on his jet. I think there are a few of us going."

Not being one to hold primal suspicions in check Mack asked, "Is he married?"

"Yeah, but I've never seen his wife and he doesn't say much about her. He has two cute little daughters that come with him sometimes. I've been getting them started learning to ride." Sam laughed and said, "They said, 'Mama thinks horses are stinky and scary.' I guess she must be pretty much a city girl. The girls love the horses though."

"Hmm," said Mack as he kissed Sam like he meant it. She kissed him back but with a preoccupied effort. *That's the way it's been lately. No need to address that right here,* he thought. He slid out of bed and went to turn on the light but went on past the switch, leaving the dawn to light the room and hopefully his mood. Something about this morning was bugging him. In an upbeat way he asked, "How about some breakfast?" as he went into the kitchen to start the coffee.

Sam stretched under the covers and moaned, "That would be great. I haven't had your good cowboy cooking in too long."

The frying bacon and the perking coffee called its aromatic siren song and Sam strolled into the kitchen, fully dressed. Mack gave her a disappointed glance as he poured her a cup of coffee. She usually waltzed around his house naked under the Indian blanket on mornings at the ranch. He chose not to comment on the change. He cooked her eggs just the way he knew she liked them and fixed her a plate. She'd already taken her mug of start the day and made her way out to the porch. Still only wearing his boxers, as a social statement, he carried the plates out so they could eat where they always seemed to end up for meals or drinks.

The two hungry conflicted lovers made quick work of the bacon and eggs. Finishing their coffee and mutely planning their day, Mack broke the silence by asking, "So, what time should I pick you up for the rodeo tonight?"

"I've been thinking about that," she said with some apprehension. "I still have a lot to do. I have to work up a feed order, do a new training schedule and finish sending out some invoices. Would it be too much of a problem if I backed out?" She had a look of question but not firm conviction on her face.

Mack let out an audible sigh and looked at the floor. He thought a minute as she looked at him, knowing she'd asked the wrong thing. He looked up directly into her eyes saying, "Yeah, Sam, it would be a problem. You told me three weeks ago we'd go to this rodeo. I've been planning on it. I ain't gonna make you go, because if you don't want to be there then it won't be any fun at all. If you don't want to go, then I'm going anyway. I'll just hang out behind the chutes with my friends. But you told me you'd go, and lord knows you need a break. You've been burning the candle at both ends for too long now. I keep telling you to get an assistant to help you, but we won't go into that again. I'll just leave it up to you. I'm going out there at seven o'clock. Do you want me to come pick you up?" Then he added, "Like we planned."

She knew she didn't have an argument and he was speaking the truth. Responsibilities had piled into a heap higher than she could shovel and she knew in her heart she needed to back off. Delegating tasks wasn't an easy thing for her; she had been doing it all for her whole professional life. There was a fight brewing she could tell — not a loud one but a silent one, and those were the worst sort. She acquiesced, "Yeah, you're right. I'll get that crap done today. The rodeo will be fun, and I've been pretty short on fun lately. Pick me up at the barn."

Mack stood and took the breakfast plates. "Good. I'll get dressed and get you back to town so we can start this day."

Samantha stood to face him and tried to reach across the emotional chasm that was beginning to form between them. She gave him a firm hug as she buried her face in his shoulder. He embraced her as much as he could with both hands full of plates. "Thank you," she said. "It will be fun."

2

THE FLYING GOAT

Unabomber stood restlessly waiting to do his job. He was a professional and this was not his first rodeo, as they say. The young cowboys cautiously circled the rosined bull rope around the big mass of muscle and brown hair. On either side of the big bull's head was about ten inches of horn that had been cut off flat on the ends. In between the horns was a small brain that was programed for three things: eat, breed, and buck.

As the cowboys went about their business, too slowly for Unabomber's liking, his bovine brain was coming up with a game plan involving spinning right, spinning left, going straight high and hard, or any mixture of the three.

Most rodeo bulls had a repetitious bucking style, and cowboys could read what the bull did and count on it. Not Unabomber, he never did the same thing twice, except put his rider in the dirt quickly. He was a winning draw if the cowboy could last the eight hard-hitting, head-snapping, arm-wrenching seconds. Tonight the pairing was a winning bull and a cowboy with moderate skills.

The young cowboy, Parker Wilson, from Lamesa, Texas stood over the bull. He'd been riding bulls long enough to know he had to get rigged up, drop down on the bull, set his spurs and quickly call for the gate to open just to begin the ride. Unabomber was not one to allow any time to dilly-dally in the chute. He wanted to get to work.

When Parker saw his name paired up with Unabomber on the list, he felt a hollow spot in his belly — the kind you get when the board you are standing on loudly cracks but hasn't broken all the way yet. True to bull rider form, he bragged to the other riders looking at the list that he had this show won with this bull. He went on to say with just a hint of trepidation, "I got it boys. I can ride anything with hair on it."

Straddling but not sitting on the bull, he put his hand in the bull rope and his friend pulled it tight. He pulled the loose skin on the bull's back in front of the rope and pulled it tighter. He had the depressing realization that he was flat out scared. His dad had told him once that courage is not the absence of fear but the willingness to face it. So now, tied to the mass of hateful muscle, he faced it. He dropped his butt down on the bull and dug his spurs in the sides of the bull. He put his free hand up in the air and yelled, "Let 'er buck!"

The gate swung open, and the bull suddenly turned and got down to business. He erupted into the arena with two straight out high and hard bucks. Parker's instincts went primal as he pulled on the rope to keep up. He kept his eyes on the bull's head, right between the horns, to maybe see which way he was going to go.

On the third explosive launch from the ground, while still in the air, the bull swung his back end around to the left and his front to the right. This move registered in the cowboy's mind and he instinctively moved his body to meet the spin. Unabomber hit the ground in a wide spin to the right. Parker was in the rhythm. The spin got tighter and tighter, but the cowboy held on tighter too.

Parker barely heard the eight-second buzzer and the roar of the crowd. He relaxed just a little. Just a little too much. It wasn't over. Unabomber heard the buzzer too, and for his grand finale he threw in a little dance move — right, left, right, left. The move forced the cowboy's upper body to his left and over his riding hand, locking his hand in the bull rope.

He lost his grip with his spurs and came off the bull on the inside of the spin. Unabomber was not through yet. He was still bucking and trying to hook a horn in the annoyance hanging on his side.

Gautier "Goat" Thibadaux, rodeo clown extraordinaire, was right there for the whole ride. He'd been running circles around the storm to get the bull to buck even better. Goat now saw he had a job to do — he needed to get this flopping rag doll of a cowboy loose from the bull. He launched himself toward the flapping loose tail of the bull rope. If he could get ahold of it, maybe he could pull it hard enough to break the lock grip of the cowboy's hand in the rope.

The rodeo announcer hollered into the PA system, "Go get him, Goat! That boy is in a storm!" Women were screaming and men were grimacing.

Just when Goat flew into the fray and got a good grip on the tail of the bull rope, Unabomber made a cut back to the right. The bull got a stubbed horn between the overall clad legs of the bullfighter and launched him into the air. The good grip on the rope and the new angle of pull provided by the bull released Parker's hand. He hit the ground in a roll and got up running like his ass was on fire and his hair was catching. Goat was airborne head over heels and flying out of control toward the arena fence.

When Goat's head hit the two-inch pipe top rail of the fence, it resonated like a cantaloupe getting hit with a T-ball bat. It was lights out for the bullfighter — he won the battle but lost the war. His unconscious body fell into the laps of the couple sitting in the Silver Star Cowboy Complex box seats.

The surprised woman had his head in her lap. The impact of the bullfighter projectile jerked open the pearl snaps on her shirt, revealing a low cut lacy bra cradling ample bosoms. When she

9

instinctively went to cradle his head, she spilled what beer that was left in her cup on his painted face. He opened his eyes and blinked three times to focus on her and her matters at hand, then said, "I must be dead and in heaven because there's beer and boobs."

She laughed and said, "You can't be hurt that bad," as she fastened her shirt back.

Goat sat up and looked around. He recognized the man holding his legs. Mack McWhirter smiled and said, "Nice of you to drop in, Goat, but you should've called first."

Goat rubbed the knot on his head and laughed. "Mack? Nothing makes for a soft landing like old friends. How have ya'll been? Nice to see you, Sam." He cut his eyes to the front of her shirt and grinned his trademark grin.

About that time, the paramedics got to him. During their patient interview, they got concerned when he said his ears were ringing real loud and he was seeing double. To check his alertness and orientation, they asked him who the president was. He said, "Chris LeDoux." When asked what day it was he replied, "Every day is Friday for me, boys."

He wasn't scoring well on the test. He was asked where he was, and still gazing at Samantha's shirt he said, "Heaven." It took some doing, but they persuaded him to go get checked out. They placed him on the cot and wheeled him out. He yelled back to Mack and Sam, "Hey, I'll see you later, depending on how pretty the nurses are!" The crowd clapped and whistled as Goat made a flamboyant exit.

Everything settled down and the rodeo continued. Sam looked at Mack and said, "There's only two more bull riders up, why don't we beat the crowd out of here and go see Goat in the hospital?"

"Good idea. I always hate fighting the crowd."

As they made their way to Mack's truck, Sam said, "Well, that box seat came in mighty handy tonight. I'm glad we were there to catch Goat."

Mack laughed. "I sure am glad you decided to come. I think there's going to be all sorts of benefits to your new acquisitions."

Samantha had inherited five hundred acres from her friend Buster Crabtree. His brother Bubba owned the neighboring land and had built the Silver Star Cowboy Complex, whose box seats they'd been sitting in. Bubba had gotten involved with some dishonest men and had angry investors literally gunning for him. He'd been shot at on a few occasions. He'd left town like a scalded cat and defaulted on his loans. Rumor had it he was running a trailer park in Monahans, Texas.

Sam had inherited the mineral rights with her land, and minerals were doing very well for her. The bank didn't want to be encumbered with the facility that had fallen in their lap, so they offered the assets to Sam for what was owed. The box seat at the Stephenville rodeo arena came with the package.

Sam was slowly getting accustomed to the change from horse trainer to large land owner. Reality and responsibility were quickly setting in. Mack and Sam were busy people. He had the Fire Department and his saddle shop, McWhirter Saddle Shop. She had her new venture, Circle Star Cowboy Complex. When they went out, though, they went together. Just not very often for the past few months. She was glad he'd forced her hand on going out tonight.

When they got to the Stephenville Memorial Hospital, they parked right outside the emergency room. The parking lot was wide open. "Looks like Goat beat the crowd," Mack remarked. "I thought it'd be pretty busy here with the rodeo in town and all."

"Yeah, I guess he'll get some good attention." She laughed and added, "I'm sure he'll be giving the nurses some, too."

They went to the triage desk and asked what room their friend was in. The bored nurse responded, "Down this hall and to the right. You can't miss him."

They went down the hall and as they entered Goat's room they saw a nurse taking his blood pressure. Goat had his arm extended for the procedure, and had her bottom cupped in his hand. When they entered the room, Mack cleared his throat and simultaneously the nurse slapped Goat's hand away.

"Not to interrupt or anything, we just wanted to see how you were doing, Goat."

Goat raised one eyebrow and said, "Thanks Mack, I'm making great progress in my treatment. Just a little concussion. They say I'm as normal as I can be, and will be cut loose shortly."

"Goat there's a room in the bunkhouse for you tonight if you need it," Sam told him.

"Thanks, Sam. I'll be out there if I have to," he said, expectantly looking at the nurse when he spoke.

The nurse didn't turn when she said, "He'll be out there."

Mack smiled and tilted his hat back. "Okay, then. I guess we might see you in the morning. We'll go get some breakfast." He could see Goat was working it, so to speak, and he didn't want to interrupt his efforts. Peripheral people were a hindrance to Goat when he was working toward a goal.

They turned to leave and as they entered the hall they could hear Goat arguing his case with the nurse, "Baby, just because I'm an old dog don't mean I can't still bury a bone."

3

SHOT DOWN SHOW OFF

Things had led to things after they left the hospital and Mack never made it back out to his place on the Dead Dog Ranch. Thankfully, he never made it past Sam's apartment in the barn. There was a good plan in place and Mack felt better about being able to spend some time with Sam in New Mexico. He kissed her good morning and left for work at the fire station a little early so he could swing by the bunkhouse to see if Goat's truck was there.

When Samantha inherited the property from her old cowboy friend, Buster Crabtree, one of the stipulations had been to build a bunkhouse that rodeo cowboys could use when they were in town. Buster always provided accommodations for cowboys on the road, even if it was only a couch or a spot on the floor.

As soon as she had the funds, she'd built the bunkhouse. When it was completed, word spread quickly in the rodeo circles and there was rarely an empty room. It was such a hit that even the world champions and high rollers of the rodeo world stayed there. They enjoyed stepping away from the high-pressure glitz and glamour of the limelight and going back to the way it used to be, just a bunch of cowboys crashing somewhere.

The camaraderie at the bunkhouse reminded them of why they got into the rodeo game to begin with. Being in the company of good and capable people was rejuvenating. The cowboy trash talk kept the competitive edge sharp, too.

Sam always kept one room open for emergencies, so Goat was guaranteed a room when he got out of the hospital. As Mack drove past the place, he could see Goat's old Chevy pickup parked in front of one of the rooms and was glad the old bullfighter didn't have to stay overnight in the clinical confines of the hospital. Evidently his arguments with the nurse for more specialized care and observation had not panned out.

As he continued on to the fire station to begin his shift, he thought, *If time allows, the fire crew can take the ladder truck out today and drive some district. They can run by the bunkhouse to check on Goat, too, and see who else is here for the rodeo.*

The ladder truck was a new addition to his fire station. When Chief Taylor took command from the previous Fire Chief, he'd done a large scale restructuring of the department. A truck was assigned to Mack's station and Mack got a promotion to Captain. He was well respected and, as they say in the fire service, well papered. Mack had certifications for Urban Search and Rescue (USAR), Tactical Medic (a paramedic to be deployed with the police SWAT team), Fire Instructor 3, and Fire Officer 2, so his promotion was an easy decision for the new Chief.

The truck crew was responsible for aerial operations at fires, along with forcible entry, ventilation operations at fires, rescue, and extrication at vehicle wrecks. Mack enjoyed the work and was able to pick his own crew to man the truck. He brought Bear, his old driver from the engine, and a firefighter nicknamed Hoss with him. Hoss was a big old boy who was farm boy strong. Nobody, including Hoss, knew just how strong he was. Tearing holes in buildings was an enjoyable effort for him. He had an easygoing attitude and didn't let much bother him, but lately Mack had sensed he had something on his mind. He didn't really seem angry, just sort of burdened.

Mack pulled into the station parking lot and parked next to a pickup truck he hadn't seen before. The fancied up four-wheel drive Ford F-250 was lifted about four inches and wore 32-inch tires. From the fancy flame paint job, he could tell the truck was never meant to take off road, but it was ready.

It had a custom rear bumper that could take an impact from a freight train and a big ranch hand grill guard that could push down a tree, and there was a winch on the front that could pick that tree back up, if need be. Mack figured one of the single guys must've got a new one. This was not a married man's truck.

He went on in the station to relieve the off-going Captain. When he got his gear on the truck, he went into the dayroom and was greeted by the tribal commotion of shift change. He found Captain Wallace. "Hey, Wally, I got ya. Ya'll do anything?"

"No, man. We didn't turn a wheel. They left us alone but the ambulance got hammered. I don't think they had dinner till about ten o'clock. They were sure servants to humanity last night. Those guys are still in their bunks. We didn't disturb them this morning."

"All right then, we'll leave them alone, too. They probably need their beauty rest. Have a good day."

"See ya next time, Mack. I think I'll go fishing today," Captain Wallace said as he left the room. He knew it would get under Mack's skin to know somebody was fishing and he wasn't.

Mack queried the room in general, "Who's driving that four-wheel drive Ford out there?"

A young firefighter Mack recognized from another station stepped out of the kitchen. He was well muscled and had perfect hair. His name was Clay. He said, "That's mine, Cap. Ain't she a beauty? I got swung over here today to ride the engine. I think the Battalion

Chief wanted me to come over and show ya'll how we fight fire on the other side of town."

Mack acknowledged the youthful bravado with, "Uh-huh. We'll see about that. On this side of town, we generally put the fire out before the news cameras get there. You'll have to pick up the pace. You had a little mud on your back right quarter panel. Might want to check that out after breakfast," he added as a little poke for a poke as he went into his office to start the business of the day.

Mack shuffled through the stack of papers on the desk to see if anything pertained to him or his shift, and then checked his email. Hoss came in and asked, "Hey, Cap, how ya doin'? We got anything planned for today?" He seemed down, just as he had for a few weeks.

Mack didn't like to pry into personal matters and was waiting for Hoss to get back in a good mood. "Looks like we have a show and tell at the elementary school this afternoon and I wanted to get out and drive some district if we have time. There's a new neighborhood going in down south and we need to go check out streets and access. You got anything you need to do?"

"No, sir. I'll just do what needs to get done."

Mack decided to press it just a little. "Hoss, you doin' okay, brother?"

"Aw yeah, Cap, I'm okay. Just got some stuff goin' on. It'll work itself out, I imagine."

"Well, if you want to talk the door's always open. How about we get out and see some country after the station duties are done? It's a nice day for a drive." Mack thought getting Hoss out of the station might limber him up a little so he could talk about what was bugging him.

"Thanks, Cap. I appreciate it."

The rookies were calling the breakfast ready, so Mack and Hoss went to the table. Mack told the table gathering the only thing they had for the day was a show and tell that afternoon. The ambulance guys said they had to go get some supplies but they'd be back for the show and tell.

Clay had to make his presence known and chimed in about the show and tell. "Man, I love to do show and tells at the elementary school. They have a couple of hot teachers over there. I've been dancing with some of 'em." He looked around the table for approval.

The group of regulars at the station wasn't impressed, but talk did turn to his truck. He wasn't shy about bragging on it. "I had the bumper and grill guard custom made. A friend of mine has a welding shop and he gave me a hell of a deal, but they still cost $1000. That flame paint job was $6000 — the factory paint just didn't look good. I took it to a place in Fort Worth and had the best Pioneer sound system they make put in, too. Man, you get that base thumpin' and it'll make the girls wiggle in the seat. Chicks love that truck, man."

Bear didn't put up with young guys bragging. "You in that truck is like having a fuzz buster on a moped, boy."

His comment generated a round of laughter from the table. Clay took it as a challenge and tried to regain his self-perceived social superiority. "Shoot, old man, that truck's just icing on the cake when they can get ahold of me." He puffed up a little bit and added, "I got ahold of this little blonde the other night at the dance hall. She was about five foot four and just the right dancing size. She had a great rack on her, and man could she spin. She had a funny little step in her dancing, but when I figured it out we tore up that dance floor. She wanted some of me, I tell ya. I got her to go out to the truck and when she saw it, she said big trucks just did it for her and I tell ya she wasn't lying."

Someone asked, "Did you even catch her name?"

"Yeah, Candy, I think."

17

At the mention of the funny little dance step and the weakness for big trucks, Hoss looked up from his plate of food and asked, "Did she have any tattoos?"

Feeling he was the center of attention now, the pretty boy smirked, "As a matter of fact she did — a lucky horse shoe with a star in the middle of it right there on her left titty. You know her?"

Hoss's dark eyes cut a hole in the braggart when he said, "Yeah, that's my wife."

Silence — silent as a one-car funeral. The two men held eye contact like two tomcats ready to fight. Clay checked his field of battle and saw a large angry man in front of him and a back door behind him with no friends around him. He thought he could make it if he had to. In an attempt to maintain his perceived alpha status, he said, "Well…" He cleared his throat and his voice almost cracked when he said, "I gotta hand it to you, you sure taught her how to screw. She didn't tell me she was married."

Mack gave Hoss a stand down signal by putting his hand on his leg. He didn't want a justified killing in his station today.

Hoss stared at the ready to run punk across the table and said, "Well, I guess she didn't tell you she had herpes and the clap either, now did she?"

The kid got pale and silent. A harder blow could not have been struck with a ten-pound sledge hammer. The entire table was amazed at the effectiveness of the come back. Not wanting to be left out, Bear cut loose with a, "Daayuum."

The now embarrassed ladies' man was demoted to end of the pecking order by raucous laughter from the table. He got up and tried to leave the room. As he was on his way to the back of the station, the alert tones came over the speaker. Everyone tried hard to stop laughing so they could hear the dispatch.

"Engine 7, Engine 5, Engine 6, Truck 7, Medic 7. Structure fire at 8081 Washington Ct. Let's roll, boys." When dispatch said '*let's roll boys*' everyone knew it meant there was a fire for sure.

The table stood in unison, like old fire horses and headed toward the fire apparatus in the bay. They were thankful for the small bit of breakfast they'd time to eat.

Clay sort of spun and grudgingly followed along with the crowd like a whipped pup. The men went to their assigned apparatus and quickly pulled on their firefighting gear. Pants folded over boots were pulled up, hoods were put on, and then finally the heavy coat. They climbed into the seats and put on the straps of the air packs held in a rack behind them. Straps were pulled tight and finally seat belts were put on.

The drivers hit the lights and siren while pulling out of the station. The engine and the truck both exited the station at the same time, turning left in a choreographed maneuver.

Once they were screaming down the road in route to the fire, Mack yelled over the siren, "Hoss I think you handled that pretty well."

Bear chimed in, "Dang, Hoss, does she really have the herp *and* the clap? I can see now why you left her. I would have, too."

Hoss laughed sort of low and said, "No, man, she's clean as far as I know. She just has itchy pants. The third time cheating on me was the charm and I kicked her out. Just the thought of her being dirty hurt that little prick way more than me wadding him up in a ball. He'll worry 'bout that for weeks till he goes to the doc, then he'll just look stupid. Hell, I can't say as I blame him though, she's a looker and mighty persuasive."

All three men were laughing at the meritorious prank until Mack turned and looked out the windshield in the direction of the address they were dispatched to. There was smoke on the horizon. "Time to cowboy up, boys. I see smoke. Looks like we've got some work to do."

No Fireground
Grudges

Engine 7 was the first to stop in front of the house that had thick black and brown smoke billowing out of the gable vents on the roof. The sidewalks were lined with helpful citizens pointing to the house on fire, just in case the firemen somehow missed it. Truck 7 was right behind the engine.

The Lieutenant on the engine checked the equipment 'out on scene' on the radio. "Engine 7, Truck 7, out 8081 Washington Court. We have a single story residence with smoke showing from the roof vents. Engine 7 will be attack, Truck 7 will have command. Engine 7 will have a water supply from a plug on the street. All incoming units continue on."

Dispatch replied, *"Engine 7 attack, Truck 7 command, permanent water supply established."*

Everyone knew their jobs and got busy. While the Lieutenant and his firefighter were getting the hose ready for the attack, the driver was hooking up to the fireplug, which luckily was in front of the house next door. Hoss carried a ladder and set it to the edge of the roof in case the order was given to vent the roof. They all worked quickly and quietly while the radio chattered and the engine revved up to power the pump.

"Medic 7 out" .... *"Engine 5 out. Engine 5 to command, do you have an assignment for us?"*

"Command to Engine 5, back up Engine 7 on the entry. Take the second line off of Engine 7."

"Received, Engine 5 backing up the entry."

"Command to truck 7 driver, get a fan to the door and prepare for positive pressure ventilation."

"Truck 7 received, set a fan." Hoss and Bear started lugging the fan and other equipment up to the front of the house.

The two Engine 7 firefighters on the first line were ready to kick the door as soon as Engine 5 crew was ready behind them. They'd stepped up on the porch to make entry when the door swung open and a screaming man with his clothes on fire came running out through the smoke. He knocked the two surprised firefighters off the porch and took off running down the street, shedding his burning clothes as he went.

The surprised Lieutenant got on his radio as he lay in the flowerbed and said, *"Engine 7 to command. A man just ran out of the house with his clothes on fire. Uh....Engine 7 will continue attack."*

Mack saw it all happening from his command position in the cab of Truck 7. He was just as surprised as the Engine 7 crew. He'd never seen anything like this before. He looked down the street to see the now naked man with smoldering hair leaving the scene post haste.

He got on the radio to Medic 7, "Command to Medic 7, drive on down the street and see if you can find the victim. He left a trail of burned clothes and seemed to be slowing down. He ought to be pretty easy to find."

Trying to stifle their laughter on the radio, the driver of Medic 7 acknowledged the assignment. *"Medic 7 received, chasing naked man on fire."* They just couldn't resist pushing the limits of proper radio protocol.

The medic unit with the two guffawing paramedics drove past Truck 7 in hot pursuit of their patient. Mack sat at his vantage point, watching the fire ground. He saw that the attack team had entered the wall of smoke coming out of the house. He could tell from looking at the smoke that they hadn't got any water on the fire yet. The now black smoke was building in intensity as it blew out the gable vents. He was looking for the smoke to turn grey or white with steam, signaling water had hit it. *I'll give them ten minutes to do it or get out. A house built like this can't stand much fire for long.*

His thoughts and concentration were interrupted by a knock on the door of the truck. He looked down out of the window to see a nasty looking, longhaired biker dude staring up at him. Mack smiled and said, "Hey, Rudy, what're you doing here?" Rudy was a friend of his and an undercover cop.

"Just tryin' to keep a low profile, but I thought I'd let you know that house was a meth lab and we were going to raid it tonight. Ya'll probably don't want to go in there. They got a lot of methylethylbadshit in there and might have some traps set."

Mack was shocked at the revelation. "You're damn right. Thanks." The ratty looking undercover officer just nodded and slunk back into the gathering crowd.

He immediately got on the radio, "This is an evacuation. This is an evacuation. Engine 7, Engine 5 evacuate the building. This is now a defensive fire. Evacuate the building. Dispatch did you receive?"

"Dispatch received." From the dispatch center they activated the hi-low warble signaling a building evacuation to all radios on the scene.

Everything on the fireground started spinning up and working a lot faster. When they heard the warble on the radio, Bear and Hoss ran to the front door and started pulling out the hose to make it easier for the crews to exit. Engine 5 crew were the first ones to get out of the doorway, and they expected Engine 7 crew to be right behind them.

Engine 5's crew was irritated by the evacuation order. They didn't know what was happening but they knew they were fixing to get water on the fire. Firefighters never like to be pulled out of a fire until it is extinguished.

There was a deep, heavy thump inside the house — a sickening sound to those who were veterans of many fires. The black smoke coming from the roof turned to orange flame and all the windows had blown out of the house like a bomb had exploded. Mack could feel the shockwave even from the cab of the truck. He quickly looked at the front of the house, hoping to see his engine crew standing there. All he could see was Engine 5's crew laying in the flower bed. Bear and Hoss were low crawling back to the street.

The radio crackled, *"Mayday! Mayday! Engine 7 at the back of the house, two men down, one trapped. Need help. Mayday!"*

Mack was shocked into acting like he'd been trained. He was on autopilot now with a considerable adrenaline dump. Civilians are always baffled by how firefighters stay so calm when things are cha-otic all around them. Training is the key. A well-trained firefighter can switch to autopilot and still have the advantage of thinking on his feet. A firefighter has seen it all before in the endless training scenarios he practices. It boils down to the old adage: you perform as you are trained.

He spoke into the microphone, "Mayday received Engine 7. Actuate your alarms and try to get out. Help is on the way."

"Command to dispatch, give me a second alarm and another ambulance." He looked to see Engine 5 crew and Hoss at the front of the house. He called them on the radio, "Command to Engine 5, take the Truck 7 firefighter and you will be rescue. Last known location was at the back of the house. Two men down, one trapped. You are rescue!"

Mack was like a dog on a chain. He wanted to get out of the truck and get in there to help but he knew he needed to stay where he was and run the show. They were just one step away from chaos. If that happened, nothing would get done.

He could see Hoss pulling on the face piece for his air pack and putting his hands on the hose line Engine 7 had been using. He crawled into the churning black smoke filling the doorway, with Engine 5 crew bringing their line in right behind him as a backup. He hoped Hoss would follow the hose line right to the downed firefighters.

As he crawled into hell's living room, Hoss kept one hand on the hose line like his life depended on it, because it did. He couldn't see anything as he crawled into the hellhole that was the house. It was hot and black so his flashlight only pierced a few feet into the smoke.

He could hear the emergency alarms on the downed firefighters and doggedly kept moving toward them. He didn't know how far in he was but knew he was less than fifty feet because he hadn't passed another hose coupling. If this were a regular house that hadn't been remodeled, this hall would go down the middle of the structure with bedrooms coming off of it every so often.

Hoss just tossed aside any debris on the hose with one hand. He was starting to get a little nervous about his situation in this blind oven but he was still determined. When he came upon a gloved hand tightly gripping the hose he felt better. He progressed a little further to find the Lieutenant, who was conscious. He hollered at him "Are you okay?"

The relieved fire officer said, "Yes, but Clay has his leg stuck under a pile." Hoss got one big arm around the Lieutenant and pushed him back to the backup crew. He found another gloved hand under some framing lumber and started digging like a badger. Hoss had to stay low because of the intense heat above him, but even on his knees he easily tossed the pile of two by four lumber off the trapped firefighter.

Clay was frantically screaming, "Get me out of here! I can't move! I'm stuck! Man, you gotta help me!"

Engine 5 crew was spraying water over them to hit the fire lapping at the ceiling above them. It was hotter than hell's backyard but the fire seemed to be momentarily contained in front of them. His confidence in their situation building, Hoss said, "Hold on, pretty boy. Are you hurt?"

"I don't think so. I'm just stuck under this pile." He desperately added, "Get me out!"

Hoss cleared the pile down to the trapped man's waist, then said, "Let's get out of here. It's getting hot."

Engine 5 continued fighting the fire burning overhead and kept it from getting closer to the firefighters in front of them. They hit the flames overhead and extinguished that fire, then twisted the nozzle to a wide fog pattern that filled the hall and kept the heat and flames at bay for a minute. Evidently, the fire had burned through the roof now and ventilated itself because the smoke was beginning to lift and it wasn't so hot.

Hoss still couldn't see very well, since he was working in the shower of water from the fire nozzle. He felt around till he found the wire frame on Clay's air pack. He got a good grip on the air pack and pulled with all he had, yanking the screaming firefighter out from under the twisted pile just like pulling an armadillo out of a hole.

Hoss knew he didn't have much time and that fire hose could do only so much, so he turned and bulldozed his way back out of the house, dragging his trophy as he went toward the hazy daylight in the front door.

The backup crew and the Lieutenant moved quickly behind him, fighting fire as they went. Hoss moved so quickly that Clay could never get his feet under him, so he just gave up and got dragged all the way to the front porch. When Hoss got out to the sunlight, he stood and pulled his air mask off so he could see better.

Still gripping the air pack, he dragged the firefighter to the waiting ambulance cot. Hoss dropped his load there and kept walking out to Truck 7. He looked up toward Mack and said, "I got him, Cap. I'm gonna take a break." With that he calmly sat on the bumper of the truck. He watched all the activity from there as they put the injured firefighter in the ambulance to take him to get checked out at the hospital.

Mack looked down at Hoss and thought, *I think they wrote a song about him, dang John Henry.* He keyed his microphone, "Command to Dispatch, both firefighters are out of the building. You can disregard the second alarm. Fire is not under control. This is still a defensive fire."

"*Received, firefighters are safe. Second alarm disregarded.*"

The fire was getting larger now, since all efforts had been for the rescue. Mack got out of the truck and found Bear. "Hey, Bear, we about have the roof burned off this thing. Let's set the water tower and just flood it."

Bear loved flowing water from the ladder pipe. He smiled and said, "You betcha, Mack. I'll put this sucker out myself!"

Mack keyed the mike on his handheld radio, "Command to Engine 5 and Engine 6, set your lines to protect exposures. We're setting up water tower operations for the main structure. Engine 6, bring a supply line to Truck 7."

As the other two fire crews kept the houses on either side wetted down and not lighting off, the house in the middle burned bigger and bigger. There was nothing to save now, so the main concern was to not lose any more property.

Bear went about his business of setting up the truck. He got a supply line stretched from Engine 6 and when the big nozzle on the ladder was in place, he called on the radio, "Truck 7 is ready."

Mack got the now rested Hoss to climb the ladder to direct the fire stream from up above. Hoss loved being on the tip of the ladder. Watching 1,000 gallons per minute rain down on the fire was like rubbing it out with a huge eraser. When he was in place, Bear called on the radio, "Truck 7 to Engine 6, send me water."

Hoss, at the ladder tip, cranked the wheels that controlled the direction of the fire stream. His efforts were so well directed that in about five minutes, the fire was basically out. There were only a few hot spots to mop up, and the crews on the hand lines could handle that.

Hoss was feeling pretty good about himself as he descended the ladder. He'd saved a brother firefighter and got to put out the fire. The day was going pretty good for him. He'd even got to use the misfortune of a wayward wife, who he knew would never come back even if he wanted her to, to put a mouthy punk in his place. Yep, he felt pretty good now.

Mack called dispatch on the radio, "Command to dispatch, fire is under control. Units will clear shortly."

"Received, fire under control."

When the hose was all loaded and the equipment back in order, Mack got everyone together. "Guys we were lucky today, this was just a routine fire that went south pretty quick. A cop told me this was a meth lab and that's why I evacuated the house. Evidently not soon enough. I expect that explosion was the lab. Your training kicked in and everybody did just what they were supposed to and now there is no funeral to go to. Hell, we barely saved the slab but we saved a firefighter and these other houses are okay. Ya'll did a great job. Let's go get lunch."

All the units cleared back in service except for Engine 7, they were short a man and not available for assignment. As Bear drove Truck 7 back to quarters, he had to say something about the rescue and its funny circumstance.

"Well heck, Hoss, that's sort of funny you and Clay having a little situation at the station. Then it all goes to crap and you end up saving his ass. I wonder what the mouthy little bastard will have to say about that?"

Hoss laughed. "I doubt he'll have anything to say. As far as I'm concerned, all arguments are left at the station when that alarm goes off. I could tell he was shocked when he found out the girl he was bangin' was my soon to be ex-wife. Him thinkin' she's got the clap and the herpes is just icing on the cake."

"I bet he was pretty shocked to see the big old hand that pulled his ass out of there was yours," Bear added.

Truck 7 stopped in front of the fire station and Hoss got off to guide Bear as he backed the big ladder truck into the bay. As he walked to the back of the truck, he saw Clay's pickup truck still in the parking lot. He didn't want to go through the awkward situation that had landed in his lap. An apology and a thank you together would just be weird. The truck came to a stop and the parking brake hissed its engagement.

As Bear got out of the cab, Hoss asked, "Do we need to do anything to it, Bear?"

Knowing full well what Hoss was thinking, Bear said, "No, man, I got it. I see Pretty Boy Clay is still here. Go on in there and see what he has to talk about now." Then he laughed that sort of laugh that says, "This is going to be awkward."

Clay was bruised up pretty bad by the collapse. He had on gym shorts, and his lower body looked like he'd been attacked by a gaggle of leprechauns carrying hammers. The emergency room doctor had recommended he take the rest of the shift off, so another firefighter had been called in on overtime to replace him. Of course, his replacement wanted to know what happened and Clay was more than happy to tell the story.

"So, there I was on the nozzle and the Lieutenant was backing me up. I couldn't see a thing — it was black as the inside of a cow in there. The farther down the hall we went, the hotter it got. I mean really *hot*.

"I could hear the fire but I still couldn't see it. I told myself I was going to put this sucker out, so I just kept going. I could barely see the glow of it in a room off of the hall. I guess it was a bedroom. Then all of a sudden, *Boom!* There was an explosion and the wall fell on top of us. The Lieutenant got out of it, but I had half the house on me.

"I'll tell you right here and now I was scared. I was stuck and couldn't move. I was stuck and the fire was gettin' bigger and headed my way. I tried to get some water on it but the hose was pinched off.

"I remember a lot of screaming on the radio. Then all of a sudden, stuff started flying all around and I look up and that big son-of-a-bitch Hoss had ahold of my air pack—" Clay noticed the recipient of his story was looking over his head. He turned around to see Hoss standing there not saying a word.

He stood and turned to face his rescuer, as the other firefighter beat a hasty retreat. He humbly extended his hand and said, "Hoss, I didn't get a chance to thank you for saving my ass. Thank you, brother."

Hoss shook his hand and said, "Aw, it wasn't nothin'. I've pulled calves bigger than you." He stared a minute at the thankful and humble firefighter then said, "You're welcome, brother."

"I sure want to apologize for that story at breakfast. I really didn't know, man."

"Hell, Clay, she was gone 'fore you got there." He added with a sly look, "But I would get tested if I was you."

5
Do You Know
Who I Am?

M ack left the fire station the next morning and went straight to his saddle shop. He was happy the fire gods saw fit to let the boys on the truck get a good night's sleep. The same could not be said for the guys on the ambulance. As soon as they bedded down from one run, the speakers would sound another one.

Mack didn't mind the momentary awakening though, it just made his bed more comfortable. He did *not* miss his time spent on "The Box." Sometimes, if the dispatch didn't say Truck 7 specifically, he wouldn't even wake up. He always thought it was strange that a firefighter could hear his assignment in his sleep and be instantly awake, but sleep through everything else.

Today, he had to get busy and finish two saddles. These were two cowboy rigs for a customer and friend in New Mexico. Mack had arranged some vacation time so he could personally deliver them and get a little time in the saddle. His customer considered himself an innovator of western equine equipment and Mack built the saddles to his unique specifications.

Mack was one of the few saddle makers that would think outside the box of their own creation and he was glad to take the job. He wanted to be there to ride the saddles to see how they worked.

A few slight modifications on a saddle, just a little change in rigging position or placement of stirrup leathers, could mean a lot to a man spending all day in the saddle.

The New Mexico cowboy had sensed Mack's misgivings about the design and told him, "You come out here and ride with me and I'll prove to you this works. We'll cover some country and you'll be sold on what I'm thinkin' this will do."

The cowboy had evidently been thinking about the design during his solitary range riding in the New Mexican high desert. He continued, "Hell, Mack, this design may revolutionize western saddlery."

Mack agreed to deliver them to see how they worked, but mostly so he could get some saddle time in New Mexico. He hadn't been to the beautiful high desert in a while.

First, he had to get the danged things finished. He always thought he could build a whole saddle in the time it took him to finish one out. Putting on the conchos, stringing it, oiling, and putting on finish was tedious and slow work for him. When he apprenticed at Joey Jemison Saddlery, the procedure was for the saddle maker to work on the saddle just to the point of beginning the finishing out process, then a finisher would takeover and do all the final work.

Making the saddle was a task of higher skill and Joey didn't want his skilled labor doing menial work. There were multiple saddle makers in the shop. With Wade, Mark, Bob, and Mack making the saddles there was a lot of production. This steady stream of work kept Jesse and Flash busy getting them ready for sale.

Now that Mack was on his own he fought old habits on finishing out a saddle. He could do it and do it well, but it was usually at gunpoint.

It certainly didn't help the inclination toward procrastination when people came by the shop to visit. The rodeo was in town and with it came Goat. The downtime during the week allowed him to make his rounds to visit, and the saddle shop was on his list today. Evidently he was striking out on obtaining more amorous accommodations and had been spending most of his evenings at the bunkhouse. With no women to occupy his time, his plan B was to visit old friends and socialize.

"I'm telling you, Mack, women are either crazy or real smart. Just about the time you think you have one figured out and get a line on her game, she'll go and change it. Ain't no way to figure it. Big ones, skinny ones, plain or pretty, it don't matter. Where do they learn that stuff? There's got to be some covert female school we don't know about." Goat took pride in his in depth research of the female psyche.

He picked up a *Western Horseman* magazine from Mack's cluttered workbench and thumbed through it. He found an ad for blue jeans and said, "Case in point. Look at this girl."

Mack wasn't really paying attention to Goat, he just let him ramble on while he tried to get the conchos strung on the saddle. He looked up from his work and said, "Yep, she's quite a looker."

"Yeah, she is. The face of an angel, bright blue eyes, blonde hair, and would you take a look at those jeans she is tryin' ta sell. In my younger days, I would give that some hard attention and try to get beside her. I'll tell you there's no shortage of men working toward that. Most guys' first thought would be if they had her they'd have it all. But I'll tell you right here and now, somewhere there's some dude that's tired of her crap."

Mack laughed at Goat's deep thought process and said, "Yep, I guess just because it is wrapped up pretty don't mean it's a good present."

"Exactly. Take Sam, for instance. Now I'm not slightin' your girlfriend or nothin' like that, but at first glance she's only sort of pretty.

She's got that fine Native American look about her but she don't do nothin' with it. I don't think I ever seen her really polished up. She don't have to. But I'm here ta tell you, she's way past this girl on the attractiveness scale. She's got somethin' magic about her.

"I think she's running a deeper sort of game, some kind of mystic thing and somethin' I can't comprehend. All you got ta do is be around her for five minutes and she's beautiful, a lot prettier than this girl right here in this magazine.

"Now if she went to the trouble of fixin' up that this girl did, well I tell ya, my friend, she'd prob'ly have to have a permit for that 'cause it'd be a threat to the entire male population. By the way, if you ever get killed, don't worry about her. I'll take care of her."

Mention of Samantha always provoked deep thought for Mack. He missed her a lot lately but she was busy with her new endeavors. They had good times together when schedules allowed, but they didn't get in each other's way. If one needed the other, though, they'd always end up together.

He was in these thoughts when he spoke. "Well, Goat, first off I don't think Sam's goin' to need any taking care of. She handles herself pretty well on her own. She's worked on ranches from South Dakota to here. She ain't your average woman. I think her game is that she don't have a game. She just is what she is. It's that plain and simple. She don't have a thing to prove. Her magic is her individualism, it's what makes her so attractive."

Considering this theory put Goat in deep thought trying to figure it out. He grew silent so Mack could get back to his task at hand. The shop was quiet while Mack worked and Goat pondered.

The front door opened and before Mack could finish the knot he was working on, Goat was up and in the showroom like a calf out of the gate.

"Welcome to McWhirter Saddlery, ma'am. How can we help you today?" He was addressing a thoroughbred racehorse of a woman, someone not unlike the girl in the jeans ad. She wore tight jeans with holes in the legs that had been made to look worn out, a leather vest and a big turquoise necklace needlessly used to call attention to her lily-white cleavage. She projected an air of new Nashville, which was her intention.

"I need to have a saddle made. I am shooting a music video at the Circle Star in a few weeks and I need a saddle," she said with great intensity.

"That's mighty interestin'. Show business, huh? You know, I'm in the biz myself. Gautier Thibodaux, bullfighter and rodeo entertainer, at your service. You can call me Goat," he said with a Cheshire cat grin as he extended his hand to her.

She stared him up and down, totally unimpressed with his western authenticity. She didn't shake his hand, and said flatly, "Nancy."

The two stared at each other for just a moment but the nonverbal communication was happening at NASA computer speed. Goat got the message, in defeat he turned and said, "Mack, there's a lady here to see you."

Mack came up front, wiping his hands on his apron. He extended his hand and said, "Hello, I'm Mack McWhirter. Can I help you?"

She shook his hand and said, "Hi, Nancy Smith. I work with Tinsley Bryant and I wanted to find out about your saddles."

Mack could see Goat had one arrow in him and he couldn't resist firing another one. "Goat, could you get another coat of oil on that saddle while I talk to Nancy?"

Not being one to fight failure, Goat excused himself and went back to the shop saying, "Yassa, boss."

She ran her hand over a fully carved saddle Mack had made. He was pretty proud of that one and it had a $10,000 price tag on it. "How long does it take to make a saddle like this?"

"That one right there took two and a half weeks. The leather carving is labor intensive. I do all the work myself. It's entirely handmade."

"Mmm-hmm. Can you do the decoration to my specifications and can you put silver on it?"

Mack could see the wheels spinning in her head and the dollar signs were adding up. "I can make it any way you want. We can use factory made silver or there's a silversmith here in town that can do custom work. What did you have in mind?"

"I want one like this with all the — what did you call it — leather carving? But I want a guitar with Tinsley's name on it right here with a bucking horse right here and some custom silver with music notes right here on the corner. The conchos will have a brand on them. Those things you put your feet in will have to have some silver with the brand on them as well. That would make a great CD cover. How much do you think that would be?

"I would be guessing at the price of the custom silver, but you would be looking at around $15 grand."

"Hmm. Okay, I want it. I can't believe you can make something like that in two and a half weeks"

Shocked and eager for the easy sale without an argument over price, Mack said, "I'll get some paper and we can draw up exactly what you want."

He drew out the saddle exactly as she described it and did a rough sketch of the silverwork with the TB brand on it for the silversmith. He was glad she knew exactly what she wanted; usually the design process was painstaking. He guessed this saddle would be ridden once then end up on a saddle stand in a living room somewhere in Nashville.

Satisfied with the drawing, Nancy asked, "You can do it exactly like the drawing?"

When he nodded and said, "It will look better than the drawing."

"That's great! I knew I came to the right place. The girl at the Circle Star said you were the man. This will save me so much time. What about payment?"

"I need half down and the remainder on delivery."

She pulled out her checkbook and as she wrote the check said, "That's fine. We're scouting the location for the music video shoot at the Circle Star today. We'll be using that location and we'll be back in three weeks for production. That should give you enough time. I'll pick it up then." She handed the check to Mack.

He was confused for a moment then it registered. She thought he was going to start the saddle as soon as she walked out the door. He explained, "I'm sorry but it won't even be started in three weeks. You're probably looking at eighteen months for delivery. I have ten orders ahead of yours. Besides, the silver work will take at least a month."

Nancy gave him the blank but searing stare of a woman accustomed to getting her way. She reopened her checkbook with a flourish and asked, "How much would it take to get to the front of the line and keep you in the shop?"

"Nancy, you don't understand. The price is the price and my work is first come first served. The next one I am starting is for a cowboy who works out of the saddle and he's been waiting a year for it. I'm sorry, but I don't move people up in line."

"No. It is you who doesn't understand. I am on a deadline. I need that saddle for the video and I need it to look good. You said it only takes two and a half weeks to make it. Your saddle will be seen by millions of people in this Tinsley Bryant music video. You have heard of him haven't you? Tinsley is *the* hot new talent in Nashville. He'll probably be the next Garth Brooks. What you need to understand is that this saddle is a key point in his new song and the project *has* to happen. It *will* happen." She slapped her checkbook on the table.

"It can't happen with one of my saddles."

As both parties had their gunfighter stare going in the standoff, Tinsley Bryant himself walked in the shop. Mack glanced up and saw a young guy who was trying real hard to look like a working-man. He wore a faded embroidered western shirt, which was the common uniform of the new country boys. It was open to reveal a T-shirt emblazoned with some catch phrase from one of his songs. A studded belt with a big belt buckle held up blue jeans that were strategically tattered, sort of like Nancy's, and the back pockets were embroidered.

Mack's conviction was that back pockets should never have anything on them other than the Wrangler W or the Levis chevron. If they did, then a guy had probably got into his sister's laundry. Tinsley didn't wear a hat, none of the new guys did, but he needed one to cover up the mop of hair that looked like he rode to town with his head out the window. When he breezed in the door, he had a look on his face that said *I'm here and, yes, it really is me.*

Goat stuck his head around the corner and, since it wasn't a woman, went back to work oiling the saddle. Mack just glanced up and went back to negotiations. Tinsley was taken aback that the crowd did not roar upon his entrance.

Without turning around Nancy said, "Tinsley, we have a problem. He doesn't want to make the saddle."

"It's not that I don't *want* to, there just isn't enough time. I don't think you'll find anybody that will do it to meet your schedule."

The singer flashed his flawless smile and said, "Dude, we gotta have that saddle. It's in my song. This one is going right up the charts, man. If you have a saddle in my video, you'll be famous. The guy that made this belt went from working in his garage to having a shop with five people working just to keep up. If anybody sees something I have, they have to have it too. I'm your ticket. You *gotta* make the saddle."

Mack was getting irritated and knew he wasn't going to do any business with these pushy people. "Even if I had all the materials here, I would *not* put you ahead of my other customers. There's not enough time to get done what you want done."

The Nashville poser got adamant and exclaimed, "Dude! Do you know who I am?"

Mack always hated it when someone pulled that out of their back pocket. He responded, "Yeah, I got a pretty good idea. You're some Nashville fabrication that was singing in the shower before a record label found you and decided to make something out of you. Without all the marketing and hoopla, you'd still be selling car parts or whatever you did before. As for the saddle, you don't know a saddle from a sofa."

Nancy snatched her checkbook off the counter and stormed out. She screeched, "Come on T!"

Truth had hit Tinsley Bryant square between the eyes. He stammered for a scathing comeback to regain his dignity. There was none, deep inside he knew he had no argument. His last futile effort as he walked out the door was, "Your loss, man."

Mack went back to the workshop to find Goat doubled over trying not to laugh. When he saw Mack and knew they were gone, he let it all out, "Bwahahaha! Mack, you kicked that pretty boy right in the seat of those five hundred dollar pants!"

Mack shrugged it off. "That conversation was doomed from the start. I hate it when people start demanding stuff. They think you just add water and poof you have a saddle. This instant gratification crap wears me out. People can't wait for anything anymore. It's been bred out of them. With all these computers and crap like that, they just hit a button and *Bam!* There it is. You don't even have to look at a book or a road map anymore. I tell ya, Goat, people are hitchin' their wagon to a blind mule — they run out of batteries or have a power failure and they'll just stand there and stare. It wears me out."

With Goat still hee-hawing about the incident, Mack went back to work on the saddles and said, "I have about five more hours of instant gratification to do on these saddles. I want to be through so I can leave in the morning. If you'll get your laughing ass to work, we can be done in time to go get Sam and cook some steaks out at the Dead Dog Ranch."

At the prospect of food and fellowship with Samantha, Goat instantly got busy oiling the saddle closest to him. "Now you're talkin'. If you're waitin' on me you are backin' up. Come on and get busy."

I'm Leaving
on a Jet Plane

The alarm clock buzzed its irritating drone. He opened his eyes and smiled contentedly. The full moon shone just enough blue light through the window to illuminate Samantha sleeping in his arms. The two lovers had been apart for too long and now he was grateful for having the past three days with her. He stared at her, relishing the moment. It would be over soon, when he had to wake her in time to get to Fort Worth and catch her ride on the private jet.

Her sleepy eyes opened and she purred, "Hey, cowboy." She smiled and snuggled in closer. "That was one fine night. I've been needing some of that quality time." She too savored the moment for a little while as she stroked his muscled chest and arms until responsibility broke the spell. She giggled and asked, "We're burning moon light. Are you going to lollygag around in this bed all day or get up and get the coffee going?"

"Well ain't you the hard-nosed wagon boss." He jumped up out of the bed, taking all the covers with him. Sam lay in the blue moon light with her arms above her head, running her fingers through her shiny long black hair. She smiled at him as he looked at her. *If the melody of a great guitar solo could be seen,* he thought, *she's what it would look like.*

She ran her hands down past her breasts and over her ribs to her thighs, where she massaged her work-hardened legs. Her hands slowly went back up and over her head as she arched her back, stretching her athletic brown body. She relaxed and looked demurely into his eyes, and then said, "Coffee."

Mack broke his trance saying, "Oh, uh, yeah. Coffee." He pulled on his jeans and shuffled into the kitchen, while the temptress declined getting dressed. She smiled to herself as she thought about how much she enjoyed these special mornings out here at the Dead Dog Ranch. Her second favorite place here was the porch, so she grabbed an Indian blanket and went out to it to start the early day and wait for that cup of coffee.

The banging around in the kitchen caused the snoring in the other bedroom to cease. Goat was more of a nocturnal creature and wanted to sleep in, the sunrise held no interest for him. He was a sunset man — when the sun went down his pulse quickened and he was ready to go to work.

As Mack went about the business of making coffee, Goat yelled from his bed, "It's the middle of the damn night! Is there any room service in this joint?"

Mack hollered back, "I'm sorry, sir, you must take your coffee on the veranda!"

He carried the two cups of coffee, one with a little milk, out on the porch where Sam waited. She sighed and said, "I sure do like it out here. Back at my place, I get up and hit the ground running. I'm not real sure sometimes if Buster did me any favors by leaving me his ranch. Life was a lot simpler when all I had to do was ride horses."

"Yeah, I've missed having you out here too. We've been real busy lately. What do you think about trying to find somebody to run it for you? I imagine you can afford it. That sure would free up some of your time," Mack said, trying to plant some seeds and then to aid in her decision-making process.

"Well, I just want to be sure everything's done right, the way Buster would want it. I'm sure he's up there on his hill, watching. If I can find the right person for the job, I might consider it, but it's hard to find the time to look for somebody. The whole thing has become a pretty big deal."

"Yeah, it seems like something's going on all the time with all the horse stuff and now shooting music videos. You have quite the thing going on out there."

"Speaking of videos, you sure did piss off those people I sent to you. They were all in a whirlwind about what they were going to do for a saddle when they got back over to the arena. What happened?"

Mack laughed and said, "They wanted a full carved, custom saddle with custom silver done in three weeks and were darned demanding about it. That pretty boy singer, Tinsley Bryant, came on like I should stop everything and do it just because it was for him. That got all over me, and was the exact wrong thing to do. I told them no and sort of pushed it when I told him exactly what I thought about him. I think I hurt his feelings."

Goat staggered out on the porch, bleary eyed and confused. "It's the middle of the night. Why are we up?" He caught up to the conversation and chimed in, "You should've seen it, Sam. That show pony came waltzing in the shop with his tore-up pants and Porter Waggoner shirt tryin' to look like a workin' fella. Hell, the only honest rip he ever put in a pair of pants was when he tried to put those tight suckers on. He said, 'Do you know who I am?' and Mack commenced to tellin' him just who he thought he was. It was great! Locked the kid up so he couldn't say nothing."

Mack sort of apologized saying, "Sam, I hope I didn't cost you any business over that deal."

Sam smiled at the thought of Mack tearing the self-important singer a new one. She said, "I guess you didn't, they're doing some scouting and still shots today. The video shoot is in three weeks, I think. It's on autopilot now and I'm gone for a week. We better get going if I'm going to catch that plane. I'll get dressed, then let's hit the road."

Goat was gradually getting his bearings and realized he was fixing to be stranded. He remembered his truck was back at Sam's place. "Could ya'll drop me by my truck? I'd hate to have to walk back to town."

Mack came out of the house carrying the two saddles to the truck and said, "Yeah, Goat, get in." He loaded his stuff in the truck as Sam came out of the house carrying her bag. The whole scene gave Mack a good feeling, almost like old and better times. *Three good friends leaving on different missions before daylight.*

He brushed the reflective moment aside and got about his business of locking down The Dead Dog Ranch so he could leave. He shut off the main breaker to the house to kill the power because he didn't trust the wiring in the old ranch house. He'd also noticed some things moved around and strange footprints around the place. There hadn't been a break in, but he'd installed a motion activated game camera off in the brush to see what was going on. He checked the battery and memory card to make sure it was all in order.

The word he got from his cop friends was that meth heads were coming into Erath county like a thieving pack of coyotes and stealing anything they thought they could sell. With everything tight and secure he threw his bag in the truck and double checked his pistol that was secure in a holster he'd made and fastened to the seat of the truck.

"Well, let's get out of Dodge," he said as he fired up the engine and pointed his pony to the north. He turned on the radio and Willie Nelson was singing "On The Road Again." All three laughed out loud at the coincidence.

On the way back to the bunkhouse, Goat asked, "Sam, would it be okay if I stay on at the bunkhouse this week? I have a rodeo to do up in Albany next weekend and thought I might just hang around Stephenville till then. Them music people might figure out they could use my western authenticity in their video. I bet they pay pretty good."

She stifled her laughter as she said, "Sure, Goat, stay as long as you want. I hope you remember all us little people when you get to be a famous star."

Goat puffed up and said, "Oh, you laugh now. That's how Slim Pickens and Ben Johnson made it. They were extras and stunt men in the movies. I got a lot to offer. It could happen. I'll have you know I've been told that in the right light I resemble Robert Redford." He thought a minute then added, "Of course, that was way after closing time."

Mack pulled up to the parking lot at the bunkhouse and said, "Mr. Redford, I believe this is your destination."

Goat got out of the truck then turned and said, "You guys just don't have no vision, no foresight. Thanks for the ride and have a safe trip." He laughed as he slammed the door on the truck.

Mack grinned at Sam and said, "Next stop for this cowboy limo is Meacham Airport."

She laughed and said, "Make it snappy driver. I have a jet to catch."

The directions Sam had written down led them to a hanger on the edge of the airport. The big sign on the hanger announced Clayson Oil Inc. Mack parked at the front door, "Looks like we made it with ten minutes to spare."

Sam was starting to act a little nervous. "Dang, this is getting real now. I was all excited about it, but now I'm really going to get on an airplane. I've never flown before. Everybody must be running late. I don't see any other cars."

"Aw, it's just like riding a bus but different — it'll be a little more cramped and you'll be 25,000 feet off the ground. Other than that… come to think of it, it's nothing like riding a bus. You'll be fine."

She gave him a concerned look and said, "You're really not helping one little bit. Do you want to come meet Jay?"

"Sure, I'd like to meet him." *Any man would want to meet another guy that was going to be traveling in a private plane with his girlfriend.* "You're right. I wonder where everybody is."

They walked in the front door of the hangar and into a front receiving area. It was decorated like something out of an architecture magazine. Leather couches, cowhide rugs and original western art on the walls, with the requisite stuffed longhorn head on the wall.

Jay Clayson entered the door from the hangar and smiled as he approached them. He looked like a male model that had just stepped off the runway at M.L. Leddy's western store. He extended his hand and said, "Hey, Sam. Glad you made it." He directed his attention to Mack and said, "You must be Mack. I'm Jay."

"Nice to meet you, Jay. Quite a place you have here."

"Thanks, we try. I have some high profile clients come through here, and we try to make them comfortable."

"Are we early?" Sam asked, "I don't see the other folks going with us."

"Well, there was a change of plans. I hope you don't mind. They wanted to trailer their own horses up there themselves. They left yesterday. I'm having my men take my horses up. I prefer to fly, twelve hours on the road just makes me antsy. We'll probably be there before they arrive."

"No, I don't mind. I guess I won't miss the drive. I've never flown before, so it should be fun."

"Oh, it's the only way to go. We'll get there quick and won't have to fool with all that TSA B.S. I despise flying commercial. Those guys are all self-important knuckleheads. We don't even have to take off our boots here." He laughed but Sam didn't know what he was laughing about. She couldn't understand why you'd have to take your boots off to fly but she wasn't going to ask.

"Well, we're all fueled up and ready to go if you're ready. Let's load up. Here, I'll get your bag." He took the bag from Mack and turned toward the door.

They followed Jay through the cavernous hangar to a sleek Gulf-stream jet idling on the tarmac. Mack had never been this close to a jet like this before — it was beautiful. He wondered how many saddles he'd have to make to pay for something like this.

Jay climbed the steps with Sam's bag and before he disappeared inside, he turned and said, "Come on in when you're ready. Nice to meet ya, Mack. See ya later."

Mack had wanted to see the interior but he wasn't invited inside.

Sam turned to Mack and wrapped her arms around him. "I guess I'll see you up there. I'm nervous."

"It'll be fun. I'll see you up there. I sort of wish I was flying with you. There seems to be room. Be careful."

Sam gave Mack a long kiss and a hug and then climbed on board the jet. The door pulled shut behind her.

MYSTERIES APPEAR IN THE STRANGEST OF PLACES

Mack had a yearning in his heart for Sam to be sitting with him in his truck watching the jet speed down the runway and into the sky. But she was on her way and he'd be in his truck driving at a comparative snail's pace to New Mexico. He wanted her back.

It is what it is. I'll catch up to her in a couple of days, he thought as he left the airport to begin his journey. He got on the entrance ramp and entered the dirt track race that was Fort Worth traffic on Loop 820 then I-35 north. The hour was still early and the traffic jam hadn't started yet, so it was a dog eat dog free for all on the road.

Finally, he exited on Highway 287 and left the maniacs to their own devices. All he had to worry about on 287 was gravel trucks and sleepy drivers heading in to work. He'd made this trip so many times, chasing the rodeos and selling saddles, that he could put his mind and the truck on cruise control after he passed through Decatur.

There was a lot of traffic on 287, which was unusual for this time of year. Sure enough on the outskirts of every little town there was a police car hiding in the shadows or behind a sign; like a predator waiting to pounce on unsuspecting prey. Out of town cars stopped on the side of the road signaled an economic boost to each little town — civic economics gauged by miles over the speed limit.

He traveled on up the road a few hours and stopped in Vernon to get some fuel. Everybody stops in Vernon to eat and get gas. There always seemed to be a mission trip church bus or a fifteen passenger van full of kids in the parking lot of the few fast food joints on the highway. *Evidently the heathens and those lost in sin in New Mexico and Colorado are in steady need of mission work,* Mack thought.

Full of fuel and a gas station burrito, he slid back on the asphalt ribbon, winding northwest through the rough ranch country of west Texas. He shot through Quanah, and pondered its namesake. Quanah Parker was the last Chief of the Comanche tribe. His mother, Cynthia Ann Parker, was a white girl captured by the Comanche when she was nine. She was adopted by the tribe and married a Comanche Chief. They had three children, one of which was Quanah.

She was recaptured by the whites but always wanted to return to her Indian family. Mack figured she must have known something the white man didn't. His half-breed girlfriend, Sam, was seeking those answers herself now — the answers of her Native roots. Cynthia Ann died in "captivity." They say she died from a broken heart. Quanah went on to progress from a war-fighting Plains Indian Chief to statesman. He was respected by his tribe and white men alike.

He flew through Childress, Memphis and Clarendon with no reason to stop. Staring blankly past the windshield and listening to the radio, he was making good time. His mind was a blank canvas waiting to be painted with whatever thought hit it, just like bugs on his windshield. When he saw the city limit sign for Claude, Texas, he thought about a man he knew a long time ago, Claude Edwards — a man he knew, loved and respected.

Claude was a man of strength and integrity. He was unselfish and always put his family and other people before himself. When

Mack was younger, Claude was like a father to him. He taught him much about life and how to be a man. No matter what troubles Mack had in his life, Claude was there to advise him or help him out of a tight situation.

The man knew about troubles, he carried horrible memories of the Korean War. Every so often, he'd let one slip out when he and Mack were in deep discussion but generally those thoughts were closely guarded.

In his youth, Mack didn't understand why Claude wouldn't talk about what happened in the war. Now, he had his own demons and he fully understood Claude's reasons for psychological self-defense.

The man bravely fought cancer for fifteen years without so much as a whimper or a question. While Mack was on the road following the rodeo, Claude died quietly. That was how the man lived, quietly but with much impact. Mack felt a great loss that he couldn't speak to the man again, especially as life got harder and more complicated.

With a tear in his eye as he rolled down the highway, he said a silent prayer for Claude Edwards. It seemed fitting, since Claude had taught him how to pray, too.

Not really listening to the radio anymore, he was lost in thoughts of his younger days — the days of seeking the truth to unanswered questions. Before he was aware of it, Mack had eased on in to Amarillo. He saw the sign for the first truck stop on the way into town and figured he'd see if the chicken fried steak was still as good as it used to be.

He pulled in and parked his pickup. Making sure the saddles weren't overly conspicuous. He locked the truck and went inside. Being the middle of the day, he avoided the big crowd of truckers so there was plenty of room available.

The hostess, Mable, smiled and winked as she said, "You by yourself, darlin'? Follow me, hon."

Mack sat in the time-warped booth with the cracked red vinyl seats and the worn wood grain Formica tabletop. The place looked like it was stuck in the fifties. Missy, his waitress, strolled over and asked, "Whatcha have, sugar?"

"Is the chicken fry still good here?"

"Honey, it's so good it'll make you wanna go home and slap your mama for never cooking it the way we do."

"Well, I guess I'll have that and a glass of sweet tea."

"You got it, cowboy. Ranch on the salad? It'll be right out." She turned and strolled back to the counter, but not before she stole another glance at her new attractive customer. She had a thing for firefighters. She figured he was the real thing, judging by his physique and the worn faded blue fire department ball cap he was wearing.

He sat in the booth taking in his surroundings. The most interesting assemblage of humanity can be observed in a truck stop — cowboys, travelers, truckers, vacationers and women looking to make a living. As he scanned the gathering, he saw a girl staring at him. She looked off when they made eye contact. This happened enough times to make Mack wonder if they knew each other, but he didn't recognize her or the big guy she was sitting with.

Missy brought him his order, and she bent way over when she set his plate down. She wanted to be sure he had a look at the desert menu down the front of her low-buttoned blouse. She smiled and said, "You enjoy." After she left the table, he noticed the mysterious girl across the way got up and headed toward the restroom.

Mack took his first bite of the supposed best-ever chicken fried steak and the only person he wanted to slap was the guy who cooked it. The breaded ground beef patty had been cooked to death then embalmed with wallpaper paste gravy. He was choking it down and washing out the taste with sweet tea when he caught a glimpse of the girl again as she came out of the restroom. She hurriedly walked past the greasy guy she was sitting with and made a beeline for Mack.

The small-framed girl with ratty blonde hair, nervous eyes and yellow teeth stood at his booth. She shifted from foot to foot as she abruptly said, "I saw your cap. Are you a fireman?"

Mack was surprised by the suddenness of it all. He coughed and said, "I sure am, down in Stephenville."

Uninvited she slid her thin frame quickly into the seat opposite him like she was taking cover from an attack. Her voice quivered with anger and fear asking, "Do you mind if I sit with you? My name is Star."

8

A DAMSEL IN DISTRESS

From her abruptness Mack took her to be a no-nonsense, forget the small talk, streetwise kid. He could tell she thought she was in trouble and she was seeking a defensive shelter. She looked to be about 24 hard years old. Her attitude, hard eyes and the premature lines on her face were a testament to the work hardening that only the road, and possibly drugs, can do to a person. *"She was probably pretty, once upon a time."*

Sitting in the booth across from him she looked desperate, like a pup at the pound. His defenses were up. He was looking for any sign that she might be a "lot lizard," (a prostitute that prowls the parking lots of truck stops looking to make a temporary friend and quick buck).

He smiled. "Well, yeah, Star. Have a seat. I'm Mack. What's up?"

"You look like a nice man and I trust firemen. There's something about ya'll. You always help people. I think I'm in sort of a tight spot. Can you help me?"

"Well, I hope I can. What is it you need help with?"

"That guy I was sittin' with? He gave me a ride about four hours ago and I thought he was okay, but now he's gettin' weird. I guess he thinks four hours in a truck makes me his girlfriend or somethin.'"

He glanced over at the man while she talked. The guy had a glaring down the gun barrel stare fixed on Mack. When he returned the stare with a "don't jack with me" inflection, the big dirty dude got up and left by the side door.

Star continued, "He was givin' me a ride to Albuquerque and he started out nice, but now he's talkin' about us like we're a couple or somethin' and tellin' me all these things he wants to do to me. I ain't like that. I have to get away from him."

"Well, he just left. Looks like you're okay now. Sit here a little while, so he can get gone." She slowly turned her head to make sure he wasn't there then surveyed the parking lot to make sure she couldn't see him outside.

"Did you get to eat anything?" Mack asked. "I would *not* recommend the chicken fry."

"No, we were just fixin' to order when I saw you come in. I didn't want him to buy me any food 'cause he might think I owe him somethin.'"

"How about I get you a hamburger? If he's waiting outside, he'll get tired of it and leave. I have plenty of time." He really didn't have any extra time if he was going to make it to the ranch by sundown, but he couldn't leave a damsel in distress, no matter how fallen she was.

Her desperate eyes softened a little as she realized she'd made the right move and she accepted his offer. "I sure would appreciate that. I haven't eaten all day and I don't have much money."

Mack got the attention of the waitress and waved her over. He told his new friend, "Order whatever you want." Then he asked the waitress for some more tea when she got a chance.

When Mack gave her full permission of the menu, it was a sort of a test. He wanted to see what sort of person she was, whether she would go for the big expensive plate with dessert or be humble and go minimal. She ordered a cheeseburger basket and a Coke, and he felt a little better about her.

While they waited for her food, Mack asked, "So, you're going to Albuquerque? Are you from there?" He knew people like her were pretty tight with revealing information so he was small talking his way into finding out more of her story.

"I'm pretty much from all over. I'm supposed to meet my boyfriend there. He's going to pick me up. Where are you headed?" she asked, still nervously swiveling her head maintaining awareness of her surroundings. Mack could see she had some other issues going on besides evading her truck driving "cabover Casanova".

"I'm headed up toward Cimarron to visit a friend. He has a ranch up there." Just then the burger arrived and she dove into it. She was hungry as a hostage. She had the manners not to talk with her mouth full, so Mack let her eat in peace. He kept scanning the room and parking lot, hoping he wouldn't see her "friend." It was Mack's experience that once weird men like that have their existence acknowledged, they usually slink back into the shadows. He wasn't too worried about him.

The hungry traveler made short work of the burger basket and politely asked for a refill on her Coke. She told Mack, "Thank you so much for that. It was delicious. I really appreciate it." She let the conversation lag a bit as she got up the nerve to ask her next question. "Uh, I'm sort of in a tight spot. Would you happen to be going through Albuquerque by any chance?" Her street hardness seemed to be relaxing a little as she sat with the sympathetic firefighter.

He could see his schedule was getting shot all to hell, but he felt like he needed to help this girl. "Well, I was going to head north just before there but I guess it's not too far out of the way. You sure your boyfriend's going to be there to pick you up? I wouldn't want to leave you stranded."

Not many men were nice to a girl like her traveling on the road. Most times, she felt like an armored sheep making her way through a pack of coyotes. She was a little shocked that he was willing to go out of his way to help her. With surprise in her voice she asked, "You'd do that for me?" Then her street suspicion came back and her eyes got direct and hard, she added, "I'm *not* going to be your girlfriend or nothin'. I'm not like that anymore."

Anymore. That word took root in Mack's mind. He was right about this girl. It was a judgment he felt bad about. Maybe not now, but at one time she was probably just a doped up hooker on the road. Probably still doing meth, judging from her looks and actions.

She hadn't hit on him, and even made it clear how it was going to be. So he believed her. There was something about her that he couldn't draw a bead on, but he was going to help her anyway. Something about her made him want to save her.

He played it off and kept it light. "Heck, I have a girlfriend. I don't think I could handle another one. It looks like you just need a little help here. This road thing ain't workin' too well for you."

With reflectiveness of her situation on her face she agreed, "Boy, you got that right. You really do. I sure appreciate the ride."

Mack stood. "Let's pay up and get on the road. We got places to be."

Mack still kept his eyes peeled as he led the way through the parking lot to his pickup truck. Star stayed close behind him. Once she was out in the wide-open air, she naturally went into her prey/predator mode, an adaptation from her years on the road.

As they weaved their way through the lines of cars, and got a distance from the truck stop, that big ole boy stood up from between two cars. He had an ax handle in his hand. When she saw him, Star screamed and ran to the other side of a car to get a shield.

Mack was surprised but stood his ground, he didn't want to run backwards over the girl and he was trapped between the cars. The big nasty man raised his weapon and said, "Nobody takes my girlfriend, mister fire man!" As the angry stack of flab started his swing, Mack stepped into it so he wouldn't take the full impact of the ax handle.

As he stepped forward, he pushed with his left forearm and pulled his right hand back. He got close enough to smell the man's stench and gave him a right upper cut just below the ribs. His hand went so deep in the fat that Mack was unsure whether he'd reached anything vital. The behemoth let out an *"Oof,"* and bent over, but came right back up, raising the stick again.

Mack caught a glimpse of the girl on the other side of the car, so he stepped back about two inches further than an ax handle's length. Just before the truck driver swung again, the scared little girl went into full spider monkey mode and jumped on his back, screaming like a banshee. She dug her dirty fingernails into his eyes and stayed on his back like she was riding a bull. She was even hitting him in the ribs with her heels just like spurring a horse. The ax handle fell to the ground as the trucker yelled and tried to get the mess of hornets off of his face.

Mack picked up the stick and quickly shoved it hard into big boy's diaphragm. That pretty much took all the wind out of him, so to speak, and he started down toward the ground. The little blonde haired bull rider did a Larry Mahan flying dismount and rolled over the hood of the car, landing on her feet.

Mack held the ax handle and stood over the gasping fella, who was trying his best to get a breath to cuss Mack. He didn't know just how long the breathless deranged idiot would be down, but Mack wanted pursuit to be out of the question so he thumped the ax handle on the guy's big greasy head and turned out the trucker's lights.

Mack looked at the breathless girl with the now wild eyes and said, "We probably ought to get on out of here." He had her in one hand and the ax handle in the other, quickly making his way to the truck. He threw the stick in the bed of the truck and opened the passenger side door for her. Once they were in the safe confines of the truck, he looked at quivering girl and remarked, "Dang girl, you got some spunk! You stuck to him like glue."

She smiled and nervously replied," Letting go wasn't an option. I knew if I let go, both of us were going to get our asses beat. You did pretty good yourself. I sure am glad you were there."

Mack let loose a laugh of victory. "Let's put some distance between us and him." He fired up the truck and got back on Interstate 40. As they made their way down the highway, he thought about how he'd get to Cimarron from Albuquerque, since he was going to pass his familiar cutoff. "Would you get that map in the back seat and look at it to see the best way to Cimarron from Albuquerque?"

She pulled it out from under the saddles and studied it a minute, then said, "Looks like you take 25 north off of 40 then to 64 and cut back west. It's pretty simple and there's no mountains."

She surprised Mack with her command of map reading. He gave her an admiring, shocked look and commented, "Most girls have trouble reading a map. Why? I don't know. You found that really quick. Pretty impressive."

"Thanks." She smiled a grateful smile and said, "At one time, I lived by the map, but that was a long time ago. I'm still on the highways a lot though. What's up with those saddles in the back? Are you a cowboy, too? A cowboy and a fireman, that's every little kid's dream."

"I made them. I have a saddle shop in Stephenville. I'm delivering them to the customer up in Cimarron and we're going to ride a while to test them out. And, yeah, I guess I'm living the dream," he said, only half kidding.

She pondered that for a few miles as she stared out the window. She put two and two together, turned back to him then asked, "Mack from Stephenville. Is your last name McWhirter?"

"Yeah, did you see the maker stamp?"

"No, you made me a saddle when I was fifteen years old. I remember your shop. That was the best saddle I ever rode."

Hearing that threw his mind into a spin. *Who is this girl? Evidently she rode a lot at one time, judging from the way she spurred that nasty fella in the parking lot, but she sure doesn't look like it now. How did this street urchin ever afford one of my saddles?* He turned to her with a bewildered look on his face and asked, "Who are you? Is Star your real name?"

Her eyes were wide with shock and surprise at what she'd just let slip. *"How stupid can I be?" Just a few minutes of small talk with this stranger and I pulled back the curtain to the past that I spent so many years trying to hide.* Nobody knew anything about her and she worked hard to keep it that way.

She constantly had to run from the truth. To even insinuate the revelation was one thing, but to hint at it to a stranger who wasn't really a stranger? He was connected to the circles she was running from. *Maybe Mack's easy-going, non-threatening offer of assistance or the familiar comfort of a cowboy's pickup truck made me drop my guard.*

She knew she couldn't evade his question for long in the confines of his truck cab going down the highway. *Hopefully he's different and I can trust him. Guess I have to now.*

Many silent miles had passed when she hesitated and reluctantly replied in a small voice, "Star is *not* my real name. I'm Phoebe Hansen."

9
CARDS ON THE TABLE

Phoebe "The Flash" Hansen, the ultimate mystery in inter-colle-giate rodeo is sitting in the front seat of my truck! He was having a hard time wrapping his head around that information. He felt like he was in an episode of the *Twilight Zone*. He wanted to hear the whole story and had lots of questions. He didn't want to scare her off, though, so he acted nonchalant about her being who she was.

The best place to start was the beginning, when he'd met her nine years ago. He eased into it, like stepping off the creek bank into unfamiliar water. "I remember that saddle. I think I made that when you won the High School Finals. Right?"

It took a lot for Phoebe to tell him who she was. She'd been running from that name for five years. Anybody that had the slightest interest in rodeo knew her name back in the day, and that's what she hoped to escape. The circles of dope heads and strippers she ran with now had no interest at all in that name or any of the many others she made up.

The fact that Mack didn't go jack bat crazy when she said it made her more relaxed around him. She felt she could talk to him. He was a good man who saved her from the crazy guy. Hopefully he'd keep her secret. Besides, it felt good to let it out, to lance the emotional boil in her mind. She had been hiding it for so long that it felt like she was talking about someone else.

"Yeah, that was my sophomore year in high school. I rode it till I got to college and started getting sponsorships and all that crap. I had to ride their saddles then, and they were junk. I never could get one broke in good. I always had to ride the newest, latest and greatest. It sucked, and Midnight never liked it either. I guess that saddle you made is still in the barn at my folks' place in Fort Worth." Emotions were welling up, but she was well practiced at not crying. Those tears dried up long ago. The road does that.

He recalled from meeting her parents when they bought the saddle, that they were high pressure and it might be a sore subject, but asked anyway, "Are they still in Fort Worth? I haven't heard anything about them for a while. They were all over the news back then, pleading for your return. Then all that quieted down."

He worried that he'd asked the wrong question because she didn't respond — she just gazed out the window at the passing sagebrush. Finally, she said, "I don't know." She paused. "And I sort of don't care." She took a deep breath and sighed. "You know, last time I saw them was at the college finals. All I was to them was another accessory to that expensive horse they bought for me to ride. Chasing Midnight was just a commodity that had to produce winning runs. Hell, I was too, for that matter."

Not knowing where to go with the conversation and surely not wanting to shut it down Mack complimented her. "Well, ya'll sure did that. You and Chasing Midnight were a good team. You won it all."

She dismissed his compliment with a wave of her hand and a "Pfffft." She turned away from the window to look at him and said, "It was all him. I was just along for the ride. Everybody thought I was some stuck up arrogant champion. I didn't have any friends because of that. Nobody knew it, but I was just shy. I didn't want all that attention. My parents did but I didn't. I just wanted to be a regular kid with a boyfriend.

"The horse did all the work — I just rode. But damn it, I *had* to ride. My parents made sure of that. They had me entered in at least three barrel races a week scattered all over the country. You said I was good with a map? That's how I learned, pulling a horse trailer all over the country by myself. Just me and Midnight, rolling down the road. Nobody wanted to haul with me. I was eighteen years old, pulling a big-ass horse trailer all over creation by myself. I was in college, too, carrying fifteen hours. I had my foot on the gas and my father had his boot in my ass."

She stared at him for effect. He felt obligated to say something, so he sympathetically said, "Man, that was a lot of pressure for a kid. I know how hard it is to get to the next show. I used to rodeo too, but we had a car full of cowboys to drive."

She turned to the window again and after a moment remorsefully said, "I guess that's when all the crap started. I had a real hard time getting where I was scheduled to be because there wasn't enough time. The push was just too hard. I remember I got some pills from a bull rider I knew. He said you could stay awake all night with them. He wasn't kidding. I didn't sleep for two days.

"One thing led to another and that was how I was getting down the road, those damned pills. I would get all hopped up on them and not sleep all weekend. That's how I made all those rodeos. I was one highway-burning bitch. Ha! Phoebe "The Flash" rollin' down the highway, zonked out of my head."

Mack understood she was baring her soul and he wouldn't insult the moment with a comment. He quietly drove as she stared out the window at the high desert. Words would come when she was ready.

"Did you ever take pills to stay awake?" she asked with guilt in her voice.

"Naw, No-Doz was about as strong as I went. Caffeine and nicotine seemed to get me along just fine."

"I can tell you that you were smart not to. The problem with those trucker pills was after a while they quit doing the job. I guess your body gets used to 'em. Once again, those bull riding sons-of-bitches turned me on to something else. Crystal Meth will get you going and keep you going like that battery bunny on TV. It makes you feel like you can conquer the world and it'll keep you up for days.

"When I used that stuff I didn't even have to stop and eat, I just kept on going down the road to the next rodeo. That's what kept my show on the road — diesel, meth and coke. Not really the romance of the west, is it?"

"No it's not. I sure hate it that it went that way for you. Couldn't you tell your parents you needed a break? Get off the road for a while?"

With a look of *are you stupid?* she exclaimed, "Oh, hell no! My father is a shyster lawyer and my mother is gold digging arm candy. With them, it's win at all costs or die trying. They don't understand taking a break, especially if it's not them taking the break."

"So, at the college finals it sure looked like you decided you were taking a break. People still talk about that night. What happened?" Mack figured he'd pushed it too far with that question.

She sat back in the seat and closed her eyes like she was checking out of the whole conversation. A few miles later, with eyes still closed, she spoke with resignation in her voice. "Most folks didn't know that Midnight was having some problems with the bones in his legs. All that hauling down the road and hard running was tearing him up. The most expensive farrier in the country would meet me at different places to keep special shoes on him. That was all that was keeping him in the game.

"My parents' plan was to run him till he just couldn't run anymore and then get another horse. Hell, all it takes is money. Right? They were going to run him till he went lame. They didn't care about him; the only thing between him and the horse killers was one bad run.

"That night at the finals he was acting like he was hurting but I knew he was willing to make the run. I hadn't slept much that week and I was pretty strung out. A week at the finals is hard with all the appearances you have to make and then the runs, too. I'd about had a gut full of the whole circus and besides that I was failing every class in college. The college had pulled some strings to let me compete."

She sighed revisiting her painful past, then continued, "All of that was heavy on my mind while I was getting Midnight warmed up and myself ready. I could tell my head wasn't in the game but I really didn't care how it went. When we were up and the run started, it was in slow motion for me. It was like every stride he took lasted five seconds.

"The first two barrels were flawless, he turned the third and when he straightened up to head to the finish I felt him falter. Like I said, everything was in slow motion so I had time to think, and I had a moment of clarity about my life. My ailing horse, the horse that I loved that had done so much for me, was about to be nothing. I was just like that horse — we were the same.

"Right there in that arena, at that moment, I decided that was *not* going to happen to either of us. I rode him out of the arena, I pulled him up a little but we loped out of the fair grounds.

"I walked him down the road to a good stable I knew of that bought horses. I sold him for one thousand dollars and the promise that he would never go to the horse killers. Then, I left. I was finished — finished with rodeo, finished with college, finished with my parents — everything."

The ultimate rodeo mystery had just been laid out on the table like a full deck of face up cards and Mack was speechless. He had the words and the questions, but like a bunch of cattle trying to get through a small hole in the fence, his words bunched up and nothing moved. He didn't even know if she wanted a response seeing how she'd been so matter of fact in her explanation. The pair rode down the sagebrush-lined highway in silence.

After many miles, curiosity got the best of him when he simply asked, "So, what did you do after that?"

Phoebe felt that explaining her past to this almost stranger was easing the guilt she'd carried all these years. The life on the road and the drugs had beaten her down so much that she no longer had any pride or self-esteem. It felt kind of good to be honest and in the moment for once. This was foreign to her since she hadn't felt anything but high for some time.

"There was this guy I bought my stuff from that sort of followed the circuit, selling to the rough stock riders. He was always a little nice to me and he had plenty of drugs, so I called him. He was in town for the finals, and he came and picked me up.

We traveled together for a while but he got to where he was getting into his inventory a little too much. When he got paranoid, he would get mean. I wasn't going to take another beating from him, so I got away from him in Vegas. Besides, it was getting harder to hide from the rodeo crowd. I didn't want to be found."

Mack bristled at the thought of a man beating on this little girl. "Ain't no reason for a sorry excuse of a man to be hittin' on a woman. What did you do for money? How did you get down the road?"

"Trying to get high and being high took away any sort of embarrassment I had, I guess. I still looked good then, not like now."

She paused in a moment of self-reflection to wipe away a rare tear. "There were plenty of places to dance and a lot of men in Vegas that wanted to take care of a girl, so I made it all right for a while.

"I hated dancing but the money was good and I couldn't do nothin' else. But that's all I did was dance. I wasn't a whore or nothin' like that. Not much, anyway. All I ever knew was how to run barrels, and I was not ever going to do that again.

"The only bad thing about Vegas was I had to leave town when the National Finals Rodeo came to town, too many familiar people around during that time. Like I said, I did not want to be found."

Mack didn't pass judgment on the failed champion. He remembered his lowest point in life. He felt sorry for her and how she let life push her down. "So, how did you end up back down in this part of the country?"

"I met this guy in the bar, he was from Dallas and had an oil company. We were sort of dating, I guess, and he took me back and got me an apartment. He said he was going to help me get clean. I was doing pretty good with taking care of myself until his wife found out about me, and that was it. He cut me off and threw me out like I was nothing.

"That hurt. He never told me he was married. He had two kids, too. She told me all about it when she tracked me down at the apartment. I thought she was going to kill me, and him too, with that little silver gun she had.

"I was real scared and he just stood there like a little boy in trouble. He wasn't no kind of a man. What kind of sorry bastard does that?

"Anyway, I've been on the road for a month trying to get to New Mexico. It's been a real hard month. I sure am glad you're a nice man and gave me a ride." Then after recognizing she had just bared her soul, she asked with a slight quiver of apprehension in her voice "You are a nice man, aren't you?"

Knowing a girl that had experienced everything she had could never trust men again, Mack looked into her deep set, hollow eyes, then said reassuringly, "Phoebe, I'm not going to do anything to hurt you. I wish I could do more than just give you a ride. You've had a tough time of it."

"Will you promise me you won't tell anyone back home you saw me? I don't want anybody to find me like this."

"I promise, but would you do me a favor? Not a promise, but a favor. Try to get yourself cleaned up. I know what you used to be, you sell yourself way too short — you were a champion. You did more than just ride Chasing Midnight. You *are* worth something. You gotta realize that."

She gave him with a questioning look, trying to figure out his angle. Nobody had given two flips about her in as long as she could remember. She wanted to believe that he believed in her. She cautiously said, "That's part of the reason I'm going to New Mexico. I met a guy in Vegas. He said he lives on a mountain. I don't know what he does but he lives there. I saw pictures. He invited me up to visit anytime, so I thought I'd get up there and try to dry out. Just get away from civilization and drugs for a while and get back to nature. Cities are *not* good for me.

"I called him and he's supposed to pick me up in Santa Fe. I won't promise anything Mack, but I'm going to try real hard." As she said the words, tears filled her eyes. She wiped them away along with a layer of road dirt and added, "I must mean it because this is the first time I've cried in a long time. I didn't know if I could anymore."

Mack wanted to cry right along with her. Life hadn't been kind to this girl who had once had the world by the tail. In the fire service, he'd seen so many lives ruined by drugs. It hurt to hear the personal account from someone he'd once admired. He wanted to do more to help her but right now the best he could do was give her safe passage to where she needed to be. "If I have to take 25 out of Albuquerque to get to Cimarron, that goes right through Santa Fe. Why don't I take you on up there? Did you really need to stop?"

She perked up at the thought of staying with Mack in this arena of safety and honesty and not having to bum another questionable ride. "That would be great! I only said Albuquerque because that's where the trucks go. I sure would appreciate that."

The substance of the conversation left the cab of the truck quiet as both gave consideration to what the other had said. Questions were answered. Trust was understood. It was a restrained ride but a comfortable one. Phoebe was convinced Mack was one of the few good men left and he was convinced she was damaged and allowed no further questioning. True to his nature he was doing all he could do for her right now.

Santa Fe, with all its square and right angle adobe architecture came into view. Mack always liked seeing this town, for some reason it made him feel creative. It must be the same feeling for lots of people here, since artists and writers seemed to gravitate to the area. He navigated his way through the streets of centuries past to the Plaza with all its tourist traffic and Indians selling silver jewelry displayed on Navajo blankets. It was a busy day on the Plaza.

He parked the truck and asked, "Are you going to be all right here? When is he supposed to meet you? I'll be glad to wait with you."

"I'll be fine. You've done so much already. You don't have to stay. He said he'd be around the Plaza all day. I'll find him. Thanks anyway. I sure do appreciate the ride and it was nice talking to you. I haven't said that stuff to anybody, ever." She looked him straight in the eye and said, "You remember, you never saw me. Okay?" She opened the door to get out.

Mack laughed. "Saw who? Your secret's safe with me. You remember that favor now. Good luck to you. Try hard. I know you can, Phoebe."

The scraggily clothed, ratty haired girl with road dirt framed eyes cleansed by tears looked directly at him and showed that she meant it when she said, "I'm gonna try real hard, Mack. Thank you for your help. I really mean it." She slammed the door on the truck and turned to fade into the meandering crowd on the Plaza.

Mack pulled the truck around the corner and parked. He knew his schedule was shot up like a dove on opening day, so he got out of the truck and became a part of the crowd. He found Phoebe sitting on a bench, waiting. He took up a post behind her and kept an eye on her as she waited for the mystery man. After a ride and revelation like that, he couldn't just leave with questions unanswered or with her unattended.

After an hour or so of waiting, she stood and waved. A guy with sharp features like skin pulled over a skeleton and long black hair separated himself from the strolling crowd and made his way toward her. He wore pointy-toed boots, faded Levis and a black leather vest over a T-shirt. They greeted each other and he wrapped a tattooed arm around her shoulders. Mack was close enough to see it was a full sleeve tat in the pattern of a diamond back rattlesnake. The head of the snake covered the back of his hand and the forked tongue of the snake ran down his middle finger.

He tensed up at the sight. He thought to himself, *Watch out for rattlesnakes, Phoebe, watch out for snakes.*

10

THE MAID'S SURPRISE

Mack had a tight gut feeling about the guy Phoebe had come to see. It wasn't just the way the guy looked, it was also about the emotional reaction he got when he saw him. His gut feeling had always proven out in the past but there was nothing he could do about it now and he knew it. Even if her boat was leaking, it'd set sail on what Mack considered stormy seas. *Let it go.*

His grumbling belly told him some fine New Mexico cuisine and a few *cervezas* might help his attitude. Even though it was not the TexMex he was accustomed to it rated a close second. Any luck at finding the ranch in dark unfamiliar country would be marginal at best, so he called his customer to let him know he'd be there in the morning.

He found a little tourist court-type hotel on the edge of town. It was a quirky little place that fifty years ago was probably full of station wagons and running kids wearing burr haircuts. Maybe back then the turquoise-colored paint was a few shades brighter. The single-story rooms were arranged in a horseshoe around the office in the middle.

The faded sign out front advertised the Comino Real Motel had air conditioning and modern rooms, evidently a big selling point a long time ago. Mack figured this place was as good as any, so he stopped in to get a room. He went into the office and paid the Pakistani man $45 for the night.

He didn't understand why in the last few years every small hotel he went into in the southwest was run by a greasy little man of Middle Eastern decent. They all looked and smelled the same; it was like it was a conspiracy or something — the curry conspiracy. But that was the way it was now and who was he to question it.

He got the key to the "modern" room and parked his truck at the front door. The first thing he did when he went in, even before he brought in his bag, was strip the beat-down bed and inspect it for bed bugs. That was a souvenir he did *not* want to take back home. Those little bastards could hide in the folds and crevices of the mattress and eat you up while you slept. If they were in the mattress, then they were sure to be in the ancient carpet too, and would end up in his clothes and luggage.

The mattress seemed clean of bugs despite its story of stains. He was satisfied there were no bed bugs, although he questioned the criminal history of the mattress. He remade the bed and brought in his bag, but he set it on top of the dresser just to be safe.

Across the two-lane highway was a little hole-in-the-wall adobe café named Abuelitas. The exterior of the building was in dire need of repair and paint. At one time, it might have been turquoise and red, but now it was adobe with flecks of history. In Mack's experience, the most authentic food could be found in the worst looking little restaurants, so he always sought out an epicurean oasis in the midst of the chain restaurant desert.

He walked through the screen door that slammed behind him and had a seat in a booth, even though there was plenty of seating available. A large woman named Carmelita happily brought him a glass of water and took his order. She sure seemed glad to have a customer. She advised, "Señor cowboy, the stacked enchiladas are my specialty. I make them special for you and I can make them with green or red. Of course if you want something else, then it is good too."

Mack knew in his heart that God never intended for enchiladas to be stacked, they were meant to be rolled. It was the natural order of things. Anything stacked was a casserole in his opinion, but he didn't want to debate that with Carmelita. "Well if they're the best, then that's what I'm gonna have. I'll go Christmas style with both red and green because I just can't make up my mind. I do know I sure would like a Modelo beer if you have it."

"Excellent choice, *mi amigo*. I am famous for my enchiladas." She laid her wrinkled hand on his shoulder. "I just got some fresh Hatch chilies today. They are *muy bueno*. I will get that beer for you."

When she brought the frosty bottle of beer she asked him, "Where are you from? You don't sound like you are from around here."

"I'm from Texas. I'm up here on some business and to see some of this pretty country."

"Oh Texas, I have many cousins there. They live in Fort Worth. I've been to visit them many times. It's crowded there and so humid. I like it much better up here."

A ringing bell and some Spanish hollering signaled his food was ready. "I will get your food."

She brought his plate of enchiladas with rice and beans and set it on the worn Formica-topped table. "You will love my enchiladas," she said and had a seat at the table next to his booth. He looked at her quizzically but said nothing. She laughed and said, "I want to see how you like them. They are different from Texas food. I make them so much better."

Once again he declined the debate. After his first bite, he agreed they were different but very tasty. Satisfied he liked her food, Carmelita stood and said, "I knew you would like them," before she went about her business in the not so crowded café.

He finished his dinner and with a full belly and so many miles behind him today he was ready to call it a day. He went to pay up and as Carmelita fished for compliments on the food, he agreed they were the best stacked enchiladas he'd ever had. She said, "Oh, you ain't had nothing till you had my *Chile Relleno*. You come back for that on Wednesday and you won't be sorry. *Vaya con Dios, señor* cowboy."

"*Adios*, Carmelita," he said as the screen door slammed behind him. He made his way across the barren highway, anxious to get on that lumpy mattress. He was in a love/hate relationship with the wore-out thing. Right now he was just dog-tired and it didn't matter. He got to the room and double locked the door in consideration for where he was staying.

Mack took off his clothes and folded them, placing them on the dresser next to the TV. He still had no faith in the bedbug situation. He found a good enough arrangement of lumps in the mattress and drifted off to sleep, but he couldn't help thinking about Phoebe and her story. His last thoughts as he drifted off were, *I wish I could help her but she made her choices and I can't change that.*

The headboard banging on the shared wall in the room next door woke him up. *Oh great, it's mating season in Santa Fe.* He lay there a minute, hoping they would either get tired or finish up, but evidently they were long-winded. He banged on the wall to try to get their attention but that just urged them on. The tempo increased for a few minutes then stopped.

The temporary silence was broken by a woman screaming, "No! No! I don't want to do that!"

A man's voice yelled, "Get over here, you little bitch! Get on that bed and quit fighting!"

A loud thump resonated from the wall and she pleaded, "Please, no! Please, just let me go! That hurts."

Having gone to sleep with Phoebe on his mind, Mack woke up in protection mode. This situation was not to be ignored. He quickly dressed and went banging on the door next to his. He heard a rough voice say, "You stay right there and don't say nothin'."

The door opened just enough for a longhaired, bearded man with a face tattoo to stick his nose out. He gruffly asked, "What the hell do *you* want?"

Mack bowed up and replied, "I want ya'll to shut the hell up, that's what I want. I'm in no mood to listen to ya'll fighting." He looked through the cracked door into the room and saw a scared Spanish girl balled up on the corner of the bed, trying to cover herself with a pillow. There was blood on the pillow and a section of rope lying on the bed. "On second thought, why don't you let the girl leave before I call the police?"

"Screw you, buddy. I paid for it and I'm gonna get it." He slammed the door.

Before the dead bolt lock even clicked, Mack kicked the door open, exploding the doorjamb. The punk was too close to the door when it blew open like a bomb and he was knocked to the floor. The girl screamed and the man spun up off the floor. Coming in low, he caught Mack around the waist and carried him to the wall.

As Mack flew backward he thought, *Damn, this dude didn't look that big.* Mack got an arm around the guy's head and as Mack's back hit the wall he made sure the man's head did too. He got in a few good licks to the guy's ribs, too, and he thought he could feel one crack from the blows.

The dude backed up and rammed Mack into the wall again, this was all he could do because Mack had him bulldogged and wasn't letting go — he just kept wearing out those ribs and tried a few kidney punches without effect.

As the big man staggered back to go to the floor with him, Mack released the bulldog hold around his neck and with the now free arm put his elbow to the base of the bully's skull before the guy could raise his head. The pair of combatants fell to the floor in a pile.

Mack slid out from under his semiconscious opponent and stood up. He raised his arms and tried to flex all his vertebrae back into the proper position. He looked at the quivering girl and said, "It's probably time for you to leave. I think it's over for the night."

The moaning hulk lying on the floor tried to get up but Mack stomped his boot heel square between his shoulder blades. Whatever fight he had left was kicked out of him right there. "Would you throw me that piece of rope?" Mack asked the girl, as she hurriedly got dressed. The girl cautiously did as she was asked and he tied the man's wrists and feet.

Mack trussed him up like the hogs they hunted back home. He was on his belly, so there was no place for him to go tied like that.

There was a bag on the dresser so Mack dumped it out on the bed. The small girl's eyes opened wide as she looked at what she had narrowly missed that night. That big boy sure did come equipped to play — inside the bag were handcuffs, other restraints and a ball gag.

As soon as Mack moved out of the passageway in the room, the girl said, "Thank you," and she was out the door like a scalded cat. She turned around, came back and kicked her customer in the head and spit on him.

Mack laughed at the assortment of toys the guy brought, he wondered if a fallen saddle maker friend of his might have made the equipment.

When that guy wakes up from his impact nap, he's surely gonna be loud and mad. I need my sleep, so I better take care of that. He grabbed the ball gag and crammed it in the guy's mouth, then cinched it tight. Handcuffs would be good insurance, so he used them, too. He put the key in his pocket. He added a fancy black leather blindfold to complete the ensemble.

Satisfied, he turned out the light and pulled the door shut as best he could. The inside was destroyed but there wasn't any damage to the outside other than the scuff mark from his boot, and it blended in pretty well with the other dirt so it wasn't apparent anything had happened here.

He calmly went back to his room and once again mounted the lumpy mattress. He fell asleep laughing at the surprise the maid would find in the morning.

11

Watch Out for Snakes

The eventful night caused Mack to sleep a little later than usual, but as soon as the New Mexico sun fell across his face he was ready and eager to meet the day. With a quick jump in the shower and a change of clothes, he was out the door. He didn't want to be in his room or anywhere near that motel when the unsuspecting maid walked in on her kinky discovery.

He paused at the door next to his as he was leaving. He could hear some skin-on-carpet scuffling sounds and muffled yelling but it wasn't loud enough to draw any attention. He looked around to make sure nobody was looking and stuck his head in the room. He couldn't resist. "How does it feel to be the bitch, big boy?" This threw the struggling thug into overdrive as he used his last bit of energy to try to get at Mack. Mack chuckled as he walked away.

He threw his bag in the truck and fired it up. He had places to be and people to see. Right now away from Santa Fe was tops on the list.

On his way out of town, he saw a handmade sign scribbled on a piece of plywood advertising tacos up ahead. A breakfast taco sounded pretty good at the moment, so when he got to the little travel trailer with a serving window cut in the side, he pulled off the road. He ordered an egg, chorizo and potato burrito with Hatch chilies in broken Spanish. Hatch chilies seemed to be the thing to eat in New Mexico. He figured the burrito and strong black coffee would at least get him on down the road and to the ranch.

He loved the dry high desert air and the smells of nature up here. Pinon Pine smoke seemed to be everywhere. He had the windows down and was soaking it all in as he drove. It seemed like the light was different up here, too. There was a different sort of clarity to it, like a woman singing on perfect pitch. Much better than Texas, where the air was heavy and the light was filtered by dust.

He'd read somewhere that Georgia O'Keefe, the painter, had moved here to paint just for this light. He could certainly see her point. Something about this part of the country made him feel very artistic. He was happy. Saddle designs and leather carving patterns ran through his mind as he watched the pastel colors of the desert flowing by.

He was well out of town, biding his time deep in thought when he passed an old man with a cane walking along the side of the road. He slowed down and thought, *What the hell was that?* as he looked in his rear view mirror. Sure enough, it was a bent over old man walking down the side of the road using a cane. He thought, *That can't be right,* and turned the truck around to see if the old guy needed some help. He laughed out loud when a movie title came to mind and he said out loud, "This ain't no country for old men."

He turned around again and pulled to a stop, just ahead of the old guy. He got out of the truck and walked toward the old Navajo man, who was dressed in the traditional way with a headband of purple cloth and a white shirt with blousy sleeves. His belt buckle was a huge turquoise and silver affair. Mack thought he was looking at a page from a calendar and asked him, "Mister, could you use a ride?"

The old Native looked at Mack a minute then gazed down the road. He took in a deep breath, huffed it out and then said, "I think I sure could."

Mack got the old Indian settled in the seat of the truck and got back on the road. He asked, "Where are you headed?"

"If you could just drop me at the trading post up the road a way, I'll bet my wife will be there. They have good coffee there and she sure does like coffee."

"If you don't mind me asking, what are you doing out here walking down the side of the road? This is a long way from anywhere."

"Well, my wife and I were going to get some pinion nuts over there." He pointed to a green area off to the east. "We started arguing about something, I don't even remember what. We stopped so I could take a leak, and before I could get back in the car she took off and left me on the side of the road."

He paused for a moment as if trying to figure it all out. "I guess it's all my fault. I never should've taken a high-spirited woman for my wife. It was a lot of fun at first. She was sure something to get ahold of. Now I have slowed down some but she hasn't. She's still real hot blooded. I think she must have some Apache blood in her I don't know about. Anyway, she will probably be calmed down by the time we get to the trading post. I sure do appreciate the ride. I was getting tired."

"No problem. I'm glad to help. What does your car look like in case we pass it going the other way? I wouldn't want to miss her if she's headed back for you."

"She won't come back. She's hardheaded. She will be up there drinking her coffee." And with that, the old Indian stared straight ahead. Apparently the conversation was finished.

Not knowing what else to say, Mack just drove in silence. He figured if the old guy wanted to talk he would. He didn't, so it was quiet in the truck. He closed his eyes and Mack thought he might be taking a nap but his lips were moving slightly like he was talking to himself.

The trading post came into view, and the old man said, "That's it right up there. I sure appreciate the ride. You seem like a real nice guy for a white man. You mind if I ask you something?"

"No, I don't mind at all. What do you want to know?"

"Are you in trouble or something? Were you in a fight?"

Mack was surprised by the question. As he pulled into the parking lot and stopped, he answered, "No, I'm not in trouble that I know of. I got in a fight last night but that's all over with. Why do you ask?"

"I'm confused. I am what your people call a medicine man. My people, the Diné, call me a singer. I know things most people don't. You seem like a good man and I think you are because you helped an old man when you didn't have to. When I close my eyes, I see two snakes. One is a big rattlesnake, as big as a man's arm, and the other is a light brown color but it has silver conchos like badges on it's back. This confuses me. I don't know what it means. Why would a good man have snakes around him? It means nothing good. If you had nine days, I could fix this for you."

Mack was confused, too. He didn't know what the old medicine man was getting at. "I don't know what it means either, but I do know I don't like snakes. I don't have nine days for you to fix it for me; I have to get on up to Cimarron to meet a friend. Do you see your wife here?"

The old Navajo man scowled as he thought about it, then his brow unwrinkled, as much as it could anyway, and he pointed to a faded green Ford LTD leaning to the right. "There's her car over there." He opened the door on the truck and said, "Thank you for the ride, my friend. Be careful of snakes on your travels. They can surprise you." He stepped out onto the red dirt and shuffled away.

He hobbled his way across the parking lot to his wife's old Ford and sat on the bumper to wait for her. Mack pulled back onto the highway, giving thought to the strange moment as he continued his journey. *Be careful of snakes is a pretty safe admonition for anybody.*

As the landscape started transitioning to brighter shades of green, Mack enjoyed the change of scenery. He'd about had enough of the pastel browns and pinks of the desert landscape. In the back of his mind he was still thinking about the snake warning and wondered if Sam might be able to decipher that symbolism for him. She knew many things and usually only talked about them if something came up in conversation.

He was always surprised at what she came up with, and the depth of her knowledge. She was being taught the old ways by a Sioux medicine man they'd met at a pow-wow in Fort Worth. She was a quick learner when she was interested in the subject.

He was deep in good thoughts of the girl he was headed to meet. He replayed the time when Sam found her Native mentor, Johnny Running Bull. Sam soaked up Johnny's teaching like a west Texas pasture in a rainstorm. She was a quick learner and was already picking up much of the language, to the delight of Johnny Running Bull.

She would talk about things so far out of Mack's grasp that he would just listen and smile. It made him happy to see her feel so good about what she was doing. Sometimes, when they rode horseback in the evenings, she would start singing Sioux songs. He didn't understand the words but it was a beautiful thing to experience. When she sang he didn't interrupt, he knew she was in her zone. Some things are like a sunrise and can't be adequately described — you just have to silently experience them.

It had been a while and he wanted those magic times back. He looked at his map, deciding to get on I-25 so he could stay out of the mountains. The only scenery he really wanted to see was his girlfriend.

12

MATCH MAKER

The map Sam had given him began at Springer. He went into
town to get his bearings then left again. The 4S ranch was
supposed to be ten miles out. He noted his odometer as he
left town, and when it showed he'd gone nine miles he started looking for it. A nondescript pipe gate with SSSS on it came up on his
right; it framed a white caliche road running off into the rolling
grasslands.

There were no ranch buildings in sight. There was nothing in
sight. Not a windmill, a pump house or a cow pen. Nothing. Since
the map showed it to be here he figured he might as well drive down
the white rock road till he found something or got told to leave.

After about fifteen minutes of seeing nothing but grass, he drove
up on a rise in the land that looked like it surrounded a bowl. As he
came up over the rise he beheld the headquarters of 4S Ranch. The
huge old main house looked out over ten out buildings. *These were
probably bunkhouses, offices and the cookhouse,* he thought.

Off to the side, and surrounded by probably a million dollars
worth of trucks and trailers, was a cutting horse arena with a giant
maze of cattle pens at the back of it. All of the horsemen were gath-
ered on one side of the arena, leaning against the fence as they listened to a presentation given by someone on horseback.

Mack parked his truck behind all the fancy rigs. He put on his cowboy hat, because the situation dictated proper headwear, not a fire department ball cap. He got out of his truck and ambled up to the crowd at the fence, marveling at the rigs as he went. *There's some money here.*

When he got there, he recognized it was Sam in the arena riding a sorrel gelding and putting him through his paces. She had on a wireless microphone and was all business as she rode around giving a play by play of what she was doing with the horse. She was pretty impressive in her demonstration. It was a side of her Mack had never seen. She was so professional sounding — completely different from the Sam he knew.

She concluded her class to a resounding round of applause. Mack made a point to note the comments filtering through the gathering of horsemen. "She sure knows her stuff." "I didn't know it could be done like that." "That's just common sense but I never thought of it that way." "She is so calm when she works, you can see the horse key off of that." Mack felt pretty proud to know her.

As the crowd dispersed for a break and a new instructor, Mack saw Jay Clayson. He had a black eye on the right and a crusty swollen left lower lip. He looked like he'd caught the losing end of something. Mack made his way over to him to say hi.

When he turned and saw Mack, Clayson had a hand in the cookie jar look on his face. He quickly tried an escape route, but he was boxed in.

Mack extended his hand saying, "Hey, Jay. I'd ask how are you but I can see that for myself. That's quite a shiner ya got there."

Jay nervously shook Mack's hand and did everything he could to not look him in the eye. "Hey, Mack. What a surprise to see you up here. Did you just get in?" He rubbed his eye and added, "Yeah, we, uh, hit an air pocket on the way up here and I took a hard lick to my head. They mean it about that seat belt sign." He gave an orchestrated chuckle then said, "Hey, I have to go check with this next presenter. Good to see ya."

He hurried off to blend into the crowd and Mack was left wondering what sort of stupid thing he'd got into that he was trying to cover up. Mack was entirely familiar with what an ass whipping looked like, and Jay sure didn't look like he got knocked around in his airplane.

He laughed about Jay's embarrassment and got on with his mission to find Sam. Saddle sales and hand shaking was pretty low on his list. He was here to see her. He looked for the biggest collection of riders, since he figured Sam would be in the middle of that crowd of hats after her successful presentation.

He found the herd of horsemen surrounding the female voice. Mack stood on the periphery, waiting for the crowd to get thin enough for him to get to Sam. When she finally saw him, she let out a visible sigh of relief and quickened her answers to all the questions from the remaining few admirers. The last guy finally filtered away, and with a hard edge to her voice she said to Mack, "Let's go over there, away from the crowd."

They got to the edge of the parking area and she turned to firmly hug his neck and bury her face in his shoulder. He didn't know what else to do but hold her till she broke her grip. Her eyes were full of anger and hurt as she looked at him. He asked, "What's wrong?"

"This has been the biggest disaster I've ever been involved in."

"What do you mean? It looks to me like you were a hit. I saw some of your presentation and you were great. You should've heard what they were saying about you in the crowd. Heck, you pretty much gave a second class right here with these guys."

She squatted down on the ground to stretch her back. Mack went down on her level too. "No it's not that, the class went okay. It was this whole trip right from the start."

"Was it a bad plane ride? I saw Jay and he said he got banged up on the plane in some turbulence."

She scoffed and said, "Hell yeah, he got banged up on the plane, but it wasn't because of turbulence."

Mack bristled as he read between the lines. His face took a serious cast as he cautiously said, "Tell me what happened."

She was relaxing around Mack but she was still trying not to lose control and let her full kettle of anger boil over. She took a deep breath and exhaled slowly, saying, "As soon as the airplane leveled out, Jay brought out the expensive whiskey. Who the hell drinks whiskey in the morning? I didn't want any but he kept pushing it on me, and that sort of pissed me off so I didn't drink any.

"Then he started talking about the horse business and all that. These clinics are a big deal now. They pay a lot of money and he said I ought to do more of them so I could become better known and probably get to be a celebrity on the circuit. Like that's something I would want to do. Yeah. I told him it wasn't that big a deal to me and the travel time would hurt my business at the ranch. That's when he started—"

"Started what?" Mack could feel the muscles in his back tensing in anger.

"He said travel time wouldn't be a problem. Do you know what the mile-high club is?"

Mack stood up and looked around for Jay. "Yeah, I think I do." He squatted back down beside Sam.

"Well, I didn't. He got up and I thought he was getting another drink but he got behind me and put his hands on my shoulders. He told me members of his mile-high club get to fly for free on his jet. So, travel wouldn't be a problem if I joined the club.

"I figured out what the mile-high club was when he slid his hands down onto my boobs. That's also when I popped him twice in the face."

Mack chuckled, his anger subsiding a little and he said, "I saw him, you got him pretty good."

"Yeah, I did. It sure made for a long plane ride to get here. But that's not the end of it. When I get here, I find out he told the other people that were supposed to be on the plane that they couldn't come. *And,* he reserved one of the bunkhouses here on the ranch just for him and me. He was pretty damn sure of himself.

"I walked right into a trap. I had to sleep in a horse trailer last night. I quit that shit a long time ago." She picked up a rock off the red barren ground, stood and angrily threw it, breaking a window on a hundred thousand dollar horse trailer. Her eyes got big as she said, "Oops, damn it!"

Mack stood, taking her hands. She looked at him with hurt in her eyes and said, "I just want to go home."

"Do you have anymore presentations to do here?"

"No, that's the real pisser. I don't have anything to do for the rest of the week. I'm gonna have to bum a ride back to Stephenville and I haven't found anybody that's leaving early."

"Well, I'm leaving right now. Hop in with me." He smiled at the thought.

"You sure that wouldn't mess up your plans? I sure would like to spend some time with you, that long ride in the truck is pretty appealing right now."

Mack knew now that to make any plans on this trip would be futile. The trip had to remain fluid and dynamic because it seemed the only plan was to change plans, but he was delighted at this change of plans.

He smiled and said, "Well, I'll tell you about how my plans have gone when we get on the road. Seems to me the best change of plans is to have you go the rest of this trip with me. We're gonna have some fun."

Sam hugged his neck with a new happiness at being rescued from a bad situation. "I'll go get my bag."

"I'm parked over there behind that 2-L truck pulling the grey and red trailer. I'll meet you there. I have to hit the little boy's room."

"Okay, I'll see you there," she said with a lilt in her voice.

Mack made his way through the crowd until he caught sight of Jay Clayson checking out the bruises on his right eye in a truck mirror. He walked up behind him and said, "Hey, Jay, have you seen Sam around here?"

Clayson spun in surprise at the sound of Mack's voice and nervously stuttered, "Uh, hey. No, Mack. I haven't seen her since her presentation."

"Well I have," Mack calmly replied and smashed his right fist powerfully into Jay's left eye. The impact snapped his head back against the truck hard enough to set off the car alarm. Mack looked down at the quivering Casanova huddled on the ground holding his bruised face and said just loud enough to be heard over the yelping alarm, "Let's just keep this to ourselves, like gentlemen. Whadaya say?"

Mack sauntered back to his truck feeling pretty smug. He hadn't hit a deserving man like that in a long time. *Damn, that felt good!* He got to the truck just as Sam walked up, carrying her bag. She threw it in the bed of the truck and got in. Mack slid in, and then pulled her to him and gave her a kiss, "Let's get on out of here."

On the way back out on the white rock road to the highway Sam said, "I'm so glad you came to rescue me. This would've been the week from hell if it wasn't for you." She slid across the seat and wrapped her arms around him. "I hope that slimy son-of-a-bitch gets what's comin' to him. Surely karma will bite him in the ass."

Mack broke a slight smile and started singing an old song., "Rocky Raccoon checked into his room, only to find Gideon's bible."

Sam looked up at him like he was on dope. *Where did that come from?* She was trying to figure it out when she saw the red scuffed knuckles on his right hand. Two and two added up and her jaw dropped. "You didn't! On the left side, too?"

Mack smiled and said, "Old Rocky Raccoon is gonna have some explaining to do about those matching eyes."

Being rescued then riding through New Mexico with Mack now cut through the merry go round blur of being a business owner and the detracting blur of responsibilities she could see how it was. They'd always had each other's backs, and she liked it that way.

OL' BOOGER AND BARNEY

The drive to Cimarron was too short as Mack readily received Sam's gratitude for saving her and leaving his exclamation mark on the event. Out on the wide-open New Mexico highway, she was relaxing and leaving all her preoccupations and business responsibilities back in Texas. She was in the moment, where Mack wanted her to be. He saw no need to interrupt the moment with stories of his trip up to this point. In a short thirty minutes, they were passing through Cimarron and on their way to the ranch just outside of town.

The gate to the Cross Bar Ranch was decorated with the sun bleached white skull of an elk and a rusty metal cutout of the brand. An elongated X was the cross and the single line of metal was the bar. The gate was open, so he knew his friend was at home. He continued up the rutted rocky road winding its way through the red sandstone hills to the ranch house. His dust cloud approach was noted by a pack of barking dogs of various makes and models that ran to meet the new visitor.

The dusty dry floorboards creaked as the man with the red beard stepped out on the porch of the old ranch house to greet his saddle-making friend. The clapboard house was original to the ranch and had been built in 1910. The wood for the house was milled from trees taken off the nearby mountain. The various colors the house had been painted could still be seen tenaciously adhering to the weathered grey wood. Each faded color represented a rancher's wife that had high hopes of sprucing up the place when she moved in. Each color was a failed effort. Paint lasted much longer than the women in this harsh country.

Booger Red Privett the Second stepped down off the porch and was grinning ear to ear as he ambled out to greet his friend and get an eye on his experimental saddles. Booger was the descendent of a long line of skilled horsemen. His great grandfather, for whom he was named, had started one of the first Wild West shows — Booger Red's Wild West Wagon Show. It had evolved from impromptu exhibition rides he would do on the roughest horses in the country to a full-blown show.

Legend had it he'd never been thrown from a horse and he had a standing offer of $100 cash money to anybody that could bring in a horse he couldn't ride. He never had to reach into his pocket on that bet.

His Christian name was Samuel Thomas Privett, Jr. An accident at an early age involving gunpowder and a hollow tree stump had severely disfigured his face and killed his friend. The cousin who hauled him to the doctor in a buckboard wagon said, "Doc, Red sure is boogered," and name stuck with him for the rest of his life.

When he was in the show ring of his Wild West show, he referred to himself as "Booger Red Privett, the ugliest man alive or dead." He figured if anybody was going to make fun of his face he'd just beat them to the punch. Booger Red the Second was well versed in this history and always had a good story ready about the famous old man. Mack enjoyed his stories about the old times and how it used to be.

Mack unfolded out of his truck and hollered, "Booger, how ya been? I sure am glad to finally get here."

"Mack, I been great! Better, now that you're here to show me them saddles." The two men shared a handshake as Sam walked around the front of the truck.

When Booger saw her, he dropped Mack's hand like it was a branding iron and immediately tipped his hat. "Ma'am, I didn't know Mack was going bringing along such pleasant company." He went to shake her slender hand with his calloused bear paw. "I'm Booger Red Privett, welcome to my ranch."

"My name's Samantha Nawaji. Nice to meet you. Do they really call you Booger?"

Booger laughed loudly and said, "Yep, that's what they call me — that or Booger Red. If I'm in trouble with the law, then it's generally Mr. Privett. I'm actually Booger Red the Second, named after my granddaddy. He was the first. I'll tell you all about him later." He winked at Mack and added, "Won't I, Mack?"

Mack looked at Sam and agreed, "He ain't kiddin'."

Sam laughed and said, "I've heard of your grandfather. Didn't he create the first Wild West show and was never bucked off a horse?"

Booger was shocked and wondered how she knew that bit of history. He removed his dust caked black hat, held it over his chest and said, "Ma'am, I don't know where you came from but I am truly impressed with your knowledge of the west."

She cracked an embarrassed smile and said, "I grew up on the Rosebud Reservation in South Dakota. I've been training horses most of my life, so I sort of keep up with stuff like that. If we don't keep up with the history then where does that leave us?"

Still amazed by this young woman, he looked at Mack and asked, "Are ya'll married?"

The couple looked at each other and laughing both said, "No," at the same time.

"Well, Mack, if you have a lick of sense you'll get back in that truck and run to town right now. I know where the Justice of the Peace lives. You need to marry this rare gem right now. I'll be the best man and we can run by the café to pick up Juanita for a matron of honor."

Mack snickered and said, "Aw, Booger, we'll get to that soon enough."

Sam spun her head and gave that "oh we will, will we?" look at Mack. He felt the water deepening around him and threw in a diversionary tactic. "We can't get married on an empty stomach. We didn't even have breakfast and I'm still waitin' for you to offer us a cold beer. I know you are hidin' some in there."

"Dadgum, you're right, Mack. This lovely lady has thrown me off my usual western hospitality. Pull them saddles out and set 'em on the porch railing so we can look at 'em while we eat. I got a smoked elk roast in there that will make some mighty fine sandwiches and I bet we can find that cold beer if we look hard enough. Sam, could you come in and help me? We got a lot to talk about, darlin.'"

Mack got the saddles out of the truck and put them on the porch railing. He shook his head and laughed to himself about how all his friends took an instant liking to Sam. She wasn't very outgoing but she had that thing about her that his kind of people liked and wanted to get to know better. He had the truck unloaded about the time they came back out onto the porch.

The screen door flew open with a kick, and Booger saying, "Now, that's just too hard to believe! Talk about a small world. Mack, you ain't gonna believe this! My granddaddy and Sam's granddaddy's brother used to work in the Wild West show together. We got to talkin' about the old times and put two and two together. Now, don't that beat all?"

Sam was beaming along with her instant new friend. "Before he married, my great uncle played a Chief in that Wild West show for about a year," Sam added. "I haven't thought about that in forever."

Mack had his eye on the sandwich coming his way but said, "That is hard to believe. Funny how things go in one big circle. I sure am glad you two met each other. My ears can take a rest," he said throwing a verbal jab at Booger.

Beers were cracked open and not much was said for about as long as it took to eat a sandwich. Booger went back in the house and returned with three fresh and sweaty bottles. Conversation switched from genealogy to new saddles at that point.

Booger went over the new saddles with a sharp eye. He knew Mack made a fine saddle but he wanted to try and catch any mistake. He went over the saddles like an English teacher with a red pen looking for a mistake. He couldn't find one.

"Dang, Mack, you made these just like I wanted. I wasn't too sure my scribblin' and directions were very plain but you hit it right dead center. I like 'em!"

Still wanting to keep Sam included, he turned to her and asked, "What do you think about them, Sam? You think they'll work on these no-withered ponies I'm runnin' out here? We go through a bunch of hills and rough country, that's why I wanted them designed like this."

Sam gave a disengaged look and said, "I don't know much about making a saddle and I don't know how he works his magic, but if Mack made it, it'll work. He makes the best I've ever ridden. All I know about saddles is they need to fit the horse and my butt."

"Well you bein' a big time horse trainer and all, I thought you might have a more intimate knowledge."

"Nope, I'm more concerned with what's under the saddle."

Booger was deep in thought as he continued to evaluate the projects. When he completed his thought he snapped his big head around and asked, "Speaking of horse training, you ever done any work with mules?"

Besides the one I'm sitting beside? she thought but didn't say. "I've ridden a couple before. They're real smart, sometimes too smart. You just have to be smarter than them and figure out how to get inside their heads, then it's pretty easy."

"Hmm, I got one out there in the pen that must be an Einstein. I'm getting nowhere with him," Booger lamented. "He's got plenty of potential, I just got to figure out how to get him goin' my way..." He was distracted as he finished his thought, and his words sort of trailed off as he gazed to the south.

Sam didn't pick up on the change in Booger or what he saw but Mack did. He, too, kept his eye on the small dust cloud coming up from the south.

"Well, with mules it's good to start with ground work. Sack them out to take the edge off and then get them to responding to the bit..." She noticed nobody was listening anymore.

Buster reached inside the screen door to get his Winchester 94 rifle. The old gun had most of the bluing rubbed off and the wood had seen better days from spending so much time in a saddle scabbard. He leaned the rifle against the wall behind his rocking chair, within easy reach. Sam looked at the gun then in the direction the men were looking and noticed the dust cloud for the first time.

"Do guns bother you any, girl?" Booger asked.

"Only when they're pointed at me."

Booger chuckled under his breath saying, "Atta girl. This probably ain't nothin' but I wasn't expectin' nobody. Better ta have one and not need it, than need one and not have it. There's been some weird goings-on out this way lately. Mack, did you leave that gate open?

"Yes, sir. Just like I found it." Proper western etiquette dictates leaving a gate like you found it.

The pack of hounds tuned up just about the time the sheriff's patrol car appeared at the base of the building cloud of dust. Booger hollered at them, sending them all back into the shade of the barn and to the cool refuge under the house. Booger took a seat back in his rocker and said, "Well, let's just see what this yayhoo wants."

"What did you get into now, Booger?" Mack asked.

"Nothing that I know of lately. I figured the statute of limitations has all run out on the rest," he said as he kept a watchful eye on the car.

The black and white patrol car with the old style light bar slid to a stop behind Mack's truck. The dust cloud billowed and thankfully was carried off to the east by the slight breeze. The three on the porch sat looking at the sheriff sitting in his car looking at them.

He finally broke the standoff and got out. He adjusted the cheap straw hat on his head and the gun belt under his overhanging gut. As he ambled toward the porch, he paid particular attention to Mack's truck as he passed.

Without getting out of his chair, a slight social statement, Booger Red said, "Hey, sheriff. What brings you out this way today?"

The sheriff stood at the base of the porch steps, waiting to be invited up into the shade. When he didn't get his invitation he said, "Mr. Privett, I'm out here on business. Who are your friends here? I don't think I've seen them around these parts before." He cocked his head to get his hat to provide just a little more shade and rested his forearm on the Smith & Wesson model 27 .357 Magnum holstered on his hip.

"These are some of my friends up from Texas, as you probably noticed when you passed the truck," Booger said, lobbing a volley in this game of verbal Ping-Pong. "Mack here is a saddle maker. He made the fine saddles you see here. And this is his lovely girlfriend, Sam." Each gave the customary nod of acknowledgement. "So what's this business you got to talk about?"

"Mr. Privett, I hear you're one of the best trackers in this country."

"You heard right," Booger replied, staring down his nose.

"I've received a report of two lost hikers, a man and a woman, over in the Valle Vidal area. I'm putting together a search party to go out in the morning and I was wondering if I could include you."

"So, you're askin' for my help?" Booger felt obliged to use the word help since the sheriff had neglected to.

Mack noticed from behind the sides of the mirrored sunglasses the corners of the sheriff's eyes squinted, signaling the impact of Booger's verbal arrow. "Mr. Privett, if we could count on you being there with your horse it would be a great help," he grudgingly said.

"Well, I reckon we could be there. I have to check with my company, sheriff. Is that okay with you, Mack?"

Mack looked at Sam, and she gave him the *okay with me* shoulder shrug. Mack said, "Sure, okay by me."

"Where do you want us to meet up, sheriff? I expect this won't be takin' too long, will it?"

The Sheriff was getting impatient with the minimal respect and import of the situation he was receiving. Plus, the sun was getting pretty hot. His crisp khaki tan uniform was losing its crease and his bright shiny badge, shining like a silver concho on a new saddle, was beginning to droop. He impatiently said, "We'll be meeting at the trail head in the Valle Vidal at 7 a.m. It shouldn't last too long, they couldn't have gone far."

"Well, we'll see you there. On your way out, would you mind shutting my gate? It'll save me a trip. We're closed for the evening."

With that, the sheriff quickly turned and retreated to the air-conditioned refuge of his patrol car. Passing back by Mack's truck, he tilted his head and paid close attention to the license plate. As he walked, he took a notepad out of his shirt pocket and jotted a note, then slyly slipped it back in his pocket as he opened his car door and got in. Having never shut off the engine, he dropped it into gear and took his dust cloud back to the south.

The three friends silently watched from the cool shade of the porch as the patrol car bounced its way down the red rutted road. The quiet was broken by the braying of the mule in the pens.

Booger chuckled. "One jackass bidding farewell to another." The porch erupted in laughter as Booger added, "How about another beer? I need somethin' to get the taste of that discussion out of my mouth. That fat Barney Fife outfit just really wads my shorts."

"He really doesn't make a very good first impression does he?" Mack asked. "I've worked with those kinds of cops before, and they always want to be large and in charge."

Booger stood in the doorway of the house and said, "That's it exactly. He wants to be the big fish in this little pond. All his deputies are a bunch of goobers." He went in the house and yelled back, "But that's neither here nor there. We got bigger fish to fry! We got stories to tell and saddles to try!"

He came back out onto the porch carrying three brown bottles of cold goodness and said, "Speaking of asses, Sam would you mind showing me some things about that mule after the sun drops a little?"

The third beer usually flipped on Sam's limit light. She was loosening up and said, "Sure, Booger. I think I can line out your ass with no trouble at all."

This coming from the fairly quiet girl he had just met surprised the big red headed mountain man. With amusement in his voice he retorted, "Darlin', I think you and me are gonna get along just fine."

14

LOOKING FOR
WHAT'S NOT THERE

After breakfast, the two horsemen tested the new saddles for fit on the horses they would be riding in the search. While they checked the physical fit, Sam watched how the horses reacted. She was working the emotional end of it.

Mack told Booger Red, "These saddles fit just like they were made for these horses." Then he jokingly asked, "Who was it did such a fine job building them?"

Booger laughed a little and said, "I got them from some old Mexican working in his barn down in Texas. I guess they'll do. What do you think, Sam? Ya think they'll work?"

He led the horses to the trailer and hollered, "They better fit us, too, I bet we're gonna be coverin' some ground today. There's plenty of places out there to get lost or hurt."

"I think ya'll will do just fine," Sam interjected. "It looks like the horses are fine with them and I've never heard a human complain about one of Mack's saddles."

As he eased the gate closed on the horse trailer Mack said, "She's right, Booger. I got a new machine in the shop I was gonna tell you about. It's new technology. They call it the ass-o-matic. I program in the customer's height, weight, pants size, diet, geographical location and general disposition. It gives me a 3D printout showing different parameters of consideration to be used in the shaping of the ground seat for the saddle. Science says these saddles are going to fit us very well. Who are we to argue with science?"

Booger Red knew full well that Mack shaped the ground seats by hand and his hands were guided by intuition and years of using a skiving knife. Technology and phraseology were lost on Booger Red. The only response he could muster was a grunt and, "Get in the truck, smart ass." Booger leaned out the driver's side window and said, "I sure appreciate you working with that mule while we're gone, Sam. Don't wear yourself out doin' it. He can be hard headed. We ought to be back just after lunch, I hope."

Mack and Sam shared an embrace. He kissed her and told her, "I ought to be back pretty soon, hope you have fun with that mule."

She hugged him back and said, "I ought to, I have fun with this one." With a laugh and a wink she slapped him on the butt and pushed him toward Booger's old truck. Mack got in smiling and the rattling truck and trailer were off in a red cloud of dust.

They got to the gate on the road and he said, "Well at least the sheriff had the decency to close the gate last night, western ways are *not* his strong suit."

Mack got out and opened the gate and after the truck and trailer were through it he closed it. It was ingrained in him to always leave a gate like you found it.

He got back in the truck and Booger continued, "I don't know what the deal is with that sheriff. I just can't put my finger on it. He always wants to be in everybody's business. Says he's keepin' a close eye on the town. I just don't buy that. Seems like he's not showin' all his cards. His deputies are a bunch of flunkies. Any time we get one out here that has any sense about being a lawman, he don't last long.

The good ones head out to Santa Fe or Albuquerque looking for better money, I guess."

As they headed down the road to the foothills of the low mountains ahead, Mack agreed, "He struck me as sort of strange too. I've met a lot of lawmen over the years. He sure seemed tense, more like a city cop than a county sheriff. Maybe you just intimidate him, Booger."

A laugh came from deep inside Booger and as it erupted, the red bearded cowboy wearing the ripped plaid shirt and dusty chaps could barely get out, "Well, I *am* a rather striking fellow."

He caught his breath from laughing and said, "Enough about me." He squinted a serious look at Mack and asked, "Tell me how a rag-tag such as yourself scored a fine woman like Samantha. I tell you what, she's really something."

Mack chuckled and said, "Hell, I don't know. I ask myself the same question. She trains horses down at Stephenville and she started coming around cozying up to me. I figured she was just lookin' to get a good price on saddle repair and such. I got to noticin' she wasn't actin' like that around other guys though, then the light came on. I've always been pretty dumb about noticin' women gettin' next to me.

"Anyway, we just started hangin' around together like friends, and then one thing led to another and here we are. The cool thing is, we're a couple but it's like we're just still friends, too. I can't explain it, man, but I sure ain't gonna question it."

Booger had a concentrating look about him as he listened to Mack. "Man, that's rare. What little I know 'bout women tells me you got a gold mine there. That just don't happen very often."

"Oh, I know. You ain't tellin' me nothin' new. She's really somethin'. I'm glad to have her with me on this trip 'cause she needed it and I did, too. She inherited a ranch from a friend of ours, ole Buster Crabtree, then she bought the horse operation next door. All that business responsibility is really coverin' her up. She thinks she's the only one that can run it right, so she's been real busy doin' that.

"I pretty much got slid to the back of the line and that's not a real good place to be. But then I've been real busy, too. We both needed to get out of town, away from it all, and remember where we were. I hope this trip'll get her back around me and put me back at the front of the line."

"It looks to me like it's goin' your way. Her eyes sure light up around you. But I tell ya, pard, you drop your guard just a little and I'm gonna take her away from ya." He laughed and slapped Mack on the shoulder.

"You'll have a hell of a time doin' that, my friend."

They were laughing at Booger's veiled threat when their old Ford pickup pulling a rickety, rusty horse trailer rolled into the parking lot at the trailhead. There were about a dozen civic-minded individuals that had nothing better to do today than walk around looking for the lost hikers there already. They all had matching yellow T-shirts emblazoned with SEARCH.

There were also two dog handlers standing off to the side trying to keep their dogs calm around the crowd. Those dogs knew they were there to work, and they were anxious to get to it.

In the middle of the group stood the sheriff and his deputy. In his baggy uniform the deputy looked like he had a pass from high school for the day. The sheriff was doing his best to look important and preside over the small search party while he distributed the gridded maps that organized the search. Mack had seen it all before, the air was full of good intentions but without firm direction the whole affair could turn into a screwed up mess.

The sheriff seemed to have a loose handle on it and Mack wasn't going let on that he had extensive training in search and rescue tactics. The Fire Department had spent some bucks on him and a few others and sent them to Texas A&M for urban search and rescue training, wildland search and rope rescue. They also sent them to New Braunfels, Texas for swift water rescue training. He'd done so well that the Parks and Wildlife Department in Texas had asked him to develop their protocols for wildland search and rescue.

Mack watched the circus from horseback on the sidelines and thought, *If they get in a tight spot, I'll step in. Right now, though, I just don't feel the love.*

The two searchers were saddled up and ready to ride. They had saddlebags packed with snacks and bottles of water. Mack had his Ruger 45, too. He was operating on Booger's principle of *better to have it and not need it.*

The sheriff handed a map to his deputy and pointed toward them. The deputy walked over, trying to look as official as possible. He handed the map to Booger Red, saying, "You're working in quadrant 1A and 2A. This is rough country so I'd advise you to be prepared."

Booger Red took a look at the map and snorted, "Hell, son, I've run that country naked and barefoot. Shouldn't be no problem." He handed the map to Mack and asked, "Whadaya think, Mack?"

"No step for a stepper my friend." For Mack reading a topographical map was as simple as reading the phone book.

Booger spun his horse and said, "Let's ride."

The deputy raised his arms up over his head in an official manner and said, "Hold on there! The group will go to the hikers' campsite to evaluate it and then disperse from there. This is an organized search."

So, the two contrarians fell in behind the group, slow walking the horses as they hiked the two miles up the trail to the hikers' last known location. When the group got there, the sheriff went into a speech as to the direction the man and woman supposedly traveled out into the rough country, and listed travel distances along with timelines. They hadn't checked out at the ranger station as required and now were missing in the wilderness.

He had it all figured out on paper. He said he doubted seriously that they went up the trail into the mountains, so the search would all be within the defined quadrants. A helicopter from the Park Service was due in this afternoon.

Mack just couldn't follow that thought process. *Why would two hikers wander out into what looked like the devil's playground?*

The campsite appeared to a basic minimalist backpacker-type site. A small two-man Mountain Hardware tent, North Face jackets; one blue the other pink, and sleeping bags were in the tent. Two good quality Osprey backpacks and a small MSR liquid fuel stove were in front of the tent. A collapsible water bag hung close by. They'd left behind a bag of freeze dried food packs, making it look like they were going on a day hike and were figuring on being back that night. Jackets left in the tent also pointed to that conclusion.

The sheriff pointed out all of what he considered influential evidence and told the crews to go search their quadrants and report back to the trailhead. If anyone found anything they were to report in on the cheap walkie-talkies they were issued.

One thing that had attracted Mack's attention and evidently evaded the sheriff's was the two empty fly rod cases leaning against the tent. As the crews were leaving to go on patrol, he leaned out of the saddle toward Booger and quietly said, "I think they went uphill to that lake on the map." He nodded his head toward the empty fishing rod cases.

Booger looked over then went back to looking straight ahead. He snuck out a, "Mmm-hmm"

They urged their horses to follow the group, but lagged behind a little. When the law boys were out of sight, they both simultaneously turned around and went back to the camp. When they got to the tent site, Booger said, "'I see,' said the blind carpenter, so he picked up his hammer and saw. A blind idiot could see they went fishing — but not that sheriff. Let's head that way. Barney might write us a ticket for not following his cherished grid system but I bet we find those folks. Heck, the fish may be in a feeding frenzy and they just didn't want to come back. I hope so, I'm getting tired of eating elk."

"I agree. They went fishing. Even so, the country up higher is a hell of a lot prettier than that rough stuff down low. It'll be a better ride."

Since he was the bona fide tracker, Booger took the lead and Mack brought up the rear. The grizzled mountain man got down to business, going slow and methodical as they progressed up the trail.

Since Booger was on point, Mack just followed along till he was needed. He was soaking up surroundings he hadn't seen in some time. The dry high desert was slowly evolving into mountain pines and green grass meadows. The air was cooler, sweeter and lacked that dusty smell it had down lower.

It amazed him how the change in elevation could bring about such drastic changes in the mountains. He was looking all around when a loud creak of saddle leather got his attention. Looking up ahead, he saw Booger getting down out of his saddle. "Ya got something up there, Booger?"

"Looks like a candy wrapper or something," he as he walked on into the brush.

Suddenly two chipmunks were fighting over a pinion nut behind Mack and he turned to watch. The battle was interrupted by, "Son. Of. A. Bitch!" He turned to see Booger dancing a jig and slinging a snake around by the tail then popping it like a bullwhip, causing snake innards to decorate the surrounding trees.

"What the hell, Booger! Did he get ya?"

"Bastard got me just above my boot top! Well that just pisses me off, man!" He cut the rattles off the snake's tail and slung the offending serpent off into the brush. He pulled his chaps back and rolled his pants above his knee to reveal two small punctures at the top of his calf, just below his knee. "I don't know how he made it through my chaps, but he damn sure got me. He was a big smart one, so I bet he didn't give me much juice. He was just giving me a warning. It's those little dumb ones you gotta worry about, they don't hold back."

Mack got off his horse to examine the bite. There were two small punctures over an inch and a half apart trickling just a little blood. "Yep, he popped you all right. We better go get that looked at. Even if he didn't give you a full dose, you're gonna be sick. Are you up on your shots like tetanus and all that? You gotta go to town, pard. Let's head back to the truck."

Mack understood what Booger was saying about the big ones holding back with their venom. It wasn't going to eat Booger. It was just telling him to get out of its living room. Still, Mack was concerned for his friend.

"Naw, I'll be all right. I stay up on my tetanus shot pretty regular, with my active lifestyle and all. I been bit so many times I'm starting to build a resistance to it, but yeah it's gonna make me sick. It sort of makes me weird sometimes. It's a long way from my heart and down low, so I think I can make it to the truck. It's only a couple of miles. You go on and get up to the lake. If I ain't back at the trailhead this evening, just hobble the horse and turn him out to graze. We'll come back for him in the morning. Catch a ride back to the ranch with somebody." Booger did not appear the least bit worried about his predicament.

Booger turned his horse downhill to leave, and Mack rode beside him for a way. "Are you sure? This could be sort of serious."

He waved Mack off, saying, "Aw hell, Mack, it would kill a normal man but I reckon I'll be all right. You go on. It won't take you very long."

"Okay, then. If that's what you think, but I'm gonna make it quick. Put some ice on that bite at the truck. I ought to be back in an hour, then we'll go to town." Booger rode back down the trail as Mack turned his horse and continued up. *That is one tough redheaded son-of-a-bitch.*

He urged his pony up the trail and rode slow, looking for any sign on the trail heading up to the lake. Mack, impromptu tracker, didn't know diddly about tracking so he just used common sense, what he'd learned in his classes and seen on TV shows. He didn't know what he was looking for, just something out of the ordinary. The classes he'd taken had not really covered man tracking.

The road was hard packed, so seeing any tracks was out of the question. The edges of the road were pushed up dirt, so maybe he could see where they left the road, if they did. He looked at that stuff just because he thought he should, but after seeing the empty fishing rod case, his money was on them being at the lake fishing. Or at least around some water somewhere.

As Mack meandered his way up over a little rise, he looked up to see the beautiful little mountain lake. It was about fifty acres of crystal blue water, postcard perfect. He could see trout dimpling the surface as they fed, but he saw no people around the shoreline. There was a little stream cascading into the lake off to his left. It looked like a place a hiking fisherman would go if he wanted to drop a line on an unsuspecting trout.

As he rode his horse around the shoreline, he stayed well back from the muddy bank. There were footprints in the mud from fishermen. It looked like the lake was fairly popular but there was no one in attendance today. A big paw print got his attention. Probably a bear or big cat. He didn't know how to identify either but he was sure glad he had his old Ruger revolver in his saddlebag. If there was a threat, he knew his horse would know before him and he'd have time to get it out.

When he got to the stream flowing down the hill, he turned uphill to follow it. There wasn't too much brush so his horse had easy passage. Up higher, he could see what looked like a beaver pond with a nice waterfall dropping into it. As he got closer, he could hear splashing, louder than the mountain run-off water falling into the pond. He wondered if that bear was up there looking for a fish dinner. His horse wasn't showing alarm and he trusted him, so Mack went on up to inspect the sound.

There in the boiling turbulence of the hydraulic beneath the waterfall was a man thrashing the water, struggling to stay afloat. His weakening struggle and the look on his face told Mack the guy was losing the battle. Mack uncoiled his lariat rope from his saddle, hopped the horse forward and yelled, "Grab the rope!" as he threw it toward the struggling victim.

The loop fell cleanly over the man and Mack dallied the rope on the saddle horn and backed the horse up, pulling the man to the bank. The exhausted and frozen fisherman lay in the shallow water, trying to get a breath of the sweet mountain air. He wore an olive drab T-shirt and waders. Evidently he'd slipped and fallen into the waterfall. His waders had filled with water and were a killing adversary he couldn't free himself from. When this happens it's a difficult predicament to get out of. Mack figured he also had hypothermia since the water was like liquid ice.

His extended arms still clutched the rope like his life depended on it. His quivering muscled arms were covered with tattoos and when he rolled over he had a fighting knife fastened to his wader suspenders. This was not your average recreational fisherman.

15
NEW FRIEND

Mack dismounted to take his rope off of the grateful fisherman. He was coiling it up when the guy opened his exhausted eyes. He looked up at Mack and said, "I sure am glad you came along. I was going down for the third time. Thank you, I sure appreciate it."

Mack smiled as he hung his rope back on the saddle. "Sure thing, bud. I can always use a little roping practice. You think you're gonna be okay?"

"Yeah, I'll be all right. I just gotta warm up a little." He slid the suspenders off his shoulders and clawed his way up the creek bank, sliding out of the cursed waders as they lay heavy on the ground. He sat there and said, "Man, that water's cold. I hate being in cold water." He tried to stand, but his cold stiff legs argued for him to stay seated. He agreed.

Mack squatted down beside him and asked, "I'm up here lookin' for a couple of missin' hikers. You seen anybody up this way in the last few days?"

He thought on the question a minute and said, "Yeah, I saw a man and a woman up at the lake a couple of days ago. They came in and fished a while, and then went back down the trail. They've been the only ones I've seen for a few days. I see everybody that comes in or out. This is my valley."

Mack wondered who he was dealing with here. The reference to *my valley* pointed toward some sort of mountain man recluse, but he sure didn't appear to be that. The beard said yes but the full sleeve of tattoos on each arm said no. So he asked him, "I didn't see a vehicle anywhere around. How'd you get up here?"

He struggled to stand on frozen legs while he replied, "Aw, I just got up here that's all. It's nice up here. I like it." Then he asked, "You said you were up here lookin' for those hikers. Are you a local cowboy or a government tracker? I haven't seen you around before." He finished by eying Mack with suspicion.

Mack laughed and said, "No, I'm from Texas. I was just up here deliverin' some saddles I made for a friend of mine. We got volun-told by the sheriff to assist with a search for those hikers. My buddy got snake bit back down the trail, so he headed back. I figured I'd come on up here to check it out before I went back."

Still wary, the tattooed man asked, "If your buddy got bit by a snake why didn't you go with him to get help?"

Mack sensed the suspicion, it caused him to wonder what this guy's story was. "He said he could handle it and insisted that I come on up here. Looks like it was a good thing I did."

The man chuckled and said to himself and partly to Mack, "All I been through and I get my ass saved by a saddle maker from Texas."

Mack heard him and wondered what he meant by *all I been through,* the mystery of the man was deepening. "Well, I'm a fireman and a paramedic, too. In case you need to validate your rescue."

Realizing his muttering had been heard, he apologized. "Oh, man, I'm sorry. I didn't mean it in a bad way. Really. I'm sure glad you came up this way. Fireman, huh? My name's Toby Fredericks by the way." He extended his hand to Mack. "Most of my friends call me Turtle."

Mack returned the strong handshake. "Glad to meet you, Turtle. My name's Mack. How in the world did you get a nickname like Turtle? You sure don't look too slow." Mack had noticed the wet clothing clinging to the guy's big chest, bulging biceps and his well-defined thighs.

Turtle laughed and said, "That's a long story, my friend. How about a cup of coffee?"

Knowing the rest of the story might be forthcoming Mack said, "That'd be great. I sure could use one."

Turtle untangled his fly rod from the surrounding bushes and took it apart so he could make it through the woods easier — through the woods was his preferred avenue. He picked up his waders by the boots and emptied the water on the ground. On the creek gravel at his feet flopped a twelve-inch rainbow trout. He laughed and observed, "Well at least I got dinner out of the deal."

Without another word, he gave the hand signal to follow. Mack did but his horse was having a difficult time in the low tangled brush. "Is there a more open path to that coffee? My horse is having a time with this brush."

Surprised by the request, Turtle said, "Oh yeah, man. Sorry about that. I didn't think of him. Follow the creek down to the open land, then cross over the creek and go about a hundred yards along the tree line. I'll meet you over there." With that directive, he silently melted into the surrounding forest.

Mack couldn't even hear him making his way through the tangled mass. *This is a man with a great skillset for the woods, or else he is part Mule deer.*

Mack followed the directions, making his way around the grassy open perimeter of the lake. He didn't move fast but he didn't move slow either. When he got to what he thought was probably a hundred yards, he slowed a little to look for a path. He passed a big bush and was surprised to hear Turtle's voice, "Come on up in here, Mack, and tie your horse in this clearing back here. He should be fine there."

How in the world? Mack led his horse around the bush and saw Turtle standing in a little clearing that was well shielded from the lake below. He wasn't even breathing hard. "How did you make it through that stuff so quick?" Mack asked. "I was walking at a pretty good clip, and you still beat me."

Turtle shrugged and said, "I got my ways, I guess. Come on up here." He waited for the horse to be tied then he took off through the brush again. After about seventy-five yards of busting brush, the two men came to a little flat spot against a rock escarpment. A little camp was set up there, and it had a permanent look to it. The bush craft shelter looked well built and weather tight. The minimal necessities were set up in an organized fashion in close proximity to the shelter. The ground around the camp had been rubbed clean of vegetation, showing the camp had been in use for a while.

Mack was interrupted in his observations by his host saying, "Welcome to my home. Let me get that coffee going."

"Nice set up you got going here. Looks like you've been here a while."

As he worked at getting the coffee going, he said, "Thanks, it's homey. I guess I've been up here a year, maybe a year and a half — something like that. So, you're a fireman from Texas, huh? I'm from Texas, too. Where are you from?"

"No kidding? I'm from Stephenville. Where're you from?"

"Corpus Christi. I joined the Navy right out of high school and I've never been back."

Take note of incoming facts, Mack thought. "Oh, yeah? I've fished all that water from Corpus down to Port Mansfield. I really like it down that way."

"I've been to Port Mansfield. Nice place, man. No other place like it. My buddy and I used to take my dad's boat and fish all the way down there and back, we'd be gone a week. We did that a lot. We'd take about three days down, then get a room there at the Harbor Bait Store to sleep and shower the salt off, then fish our way back. It was a blast. I was really a son of the sea." Then he added with a hint of wistfulness, "But that was a long time ago."

Mack knew the room he was talking about well, he'd had a pivotal moment in his life there with Samantha. The memory caused him a moment of regret that things weren't as good now as they were back then on that deck over the water. Still curious about his new friend he asked, "So, is that why you joined the Navy, you were a son of the sea?"

"Yeah, you know join the Navy, see the world and all that crap. My best friend and I joined on the buddy plan." Trying to divert attention away from himself he asked, "How long have you been a firefighter? That seems like a really cool job. I really admire ya'll." The coffee was ready so he poured Mack a cup in a tin can with the top cut off. He poured himself a cup in an old beat-up tin cup.

Mack took his coffee and said, "Thanks, I've been doing it for eighteen years. It's a hell of a job. It's got its ups and downs but overall it is great. Can't see myself doing anything else. Are you doing anything now? I guess you're out of the Navy."

Turtle stared off down the valley and said, "Right now, I pretty much just watch this valley. I'm up here by myself and I like it like that." He thought a minute then got back to the conversation, "You know, one of the guys on my team was a fireman before he got in the Navy. He had some great stories. Ya'll do some crazy stuff. I just can't see myself running into a burning building though, that shit'll get you killed. I met some firemen at a funeral for a friend of mine that were playing the bagpipes. They were cool guys and real easy to talk to. It was like I was talking to my buddies — they knew what I was talking about."

"Do you ever get off the mountain?" Mack asked, trying to get away from the fireman stuff and get this guy to tell his story.

"No, I don't see any need to. A friend of mine brings me some supplies every now and then. He's the only one who knows I'm up here. He got thrown off his horse up here one day and I saw it happen. I went and helped him because I'd seen him up here a lot before. Sometimes, we sit and talk. Keep it safe, you know. But that friend of mine, he makes up for not talking to anybody — that guy can talk your ear off. His name's Booger Red. He was named after his grandpa, some famous cowboy. He has a million stories."

Mack was astonished at the small world. "You gotta be kiddin' me. Booger Red is who I was coming up here with. He's the one that got snake bit. He didn't tell me anything about you bein' up here."

"That's because I made him swear not to tell. I don't want people to know. Man, that is just crazy that you're friends with Booger. Is he gonna be okay from that bite?" Turtle seemed to warm up a little more to his new friend at this revelation.

"He seemed to know how to deal with it, so I just followed his lead. I'm a paramedic but I've never dealt with a snake bite and he has. I figure he knows what's best for him. I'm gonna go check on him this evening. I'll tell him you said hello. It'll get his goat when he finds out I know one of his secrets. It's my secret too, by the way."

He had a serious look on his face when he said, "I appreciate that."

Mack looked Turtle straight in the eye as they spoke and saw a man who'd seen things that couldn't be unseen, and done things that couldn't be undone. Things like that changed a man's eyes and marked them as members of a secret society of hard men.

With the connection established, Mack had to satisfy his curiosity, "Tell me how a guy that was so in tune with the ocean ends up here on a mountain." He purposely left out the word hiding.

Turtle looked at the ground, rubbing and wringing his hands. He haltingly answered, "Well, Booger knows all this stuff anyway so I guess I might as well tell you, being that you're a firefighter and you saved my life and all. As long as you can keep the secret." He raised his head and squared his shoulders. "Like I said, my buddy — his name was Freddy — and I joined the Navy because we loved the ocean. We got assigned to a ship and the first six months was a blast, but being stuck on a ship can get pretty old after a while. We wanted to see more action so we decided to volunteer for the SEAL program. We thought we were pretty tough and we could swim real good, so we figured it was a no-brainer. Being a SEAL is about the coolest thing there is."

Mack was intent on hearing the story now. "Yeah, those are the toughest guys around, from what I've heard."

"Yeah, they're tough. That training was the hardest thing I've ever done in my life and those instructors just dance through it every day like it's nothing. Just getting ready to be considered was awful. That's how I got my nickname, Turtle. We were doing a ten-mile run with full packs and it was kicking my ass. I only thought I was in good shape.

"At the end of that run my legs gave out on me but I wasn't going to quit. My friend was right beside me, screaming at me to make me keep going. I crawled over the finish line. Under that full pack they said I looked like a turtle. You probably know how that goes, the name stuck. But anyway, I got in better shape — I had to."

He stopped to pour himself another cup of coffee then walked over to his shelter. He pulled a piece of venison jerky out of a coffee can and offered Mack some, but he declined. Turtle drank his coffee and chewed the dried meat as he thought about how to continue. Mack felt there was a bigger story coming on, so he kept silent to let the man think.

Turtle looked at Mack with hard and heavy eyes that had seen so many things and said, "You know that stuff they say about Mother Ocean and all that?"

Mack nodded. "Yeah."

Looking Mack straight in the eye for emphasis he said, "Well, that's a bunch of crap. Mother Ocean is a bitch. She's a beautiful woman that will draw you in and make you fall in love with her, and then she will kick you in the balls, take everything you got, and leave you crying in the sand like some little boy."

He broke the stare, paused, dropped his head and then continued, "We were on small craft maneuvers late one night. We had to paddle off shore forever then bail out of the boat and swim back. My friend Freddy was my swim buddy, and somewhere during the swim he slipped under and never came back up. Just like that he was gone, just gone, man. I searched for him out there in the dark but I couldn't find him. That bitch took him from me. That's why I'm up here on this mountain. I want to be as far away from that bitch of an ocean as I can be."

It was quiet in the secluded camp for a while as the weight of the information sank in. Mack had no idea why the soldier was opening up to him. He didn't know what it was like to be a soldier but he did know debilitating loss, and he knew that well. Maybe it was because he was a firefighter and in some small way could relate to loss or maybe Turtle was lonely and needed to vent his burden to someone. He certainly hoped it wasn't because his new friend had lost his mind in his self-imposed seclusion. Whatever the case, Mack listened and let Turtle reveal his story at his own pace.

"I crawled out of that cold damn water and I was headed directly to the bell. I was going to hit that bastard three times and DOR (drop on request) right there. I was finished. One of the instructors saw me though, and he got in my face and told me about loss in a not so sensitive way. He had lost more close friends, in worse circumstances, than I had ever had. He said he wasn't going to let me DOR and he was going to make me into a Navy SEAL."

Turtle took a stick and scratched in the dirt a while as he replayed the past in his mind and thought about what he was going to say next. He threw the stick and said, "That hard-nosed son-of-a-bitch did me three favors though. He got me through BUD/S and I finished in the top half of my class. I don't know if he had anything to do with it but I also got sent far away from the ocean. I ended up on a mountain in Afghanistan." He laughed a low laugh and looked up from the dirt.

"What was the third favor?"

"He redirected my grief about Freddy into anger." His eyes squinted and his face took on a fearsome chiseled look that made Mack uncomfortable. "That anger rained down on those rag-headed sons-of-bitches like fire from heaven. I was a sniper and my team had an overwatch of a valley. A valley a lot like this one. We kept it safe, at least as safe as it could be. We were *very* good at what we did. Doing that was the most important thing I've ever done in my life and I was really good at keeping my brothers safe. I did that job for four tours. It was all I really wanted to do. Ain't that somethin'? You get real good at somethin' then there's just no call for it in civilian life."

The pieces of the jigsaw puzzle were falling into place for Mack. This man was war damaged and seeking his comfort zone by living on the mountain — a place geographically comparable to the place where he'd been the most useful in his life. It was a shame that a man with such a guardian spirit would sequester himself like this, but Mack knew society could be a very difficult place for him right now. "So why did you get out?"

"I got promoted and shipped back stateside. My new assignment was going to be administrative. It was time for me to re-up, so I just didn't. I was a warfighter, not a paper-pusher. Just couldn't see myself doing that. My life was full throttle, a desk would've killed me."

Mack chuckled at that and said, "Yeah, I know what you mean. When I was promoted to Lieutenant I had to go to a downtown office for two years, it was the only time I hated going to work."

A flash of surprise crossed Turtle's face as he assessed the dust-covered cowboy in front of him. "You're a Lieutenant?"

Mack wasn't one to flaunt his rank but it had come up in conversation. He admitted, "Well, I'm a Captain now. That was a while back and I never want to do that again. I would rather be in the field."

There was a hint of increased respect in Turtle's voice as he addressed his new friend and confidant. "Yeah, I guess some of us were just meant to be on the front lines."

The mood seemed to be a little lighter, so Mack asked, "How was it coming back?"

"Aw man, it sucked big time. Everything was different with me and my girlfriend, so that didn't last very long. Hell, for that matter everything was different from when I left. Home, friends, what I did for fun, everything was just different. Every job I had was stupid and pointless, so I traveled around a while seeing the country and then I found this place. It was just like that valley over there, except for the lake. I was comfortable here, so I just set up shop. Now, I watch the valley."

"Do you think you're going to stay up here? Do you ever consider going back down to try it again?"

He had a *why would you ask that question* look on his face when he answered, "I'm doing fine up here. You and Booger Red are the only ones who know I'm here, so nobody bothers me. That Sheriff might have an idea though. I see him pokin' around sometimes. He might have had reports or something. Sometimes, if I make a mistake, a fisherman might see me and maybe report it. Evidently, he doesn't know where to look, he usually stays lower and doesn't make it all the way up here. I see him park and go walking around in the woods for a while then he leaves. I don't see a reason to go back down unless I get found out or have a damn good reason to."

Mack thought he might try to expand Turtle's vision a little bit. There seemed to be a mutual respect building between them, so maybe some subtle advice might be beneficial. He knew all to well how weird a man's mind could get when he was away from people, either on a mountain or in a bottle. When you only have yourself to talk to you only get one skewed point of view. He never ever wanted the story about his bad time at Port Mansfield to be told again but he felt like it could help Turtle to know he had a friend who had a somewhat similar story. "Turtle, I want to tell you my story, and you can take it or leave it. Only two other people know it."

Mack told him how he'd lost his fiancé and her son, Sarah and Little Jake, to a fire set by an arsonist. He laid the truth right out on the red New Mexico as he confessed to Turtle how he'd climbed into a bottle and how it almost killed him.

Turtle was enthralled as Mack told about the fire that killed his rookie and indirectly killed his old friend Buster. He compared his road trip down to Port Mansfield with Turtle's travels that led him to his lofty perch on the mountain.

Turtle's attention was riveted to Mack's story of how he figured out who had set the fire. When Mack got to the end, where he orchestrated a final reckoning, Turtle was slapping his leg and laughing. "Dang, Mack, you went total frogman on his ass. That's like somethin' I'd do, but I'm trained for it." With a bit of unsolicited admiration, he said, "You can be a bit of a bad ass. I like your style, dude."

Mack was still a little embarrassed about what he did down on the gulf. "Well, I ain't proud of it but that's what happened." He glanced at the sun getting closer to being behind the mountain and said, "Man, I gotta get goin'. I bet Booger's waiting on me at the trailhead."

He stood to walk toward his horse that was tied in the clearing and Turtle walked with him, asking questions of clarification about his exciting secret. Mack got to his horse and mounted up because he was running late. He told his new friend, "I'll be back up in a day or two, and we can talk some more. Sorry I have to run off."

He turned his horse and looked down at the battered warfighter standing beside him. "Turtle, I only told you that story so I could tell you this, sometimes you just have to get back on that horse that bucked you off and ride it out into the arena again — in front of God and everybody — just to show them you can."

16

WATCH OUT FOR SNAKES

Mack reluctantly rode back down the trail, knowing his new warfighter friend was battling his demons in his own way. There are as many ways to wage the emotional fight as there are damaged men that fight that battle. He'd faced his own struggles and with the help of good friends like Samantha, and his fishing guide buddy, Cody, he'd won the war. He'd won his sanity courtesy of these friends and an event of explosive vindication. The right way to fight it is to win however that may be, the wrong way is self-destruction. Turtle seemed to be circling his wagons away from self-devastation and was in a self-imposed rebuild phase. He was glad about that.

Since he'd scoured the ground for signs on the way up the trail he was only half aware of his surroundings as he returned to the trailhead. Hopefully, Booger Red was back from the doctor and waiting for him with the horse trailer.

He was mulling that probability over in his mind when something shiny, an object other than the glistening quartz rocks on the ground, caught his eye. He stopped his horse to take a closer look. It was the slender top section of a fly rod, with its gold line guides sparkling in the clear mountain sunshine. He dismounted and tied his horse to a branch. The fishing rod section was in a pile of brush at the side of the trail, probably left by a trail clearing crew. "Now, why would a trail cleaning crew pile all that brush right here?" he asked his horse.

He explored behind the brush pile and found a rough jeep trail the pile seemed to have been purposely obscuring. The trail went uphill until it disappeared into the pine trees and scrub growth. Some of the newer growth had been mashed down, so he knew the trail had been used recently.

As he progressed up the trail, he found a piece of cloth hanging on a tree branch and then a fishing fly box. *The water's in the other direction. Why would a fisherman go bushwhacking up this way?* He consulted his topographic map and saw there was a little secluded lake further up the mountain. *That's what they did. They just wanted to have some very private time. Hope I don't surprise them too much.*

He looked up the hill and saw a trail that went up and over a small rise. He climbed up the moderately inclined trail, and when he dropped off the back side the of the rise he shuddered as he discovered something he didn't want to see — a man's battered and twisted body was laying roughly concealed under a bush. His bloody hands and arms bore signs of a life and death struggle, evidenced by the deep defensive wounds. His attacker had hacked him to death with a big and powerful blade. The deciding blow was probably the deep cut running from the side of his neck to his Adam's apple — it nearly severed his head.

The goriest wounds were the deep cuts on the man's legs. They showed no blood loss, meaning the slicing blows had been delivered after he was dead. Whatever depraved beast did this attacked the body with a crazed and morbid enthusiasm. The victim's pockets were turned inside out and his boots were missing, as were his toes. Mack had seen plenty of men killed by various means in his career and had regrettably built a tolerance to the scenes, but this grizzly sight was just too perverted and is stomach involuntarily retched.

Mack knew not to disturb the crime scene and he also knew he should leave and alert the sheriff. He also knew there was another person to be accounted for and he had to find her — alive or dead. The sheriff was a long way away and Mack was the only one here for the search.

He silently backtracked to his horse and pulled his Ruger 45 long colt out of the saddlebag. Before he stuck the gun in his belt at the small of his back, he looked at it praying to all that is good he wouldn't have to use it.

He proceeded as carefully as a naked man crossing a barbed wire fence. Silence and awareness of his surroundings were the important things to consider now. He was comfortable with stealth. He preferred to hunt deer like this back in Texas. Hunting from a deer stand had never been appealing. He didn't move as he listened to the woods around him. Quietly he advanced up the trail to another little rise.

When he got close to the top he caught a whiff of a sweet solvent smell alien to the woods around him. The smell triggered an alarm in his mind that urged caution, but he couldn't associate it with a particular danger.

When he got close to the top, he belly crawled the last few feet to poke his head over the crest. He'd smelled that scent before but couldn't place it. He just knew it didn't belong in a pine forest. It was frustrating, and he should know the answer.

He peered over the crest and saw a clearing. An old miner's cabin not much bigger than a small travel trailer sat on the only flat spot. The cabin had been dug into the side of the hill. Dirt and rocks covered the roof. From above, it looked like part of the landscape. The only giveaway was the smoke stack from the wood-burning stove inside. *Maybe the hikers had seen smoke and were curious.*

The only opening was a doorway in the front. To the side of the cabin on some flat ground was an army surplus wall tent set up. Tan camouflage netting covered the olive drab tent fabric, and the foliage surrounding it — trees, grass, everything — was dead.

Mack lay still on the ground, the only thing moving were his eyes as he looked for any movement or signs of life. The only activity he could see were the birds flitting around on the ground. A slow lethargic motion from under a pile of sticks drew his attention, causing him to focus on it. The pile seemed to be a crude lean-to and underneath it was a blonde girl dressed in torn, bloodstained hiking clothes. She had her back to him. When she painfully rolled onto her back, Mack could see her hands and feet were tied.

Mack didn't know what his field of battle would be as he began to formulate a rescue plan. First he had to be sure there was nobody other than the girl there, so he just lay there like the calculating animal he needed to be and watched. He tried to become part of the dirt he was laying in.

As he lay flat, observing his surroundings, he noticed it. In the crotch of a tree was a trail camera, the type used by hunters to record animal movement. He was pretty sure his image had been recorded but was worried that maybe this was also a warning device. There were no wires extending from it, which was comforting. He made a mental note to grab it on his way out. He didn't want his picture floating around in a criminal investigation.

It felt like forever before he was satisfied they were alone. He inched back off the rise and skirted around the clearing so he could approach the lean-to from the back and use it as a shield for his cautious movements. Silently he crawled around to the back of the lean-to until there was just a wall of twigs between him and the girl.

He watched her through the twigs. She was semi-conscious and extremely banged up. She'd taken a beating and from her closed and sunken eyes, he figured she was dehydrated too.

He whispered to her through the twigs telling her he was there to help and not to speak to him. She only half opened her eyes and mumbled incoherently. It would be too loud to get through the twigs, so Mack crawled around the barrier to get to her.

As he moved low to the ground he kept a watchful eye on the cabin, alert for any movement that would cause him to pull his gun. Using his knife to cut the rope would be too risky — it might cut her. Plus, if she screamed anybody close would hear it.

He still wasn't convinced he was alone in the woods. He focused his attention on quickly untying the amateurish knots while the girl blankly stared at him like a critically injured animal in a trap.

Suddenly her eyes grew wide with fright and she squeaked a small scream. As Mack spun around reaching for his gun the last thing he heard was, "Gotcha" before the hard thump to the side of his head knocked him out cold.

Mack awoke lying in the dirt beside the girl. His hands and feet were tied with the same stupid knots that bound the girl. His throbbing head lay heavy on the ground. When he grimaced, he felt a crust of dried blood on his face and figured he'd been out for a while.

The sun was on its way down, just beginning to touch the tops of the surrounding mountains. He knew it was going to be a long night. Without raising his aching head, he yelled at the cabin, "Hey, how about some water out here?"

A man with greasy long black hair appeared in the doorway, carrying a bowl. Mack had a limited field of view, so he could only see the scuffed black boots shuffle toward him, kicking up dust. Their captor said, "I'll feed you like the dogs you are." The hand carrying the bowl was at the end of an arm with a full sleeve tattoo of a snake, with the man's middle finger bearing the snake's tongue. He set the bowl down and lazily ambled back to the cabin, muttering incomprehensibly.

"Hey you son-of-a-bitch, get your ass back out here! Why the hell did you tie us? Get out here, you bastard!" Mack recognized that arm. Fury burned within him as he struggled with the knots. He was mad at himself for not trusting his gut, grabbing Phoebe and leaving Santa Fe.

Where is Phoebe? Is she still with this scum? Who is this snake armed son-of-a-bitch? He was enraged and swore if he could just get loose he'd cut the head off that snake and choke the bastard with his own tattooed hand. He could feel himself losing control, and knew he was no good if he got past that point. A mad dog on a chain can do nothing. He tried to calm down, take some deep breaths and reevaluate his situation.

Mack nudged the dazed girl and she only moaned. He knew she needed some water but it would be a trick getting her to drink. Disregarding his pulsing head, he rolled over to the bowl and slurped up a big mouthful. He rolled back and put mouth over her dried cracked lips and trickled some water into her mouth, like a mother bird feeding a baby.

He was thankful she still had the capacity to swallow and not choke. He emptied the entire water bowl like that, taking only one sip for himself. The effort seemed to pay off because she managed to audibly say, "I'm cold."

He snuggled up to her as best he could with his hands tied and shared his body heat. New Mexico nights can be chilly, and what little heat she returned he was grateful for. When he felt her shiver, he was glad her body was trying to make its own heat. He spent the night trying to keep her warm and work on the knots. Sleep was out of the question.His mind was spinning at maximum RPM as he tried to figure a way out of this predicament.

Finally, on the brink of exhaustion, Mack drifted off to sleep. He had a dream about himself and the old Navajo man sitting in the cab of his truck. The old man was saying, "I figured it out about the snakes around you. I told you so."

The girl shuddered and squirmed closer, and he woke up before the old man could finish the explanation. His dehydrated mind was a blur of thoughts as he considered how he was going to escape and help this girl.

The other girl, Phoebe, was on his mind too. Could he help her? Could he even find her? Even if she needed help, surely she wasn't in on this. Mack didn't want to consider the fact that she might be dead.

When he got loose he'd make Snake Arm tell him where she was. If the unconscious girl could spare fifteen minutes he'd have free rein to convince the guy to talk. She'd be an unreliable witness, even if she did want to fess up to the truth about what happened to her captor. But first Mack had to get free of these ropes. The thought of beating the snake man to a bloody pulp gave new vigor to his efforts.

The worst part of the night came during the hour before the dawn. This was the darkest and coldest part of the night, and it just about froze the fight out of Mack. He held fast to his job of giving his body heat to the girl, and was glad to see the sun start to peek over the mountain. Usually the sunrise held a special place in Mack's heart, but today it rang hollow. He'd hoped it would shine on his freedom and see him leaving the mountain. This morning all it brought him was some warmth, which he was grateful for.

About an hour after the welcome sunrise broke over the mountain, Snake Arm came out of the cabin. Mack never smelled any coffee brewing. He must have had a morning dose of his drug of preference, because he was feeling pretty chipper and talkative.

"Good morning, campers! I trust you had a good night? It looks like it's gonna be a great day, for me anyway. Not so much for ya'll." He snickered at himself as he waltzed over to the woodpile to pick up a machete from a stump. A machete that still bore blood stains.

He stood in front of his bound captives and continued his deranged oratory while he waved the machete around. "I've been coming up here for three years now, just doing my job cooking up some fine pharmaceuticals and nobody's bothered me. Now in three days, I've had three nosey intruders snooping around. I just don't understand it, dude. Why the hell are you people here? I just want to be left alone to do my thing, man. I got people depending on me. When I let them down, they get a little testy."

The tweaking attitude of the doper plus the sweet stink of the camp solved yesterday's riddle for Mack. He'd been to a few fire calls on clandestine meth labs. This was a lab and the guy was a cook. *That explains the stink and the dead foliage around the tent. He acts like he's been sampling the product this morning.*

"I just can't have my little camp become a tourist destination, you know? I can't afford for word to get out, not that anyone who counts would listen to you anyway. Looks like I got one down and two to go.

"That girl looks like she's close to gone anyway. She just didn't have any staying power, but oh man she did wiggle for a while till she got tired. What about you, cowboy? You got any staying power? You think you're gonna save the day and make it out of here? I bet you're sorry you got off the beaten path. Why'd you even come up here, man? "

With rage on his face Mack looked him straight in the eye and said, "You take this rope off me and I'll show you some staying power. You're pretty tough talking to a guy that's tied up. Where's Phoebe?" For the life of him Mack couldn't remember her street name. "You ain't getting away with nothing, boy. People know I'm up here and when I didn't show up last night they're darn sure lookin' for me this mornin'. My horse is tied on the trail right by your crappy camo job of that jeep trail."

Snake Arm strolled over behind the tent and came back leading Mack's horse. "Oh, you mean this horse? And who is Phoebe? You must be out of your head, man. I don't know no Phoebe. No sir, I don't think anybody's gonna find you. Ever."

"Phoebe's that girl you picked up in Santa Fe you stupid son-of-a-bitch."

Wide-eyed surprise replaced the taunting sneer. "How'd you know about that, boy? Man, you sure get around. Are you stalking me or something? Did they send you? Is Phoebe what she told you her name was? She told me her name was Star. You just can't trust these meth head bitches."

The sneer came back as he bent at the waist, provoking his captive. "You can't trust them but they sure are fun when they're trippin'. You ain't got to worry about her, man. She loves my stuff. She's off in her own little world."

Mack's heart sank. *Maybe this son-of-a-bitch is right. Maybe nobody will ever find us.* It deeply saddened him that it would end like this, with Sam never knowing what happened. His world was falling down around him.

The thug dropped the reins on the horse and walked back over to his captive audience. "Well, let's get this over with. Whadaya say? I got a new batch to start today and ya'll have held me up long enough."

Mack had never felt so helpless in his life. He wasn't going to take it like a coward though. He was going to make this piece of two-legged trash look him straight in the eye. His only thoughts were of Samantha and how he would kill this guy if given half a chance.

Snake Arm lifted the machete and an evil grin spread across his face. He looked at his tied hostage defiantly staring him down with hard eyes and thought, *Man, it's never been like this before. They usually cry. What a trip.* He held the blade there a moment to savor the feeling of power; malicious joy filling his face.

An explosion shattered the mountain quiet, changing the evil grin to a slack jaw. The squinting sinful eyes fixed in a thousand yard stare across the valley. The blast of a second a gunshot sent him to his knees and he fell on his face, still clutching the machete. Blood spread underneath him and soaked into the sand around his useless body.

As he fell from Mack's view, in his place, farther back Mack saw Phoebe standing on top of the cabin holding his Ruger 45, smoke curling from the barrel. She climbed down from her perch and walked over to her bound and helpless friend. As she got closer, he could see she'd been hitting the drugs pretty hard, whether by choice or that of the snake-armed villain he didn't know.

The teeth she had left had yellowed more and she now had open sores on her drawn, skeletal face. She was a wasted pitiful case, but also an angel of mercy. She laid the gun down and her hands shook as she started untying the knots. She seemed disoriented, but in a matter of fact way, "He was not a nice guy like I thought. He was mean. You were nice to me."

Mack sat up and tried to give her a hug, but she pulled away. "Phoebe, thank you. I thought it was about over. I'm sure glad you were here. Let's get out of here!"

"Tend to the girl, he hurt her bad and I couldn't stop him." She turned and delivered a hard kick to the lifeless head of the dead waste of humanity. As Mack untied the girl, Phoebe walked to Mack's horse and climbed on. She looked down from her throne of days long passed with sad, hollow eyes and said, "You're gonna need the jeep to get her down the mountain. It's behind the tent. I'll leave your horse at the bus station in town. I started this mess on horseback and I'll end it that way.

"I'm in a bad way, Mack, but I remember the favor you asked. I'm going home."

Mack watched her as she turned the horse and faded into the trees. Mack called out, "Phoebe, wait!" She didn't turn, she just raised her hand, gave him the okay sign and rode on.

17
COMING DOWN THE HILL

Mack stood in shocked disbelief pondering what had just happened. As Phoebe rode off into the rising sun, he said in a low tone, "God be with you, my friend. God be with you."

A whimpering sound behind him brought his attention back to matters at hand. He switched gears in his head and went from almost killed hostage to paramedic care-giver. He had to get the girl a little more stabilized and off this mountain of hell.

He pulled out his crushed can of snuff, put a dip of Copenhagen in his lip and quickly evaluated his surroundings. The sting in his lip reminded him he couldn't raise a spit and he probably needed some water. He did manage to work up a good enough hocker to launch a liquid brown projectile directly onto one of the bullet holes in Snake Arm's back.

He picked up his gun and ejected the two spent rounds. He had some bullets in his pocket to replace the two Phoebe fired, and he threw the spent brass off into the brush as far as he could. There was no telling if he'd need all six rounds but he wanted them if need be. After that, the gun went into his belt.

He figured he was alone out here. If there was anyone else around, they would've either come running or hightailed it out of there at the sound of gun fire. Any sort of supplies would be in the cabin, so he went in to find water. New Mexico's low humidity will suck the moisture right out of a person, and the two survivors here desperately in need of a drink.

He'd been around enough crime scenes to know not to touch or disturb anything. This was certainly a crime scene.

The inside of the cabin was dark, stinky and sparse. There was a mattress on the dirt floor, a small table, and a shelf holding canned goods with an ice chest underneath it. He opened the ice chest and was elated to find some bottled water. He grabbed his wallet, cell phone and pocketknife off the table then took a granola bar off the shelf and all the bottles of water he could carry.

He went back outside, leaving the door open, just like he'd found it. Under the lean-to, the girl was still in the same position. He went to her and sat her up, she was barely coherent but enough so that she could hold the bottle of water and drink.

 Once she figured out what it was, she started gulping the water too quickly. Mack took the bottle from her grabbing hands. She made the sounds a baby would make when its bottle was taken away. Mack calmly and quietly told her like a father speaking to a child, "You have to go slow darlin'. Too much too fast is gonna hurt you."

She turned her sunken eyes toward the sound of his reassuring voice and again made baby sounds. He gave the bottle back to her and watched to make sure she took it slow. He sucked down a bottle of water too, never minding he still had that big wad of snuff in his lip. Drinking and dipping was an acquired skill he'd perfected.

When the girl had two bottles of water in her belly, Mack gave her the granola bar. She pretty much devoured it in one bite. He could tell from the returning color on her dirty face she was improving physically but she hadn't uttered a word other than the baby sounds. He thought she'd been through a horrible few days, so he just let her move along at her own pace.

The two sat in silence there under the lean-to, as he waited for her to make the first move to stand. As long as they had decent daylight, he was in no hurry.

Finally, she had a little more movement and inclination to her body. She broke her downward stare and timidly asked Mack, "Are you a good man?"

"Yes, I am. I'm a fireman, hon. I'm here to help you."

"Mmm-hmm." She vacantly stared, with very little regard, at the dead man in front of them. "Did you kill him?"

"No, someone else did. He's not going to hurt you anymore."

"Was it that other girl? He was real mean to her, too."

"I'm not sure how it happened. Do you think you can stand up now?"

"Yeah, I think so." She stood up with his help then looked back down and said, "I would've done it, too. He hurt me a lot. He was a monster." She turned her head and spat on the dead body.

He led her behind the tent and the old jeep was right where Phoebe said it would be. He lifted her into the passenger seat and belted her in. He sat beside her, turned the key, pulled the choke and stomped the foot feed, coaxing the old worn-out thing to life. While he let it warm up, he told her, "Stay right here, I'll be back in a second."

He had a vague understanding of crime scene investigation and wanted to hedge all his bets. He had no confidence in the sheriff and his boys. He ran back to where he'd been hiding on the trail and snatched the trail camera off of the tree. He was interested in what sort of pictures would show up on the camera.

He ran back to the jeep and climbed in. The exertion combined with his decreasing adrenalin levels let his head remind him it was still there. That couldn't slow him down though. He had to get down the hill.

As Mack maneuvered the vehicle out of the little hellhole in paradise, he asked the girl, "What's your name?"

"Sandy." Her voice had a hollow sound to it and her face was vacant, devoid of expression. Mack figured she was in shock from all she'd been through, so he wasn't going to press her. He didn't want to trigger some hysterical reaction while he was driving the Jeep down the rough road.

"Sandy, my name's Mack."

"Hi, Mack." Her vacant eyes scanned the road in front of them. Her gaze went constantly side-to-side for about thirty degrees. Never up or down, not to the side and she didn't look at Mack when he spoke — just that thirty-degree cone of vision in front of her. Eventually she asked, "Have you seen my boyfriend?"

"No, I didn't see him." He certainly didn't want her to know the boy had been hacked to death with a machete and stuffed under a bush. That information could come later in a more clinical environment.

Still in shock, Sandy absently said, "We got separated when the bad man surprised us. Jimmy told me to hide so the bad man would chase him. I heard them fight. I don't know why Jimmy didn't come back for me. I don't know. Then bad man found me and tied me up. He hurt me real bad." Silent tears were running down her face, making mud trails. She continued to scan side to side as she talked. "I don't know why he didn't come back for me. Did you see my boyfriend? His name is Jimmy. He was supposed to come back for me."

"No, Sandy, I didn't see Jimmy but we'll find him I'm sure." He placed a reassuring hand on her shoulder and she flinched like a scared cat and let out a piercing scream that could only come from deep within. It made Mack flinch, too. He took his hand away and she instantly quieted and went back to scanning the area in front of her.

That primal scream scared an animal out of the brush off to Mack's left. His mind instantly thought deer, but when he glanced over at it he could see it was a horse. The horse trotted through the short brushy trees and he could see it had a saddle and bridle. It was Booger Red's horse.

Mack stopped the Jeep to see what the horse would do. It trotted in a wide arc and went back to the small tree it had been behind. He gave Sandy another bottle of water and told her to stay in her seat. She just nodded and kept scanning the road in front of her. Mack walked over to the tree and beneath it he saw Booger Red, sitting cross-legged in the shade. He was carrying on a conversation with whoever he thought was beside him.

"That's what I'm saying, Pops. If the Indians still had control of this land, it would be a lot better.

"No, they wouldn't be killin' the white man because the white man wouldn't be here. Good gosh!

"The buffalo would still be here and they are way better than cattle.

"Why, hell yeah, I'm a cowboy now, but if they were still here I'd marry an Indian woman and adopt myself into the tribe. I like Indian women."

Mack moved around to in front of Booger, but his babbling friend never acknowledged him or broke his conversation. Mack could see he was pale and sweating heavily. The side of his face was skinned up and the palm of his hand was shredded. He most likely fell off his horse. "Hey, Booger, you okay, man?"

He fixed his gaze on Mack as if he was trying to figure out who he was and what he was doing there. He squinted and scowled as his confused mind tried to put two and two together. Finally, a couple of brain synapses clicked together and wide-eyed he asked, "Mack? That you?"

"Yeah, Booger, it's me. Who are you talking to?"

"This is Pops. He's my grandpa. We were just discussing buffalo and such like that." He looked to his right and said, "Yeah, this is the guy I was telling you about, Pops. He's a hell of a saddle maker."

"Booger, you want a drink of water and a ride to town? I think we ought to be getting on out of here."

He looked at Mack with confusion, like he was speaking a foreign language, then he looked to his right again and said, "Yeah? Probably so. You gonna be all right out here? Well, tell her I said hello." Then he looked at Mack and said, "Yeah. A drink would be nice. Got any whiskey? Buttermilk would be good, too. Help me up. Something's wrong with my leg I think. It don't work too good."

"Well let me look at that leg first." He took his pocketknife and cut the pants leg up the side. Booger's calf was red and swollen so it flowed out over the top of his boot. Without asking, Mack ran the razor sharp blade down the side seam of the boot and the swollen calf muscle popped out.

The puncture wounds from the snakebite had started to blacken around the site and red streaks extended up and down from the wound. Mack tried to remain calm when he saw the advanced stage of the injury, though it was doubtful Booger would've noticed any concern in his current state of mind.

"Well, let's get you up and see if you can make it to the Jeep. I'll help you." He grabbed him by the wrist, and when he did he could feel his radial pulse racing pretty fast. When he pulled him to his feet, Booger said, "Hoo, boy, we must've had a hell of a night! I'm on the merry go round, and I must still be pretty drunk."

Mack knew that Booger was dehydrated and in shock. It was a wonder he was still conscious after spending the night out in the elements with a snake bite. His body was compensating for the shock but that couldn't last much longer. He had to get him to a hospital quick.

They hobbled and staggered to the Jeep where Sandy still sat wearing a blank stare and nursing her bottle of water. She barely acknowledged their approach.

Mack managed to get his patient into the back of the jeep, and when he gave the delirious man a bottle of water, he hollered out, "Whiskey!" and downed it without taking a breath. Mack went back to get Booger's horse and tie it to the back of the Jeep with a lead rope. They weren't going to be moving very fast on this rough road.

As Mack made his way down the road with his two patients, he was steadily checking his cell phone for any sort of a signal. Booger took the second and last bottle of water and downed it in two gulps, then started singing "99 Bottles of Beer on the Wall."

Mack was glad to see it was annoying Sandy. She was becoming a little more aware of her surroundings, however loud and off key they might be. As he descended toward the trailhead, he could see Booger's truck and trailer in the distance. He checked his phone again and saw he had two bars, so he dialed 911.

"911 emergency for Colfax County, what is your emergency?"

"My name is Mack McWhirter. I was working with the search for two hikers in the Valle Vidal. I have one of the hikers and an injured searcher with me. I am a paramedic in Texas. I need a ground ambulance and a helicopter to meet me at the first trailhead in the Valle Vidal. The hiker is dehydrated and was assaulted and the searcher has been snake bit. I'll be at the trailhead in about fifteen minutes."

"You have two patients? I can dispatch an ambulance and they'll make the determination as to the need for a helicopter. We don't automatically send one."

"Listen. Do you understand I'm a paramedic and I'm making that determination right now? The snake bite victim was bit yesterday and is in decompensating shock right now. He won't make the trip to the hospital in an ambulance."

"*Sir, I don't know who you say you are.*" The dispatcher said in a pissy and condescending tone.

"My name is Captain Peyton McWhirter. I'm a nationally registered paramedic in the state of Texas, badge number 081, Stephenville Fire Department. What is *your* name?"

All he could hear for a moment was clicking on a keyboard then the voice said, "*I have a ground ambulance and a Medivac helicopter coming to your location at the Valle Vidal trail head. Please remain at that location to direct the units when they arrive.*"

Click.

Mack was furious at the self-important button thumper. He hadn't even had a chance to say he needed the sheriff out here for the two dead guys up on the mountain. With such a medical response, though, he figured the sheriff would respond to the location out of protocol. The dispatcher would probably send the New Mexico sheriff anyway, to adjust the attitude of the angry man from Texas. *Bring it on!* he thought. *I have just about had my fill of New Mexico and everything in it.*

He didn't know where the medical resources were coming from, but in the fifteen minutes it took him to get to Booger's truck and trailer he could hear a siren echoing through the mountains. The ambulance was on its way.

He parked the Jeep beside the trailer, away from where the "bird" would land. He didn't want to have everyone sandblasted by the prop blast from the landing helicopter. He shut off the raggedy old Jeep and he could hear the wop-wop-wop of the helicopter coming along with the ambulance.

His patients appeared to be calm and secure where they sat. Booger was down to 49 bottles of beer on the wall. He figured he'd better tend to the horse, since a run away horse would just add to the impending commotion. He looked in the trailer and saw the horse he'd been riding standing calm in the shade. *At least Phoebe made it this far. She must've hitched a ride to town.*

He put the trail camera in Booger's saddlebag and opened the back gate of the trailer. He led the horse in and just had it secured when the helicopter came overhead and did its circle to inspect a landing spot.

The screaming ambulance was just coming around the corner on the road. It was all upsetting the horses so he quickly exited the trailer to keep from getting smashed.

Mack crouched behind the truck to take shelter from the landing helicopter. When he heard the engine spool down, he stood up to see two flight nurses headed his way. They came to him and he introduced himself, "I'm Mack McWhirter. I'm a firefighter paramedic from Texas."

The lead flight nurse brusquely asked, "So, what do you got here?"

He led them around the truck to the patients. "This girl's name is Sandy. She was the object of the search yesterday. She was abducted and assaulted. I got some water into her and she appears stabilized, except for the psych trauma.

"This man here is Booger Red Privett. He was snake bit on the left lower leg yesterday by a big rattlesnake. He thought he could make it back down the mountain, but I found him incoherent about an hour ago. I figured he was the higher priority. What do ya'll think?"

Booger was mumbling, "Nineteen bobbles ob beer on old McDonald's farm," and was not as animated as the second flight nurse took a quick set of vitals on him. He looked up at his partner and said, "That was the right call. We gotta go now. He's sinking. The ground guys can take her to Raton General."

His partner ran to the copter and got the cot. He returned and the two wrestled Booger onto the cot and they were rolling it to the helicopter just as the ground ambulance was pulling in. The two medics got out of their rig and were walking toward the helicopter, but the flight nurse waved them off, pointing to the truck where Mack was standing.

The cot was pushed into its fixed position and the nurse climbed in to shut the door as the pilots was increasing RPMs to take off. In less than a minute, they were airborne and on their way to the hospital in Raton.

The two medics from the ambulance veered toward Mack, and seeing his beat up head asked, "Are you the patient? Did you call?"

"No. I called, but it's for her." He guided them around the truck to Sandy. As he walked, Mack had his head turned telling the medics, "She was the object of the search yesterday. She was abducted on the mountain, beat up pretty bad and she's really dehydrated. I found her and brought her back down."

As they got to the Jeep, one of the medics asked, "Where is she?"

Mack spun his head and a shock of fear hit him. The Jeep was empty. "She was just here! Where'd she go?" He scanned the area all around then he heard a whimper from under the Jeep. The medics just stood there waiting to be convinced they were on a valid call. He got down on the ground, even with her face and said to the frightened girl, "Sandy, it's okay, hon. Come on out. It's quiet now."

Her sunken eyes were open wide and she was shaking. "I'm scared. Where's Jimmy? I want to see Jimmy."

"We're looking for him, Sandy. These guys are here to take care of you. Will you come out and let them help you? They're paramedics."

Mack looked up at the medics and one them mouthed, "Jimmy?"

Mack looked at Sandy to make sure she wasn't looking, then mouthed back, "Dead."

At Mack's reassuring beckoning, she hesitantly edged out from her hiding place under the Jeep. She crawled over to where Mack still sat on the ground and leaned against him. She looked up at the two smiling paramedics and instantly threw her arms around Mack's neck and began sobbing into his dirt -caked shoulder. Mack picked her up as he stood and carried her to the waiting ambulance.

The two paramedics knew they were dealing with a delicate situation and just let it play out, wisely following Mack's lead. He climbed into the back of the ambulance, still carrying her in his arms, and gently laid her on the cot. After a moment she relaxed her grip on his neck and looked at Mack. "Am I going to be all right?"

"Yeah, Sandy, you're going to be fine now, darlin'. These guys are here to help you. You've been through a lot and you're dehydrated. You're safe now but you need an IV to get some fluids into you. Will you let them start an IV? Once they've done that, they'll take you to the hospital to get checked out. Okay?"

She slowly nodded her head but when the paramedic took her arm to prep for the IV, she started slapping at him, screamed and jerked it back holding it close to her chest. The shaken paramedic knew this would be problematic. He looked up at Mack and asked, "Are you really a paramedic?"

Mack knew what he was getting at and said, "Sure am, in Texas. I seem to have a connection with her, you want me to give it a try? She really needs that IV." As Mack went to kneel on the floor beside the cot, he tapped his finger on a small bin that held a sedative called Versed. When the medic looked up, Mack raised his eyebrows silently communicating, *How about some of this?* The medic gave a half a smile and an imperceptible nod of his head. He knew this Texas cowboy medic knew what he was doing.

Mack knelt down beside Sandy as she lay on the cot and took her hand. He held her small hand in his and rubbed up and down her arm with the other. She allowed this, as she looked into his eyes with a 'please help me' look. "Now, Sandy, I'm here to help you. You understand that. Right?" She nodded. "We've been through a lot together. We just need to do a little more."

Her eyes teared up and she nodded her head and relaxed her arm.

"Okay, I have to rub this stuff on your arm to clean it," he said, making sure to maintain eye contact and hold her trust. He cleaned the site at the crook of her elbow with Betadine and then an alcohol prep. "Now, I have to put this rubber band on your arm for a minute. Okay?"

She watched his movements closely as he worked. The previous paramedic had unwrapped a 20-gauge IV catheter and held it ready for Mack to take. Mack looked for a good vein and could barely see the pale blue line on her arm. She was pretty dehydrated so her veins weren't popping up very well. He took the needle and told her, "Okay. Now, you're going to feel a little prick then it will be over. Okay?"

Sandy closed her eyes and clenched her teeth as she nodded to go ahead. He touched the point of the needle to her arm and pushed it in. He saw a flash of blood in the chamber so he advanced the catheter into her vein. The paramedic had the flushed IV line ready. Mack connected it, popped the tourniquet loose and confirmed a good flow, then he taped the catheter and IV tubing in place. He looked back at her and she still had her eyes closed and her teeth clenched. "That's it. We're through."

She opened her eyes with surprise and said, "I didn't even feel it." She began to relax a little more on the cot knowing she was safer now.

As the paramedic started to inject the Versed into the IV line to insure their precious cargo would be even more relaxed on the ride to the hospital, he said, "That was a good stick, man. It looked like it was going to be pretty difficult with not much of a target."

"I figured I only had one shot at it, and it had to be good." Mack said as he stiffly stood up.

The Versed was flowing into Sandy's vein. Her eyes were getting droopy and she was less aware of what was going on around her, so the paramedic moved to where Mack had been and began a head to toe assessment of the patient to find all her injuries and treat them.

Sandy didn't fight this, so Mack felt it was safe for him to leave. As he opened the side door of the ambulance to step out, one of the paramedics said, "We'll take good care of her. You'd better get your head looked at, bud."

Mack stood the side with his eyes closed as the ambulance drove away to the hospital in Raton. When he opened them and raised his head after the ambulance's dust cloud diminished, he saw the sheriff sitting there in his car. He certainly didn't want this conversation but he knew it would come eventually.

Right now, he was tired, hungry and needed to take care of the horses but he walked over to the patrol car, anyway. The sheriff rolled down the car window and said, "Boy, we need to talk."

18

THE QUESTIONS

Through the window the Sheriff said, "The dispatcher called me on the radio and said you found the lost hikers. How are they?"

"The girl that was lost just left in that ambulance. She's pretty beat up but stable. Her boyfriend's still up on the mountain. He's dead." Mack said with exhausted resignation.

At that news, the sheriff shut off his car and clumsily got out. He got up in Mack's face and shouted, "What the hell do you mean he's dead? What was that helicopter for?"

"That was for Booger Red. He got snake bit yesterday and thought he could make it down okay, but I found him this morning. He was delirious from the bite, dehydrated and in worse shape, so I called for a helicopter. I found that boy right before I found the girl. He was hacked up pretty bad."

"Okay, wait just a minute. Why don't you tell me what happened from the beginning, starting with why you didn't search the assigned grid coordinates I gave you? We had a system here and evidently you and Mr. Privett totally disregarded my instructions. Also, why the hell'd you spend the night out there without notifying anybody?"

Mack decided not to say what he really wanted to. He figured he should just stick to the facts. "When the group went to the hikers' camp yesterday, I saw an empty fishing case laying by the tent.

Everybody was so wound up and focused on your grid coordinates I figured nobody would listen to me about it. Booger agreed they probably went fishing, so we headed toward water. Speaking of water, you got any?"

The sheriff opened the trunk of his car and got a bottle of water out of a cooler he kept there. He handed it to Mack, who downed it in one gulp, and then he gave the Sheriff an '*is that all?*' look. He pulled out another bottle and handed it to Mack. Since he could raise a spit now, Mack put the bottle under his arm and got his can of snuff out of his pocket.

"So, on the way up there to the lake Booger got bit by a big rattlesnake. He wasn't too worried about it and said he could make it to the hospital. He told me to go on up and check out the lake."

"So, you just let him ride back by himself? That was pretty stupid." The sheriff was entering intimidation mode, trying to remain the Alpha in the conversation.

Mack let that slide, thinking the sheriff was pretty intimate with stupid. "He's a lot more knowledgeable about snake bites than I am, so who was I to argue? Anyway this is pretty hard country up here and I figured we needed to find those hikers. So, I went on up to the lake, but didn't see them up there."

The sheriff interrupted and anxiously asked, "Did you see anyone else up there? I've had reports of someone camping long-term up there."

Keeping the secret, he said, "No, I didn't see anyone."

"No other hikers or campers or anybody? You're sure?"

"I'm pretty sure of what I didn't see when I was up there, but I'm getting to that if you'll let me finish." Mack was getting exasperated. "Is this an official statement or something? I figure it is and that's why I'm trying to keep it all in order. Quit interrupting."

The sheriff didn't like to be told anything. He laid his forearm on his holstered revolver, squinted his eyes behind his mirrored sunglasses and replied, "Everything you say to me is an official statement, bud. I'll ask any question I want."

Mack now understood the gravity of the conversation. This was not a good-natured cop and he was not to be trusted. He refused to apologize as he continued. "On my way back down from the lake, I found the top section of a fly rod laying next to the trail. I got off my horse and started looking around for anything else. I found a jeep trail concealed behind a stack of brush, so I went up the trail and found a few other bits and pieces. Then, I found the guy. He'd been hacked up pretty bad and it looked like it was a long fight — he had lots of defensive wounds. He'd been killed and hidden under a bush. I went on up the trail and started to smell something like meth cooking, so I got really careful."

Mack saw a quick flash of surprise, fear and anger on the sheriff's face all in one fleeting moment. He blurted, "Are you saying—?"

Mack held his hand up to stop the interruption and for some reason the sheriff complied.

"I was laying low behind a little rise and I saw the girl — Sandy — tied up under a lean-to. I couldn't see her face but she never moved the whole time I was scoping out the camp. It looked like an old sheepherder's camp. There was a dugout cabin in the side of the hill and a military tent off to the side. I didn't see any activity for a good while so I snuck down to untie her. That rat faced, snake tattooed son-of-a-bitch caught me and hit me in the head.

"I woke up tied up next to her and we stayed that way all night. That's why I stayed all night on the damn mountain. Sorry I didn't call!" His patience was evaporating like the sweat off his brow.

The sheriff was taken aback at Mack's building irritation as he told the story. "Well, how did you get away?"

"The next morning that bastard came out of the cabin with a machete and was going to kill us both. Said he'd been cooking on the mountain for a while and couldn't have any witnesses. He admitted to killing the girl's boyfriend. He was just fixin' to do it and I was trying to shelter the girl when somebody shot him. My back was to him. When whoever did the shooting came to untie me, they stayed behind me and I couldn't see who it was.

"I was pretty much delirious from that thump to my head and dehydration. They untied my hands then ran away. All I saw was somebody with long black hair runnin' away. They took my horse and rode away, but when I got down here I found my horse in the trailer.

So you got two dead guys up on that mountain. I didn't disturb the crime scene other than to take that Jeep to get the girl back down here."

The sheriff had a hint of anger on his face as he tried to be official. "So, you have some familiarity with meth labs, do you? You also used the term crime scene, so you know how to preserve one? And you knew enough to call for a helicopter. Are you with law enforcement? Who the hell are you? You ain't just any old saddle maker."

"I imagine your dispatcher told you I identified myself by rank and certification. That's how I know that stuff."

The sheriff had a contemplative scowl on his face, like he was trying to figure out an algebra problem. He sneered when Mack mentioned rank and looked at the old ratty Jeep. "Why don't we get in that Jeep right there and go back up the mountain? You can show me right where everything is and how it all went down."

Mack had a gut feeling something wasn't adding up right but he couldn't put his finger on it. He went with his gut. He wasn't going anywhere with this guy. "You can go up there yourself, it's not hard to find after I pulled that brush off the trail. The crows will show you where the dead guy is. They were pretty thick when I came by. I have to get these horses some food and water. It's been two days for them.

"The medics told me there was a doc in town. I need somebody to take a look at my head, I didn't want to go all the way to Raton with the ambulance and leave the horses."

The surly law officer pointed his finger right at Mack's nose and said, "No, sir, that's where you're wrong. You're going up there with me and we're going right now."

Mack went into fire officer mode and asked, "Sheriff, are you denying me needed and advised medical treatment? The only way I'm going up there with you is if you arrest me. If you do that, you'd better damn well take me to get looked at first. I've gone about as far as I can go with my head fixin' to explode."

Then to emphasize his point and remind the lawman that there were records of Mack being there, just in case things were going to get really dramatic he added, "The medics on the ambulance and the flight nurses on the helicopter all have my name and certification on their patient reports. They both told me to seek medical treatment. Now both you and I know that trumps whatever plans you have for me.

"I'll be glad to go later, but right now I'm going back to Cimarron. Those dead guys aren't goin' anywhere. As far as the shooter is concerned, I'm pretty sure they're well on their way to somewhere else right now."

Mack turned and walked away from the indignant officer of the law who knew he couldn't do anything to keep Mack there, short of arresting him.

As Mack walked up to the side of the trailer, he checked to see the horses were tied properly. As he opened the door to Booger Reds truck the sheriff yelled, "You just make sure to come by my office in the morning to finalize this report! I'm goin' up there to inspect the crime scene. I'm not finished with you yet, boy!"

Mack just stuck his arm out the window and waved as he pulled the truck and trailer back onto the paved road. He made sure to spin the tires and leave the maximum dust cloud for the sheriff to stand in.

The events of the past two days replayed in his mind as he drove back to Booger's ranch and Sam. He figured Sandy would be okay physically but she'd have a long row to hoe in her emotional recovery. Booger was too mean to die but he was going to have a long trip to come back to normal from that bite, too.

Mack couldn't come to a decision about whether he'd had a close call with the sheriff or not. The conversation and attitude puzzled him. He wasn't scared, but he didn't feel secure either. He was beginning to see a lot of odd goings-on. Seeing Samantha walking out of his front door in nothing but an Indian blanket just as the sun was coming up would go a long way in making him feel secure.

He'd been too busy surviving to think of her, except when he was about to get his head cut off. He remembered thinking just before the gunshot that his biggest regret was he would never see her again. That's when he knew he loved her and needed her in his life. Now as he pulled the truck and trailer through the gate at Booger's ranch, he thought, *I sure hope she's okay.*

MEANWHILE,
BACK AT THE RANCH

His late arrival at the ranch house was announced by the cacophony of barking dogs. When the pack recognized it was Booger's truck they lost interest and assumed their positions under the house and around the barn. Before Mack could get out of the truck, Sam came stomping out onto the porch and stood there with her hands on her hips.

She had the ability to convince the receptor of her wrath to visualize a third eye of anger in the middle of her forehead. She was seeing through that eye as she glared from the porch, loudly asking, "Where the hell have you been?" Her other eyes showed both love and angered concern.

When Mack, dirty, bloody and looking like he'd been beat with a bag of nickels stepped stiffly out from behind the wheel, her third eye blinked and receded. She jumped off the porch and ran to him. "I was so worried. What happened to you?"

Mack held her tightly in his arms, like he hadn't seen her in years. He buried his face in her shiny black hair, and savored the moment. "It's a long story. I'm sure glad to be back with you, sugar."

He broke the embrace to take care of the horses before he tended to his own needs. "Would you help me with these horses? They been missing food and water for two days. Let's get the saddles off them, then we can talk."

They quickly set about the task and got the horses turned out for feed and water. Sam carried the saddles up to put them on the porch, and as she walked she asked, "Where's Booger? Why didn't he come back with you?"

Mack walked toward the garden hose at the side of the porch, saying, "He's in the hospital up at Raton. I'll get to that in a minute." He stood by the water hose and started taking off his crusty clothes, throwing them on the porch. He turned on the water, and after the initial shock of the frigid well water, he stood there and let it wash the past two days off of his body but not out of his mind. He'd get to that part with Sam — she was good at clearing his mind.

Sam sat on the porch steps watching him, naked in front of God and everybody. The sight of the man she'd missed so much stirred a burning desire in her heart. Absence makes the heart grow fonder but the threat of loss creates a passionate desire. She watched his naked muscled body as he let the water cascade over it.

Feeling herself getting carried away in the moment, she sought to lighten the mood. "Did you get in a fight with a grizzly bear? You even have bruises on your butt."

Feeling just a little more refreshed, he smiled and said, "If you'll go fix me something to eat, I'll tell you one hell of a story. I haven't eaten in two days. I hope you didn't drink all the beer while I was gone. Would you see if there's any aspirin in there, too?"

"Comin' right up," she said as she stood and climbed the steps. Before she stepped in the house she turned to steal another glance at him as he ran the cold water over the knot on his head.

He noticed her looking. The promise of food and her company overcame his pain and exhaustion. He still had enough wind in his sails to be a little feisty, so he turned toward her and swiveled his hips from side to side. She giggled and blushed a little as she went in to fix her man some dinner.

Sam came back outside with a plate of smoked elk roast and some leftover green beans, along with a bottle of beer. She handed the plate to Mack and kissed the knot on his head. He was air-drying in a rocking chair, still buck-naked.

She sat there watching him eat for a minute before going back inside. When she came back out to the porch, she was carrying some fresh clothes. She put them in the chair beside him and said, "If you want to finish that meal, you'd better put these clothes on, cowboy. I'm getting pretty hungry myself."

He finished the last bite of his food with a big grin. "Mmm-hmm." Standing up directly in front of her, he slowly started to dress.

When he bent over to pull his pants up, she slapped him on the butt and said, "Quit playing," and went back into the house.

He called inside, "I'm not playing, my little Indian maiden. I missed you."

Sam returned with a fresh cold beer in each hand. She sat down, handing one off and said, "Enough of your teasing and stalling, tell me what happened to you."

Mack was feeling back on track now. He had a full belly and was with Sam. He felt like he could use a nap but he never did have much luck sleeping during the day, besides he didn't want to take his eyes off Sam.

He took a big draw off his beer and said, "I tell ya, it's been a weird two days. Booger and I got to the trailhead to start that search and we could tell it was going to be screwed up as a football bat. That sheriff had it so organized that nothing was gonna happen. We just sort of started thinking outside the box."

Mack started telling the long story, and the further he got into it the more engrossed Sam got. She grimaced at the gory parts and had the start of tears in her angry eyes when Mack got to the end, where the gunshot saved his life.

"Who fired the shot?"

"Remember, I asked you if you'd ever heard of Phoebe Hansen?"

"Yeah, she was that barrel racer who just vanished. I seem to remember somethin' about that, but I never was into rodeo much. What does that have to do with anything?"

"I was gonna tell you about her story when I picked you up in Springer, but those other things came up and I didn't get a chance. Anyway, I ran across her in Amarillo on the way up here. I rescued her from some truck driver scum who thought she was his girlfriend.

"I guess she started to trust me and she knew who I was, so she told me the whole story about what happened and why she vanished. Swore me to secrecy too, I'm the only one who knows.

"Long story short, while she was on the road, she got hard into drugs. I dropped her off in Santa Fe to see this guy. She thought he was gonna help her get cleaned up, but he just took her up on that mountain and got her more strung out. When I dropped her off, I figured I'd never see her again."

Sam was confused when she asked, "So, again, what does she have to do with all this?" She thought a minute and said, "Wait. She was there?"

"Yep, karma, baby. That doper took my pistol when he smacked me. Somehow she got ahold of it. Just before he was gonna kill us, she shot him twice in the back." Mack composed himself as he looked deep into Sam's loving eyes and said, "She saved my life."

"Thank God for that. What happened to her? Why didn't you bring her back here?"

"After she untied me, she got on my horse and rode off down the mountain. She said she was goin' home. It sounded like she finally wanted to clean up. That was pretty much rock bottom for her, I imagine.

"I drove a jeep down the mountain with the girl, and my horse was at the trailer. She said something about catching the bus back home, I think. I was still pretty fuzzy in my head at that point."

"And you didn't see her again? Hmm. Well, how did Booger make it to the hospital if his truck was still there? Did somebody take him?"

"Now that he's safe it's all sort of funny in a twisted sense. As I was driving back down, I saw his horse walking around in the brush. I went looking and found him under a bush, delirious. He was talkin' to his dead grandpa, and they were havin' quite the conversation.

"His grandpa and I convinced him to get in the Jeep. On the way down, as soon as I had a cell signal, I called 911 and asked for an ambulance and a Medivac helicopter to meet us at the trailhead. Booger wasn't doing so well."

"They sent a helicopter just because you asked? I thought that was a pretty big deal."

"It *is* a big deal and it's like pullin' teeth on a gorilla to make it happen. It took a little convincing of the dispatcher to get one in the air. Booger needed help fast. Either way, they came, both the ground ambulance and the bird. Problem is, that got the sheriff out there, too."

"What did that pompous ass think about you savin' the girl?"

"He acted weird about the whole thing. He was mad because Booger and I deviated from his precious search grid. He tried to order me to go back to the scene with him, but I told him unless he arrested me, I was going to take care of the horses and then my head.

"I had him there. He knew I had witnesses and he knew he couldn't make me stay, so I just left. That really chapped him. He did tell me to come by his office to make a statement.

"I'll give him the story, but I ain't gonna tell him about Phoebe. I guess I need to go do that, but I bet him and all his deputies are still up on the mountain doing a murder investigation. No need to go to town just yet."

Sam was pretty eager to be somewhere besides Booger's ranch. "Let's run up to Raton and visit Booger, just to see how he's doin'. I bet he'd enjoy the company."

"That's a good idea. We do need to go see him. We could get a hotel room up there and eat some Mexican food. It'd be a nice night."

"I'll get cleaned up and we can hit the road." Sam stood, popping open the snaps on her plaid shirt as she did. Her belt came undone and she shimmied out of her Wranglers, as she grinned at Mack's wide and wanting eyes. "Just how cold was that water?"

20
HOSPITAL VISITS

The grizzled red haired mountain man was rarely seen in white, he felt it was a color reserved for new brides and the dead. He was doing his best not to earn the color. His colors were more along the lines of dirt, rust and broken wood.

The clinical environment where he lay was as unnatural to him as a fish in the desert. Mack and Sam quietly stood in the hospital room watching him as he napped fitfully. A little episode of apnea scared Mack, and as he reached to jostle him back to breathing it woke him.

Booger jerked awake with a snort and a gasp, confusedly looking around to get his bearings. He locked his gaze on his visitors, trying to make sense of it all. Finally, his glazed eyes focused and without his usual vigor he said, "Hey, Mack, how's my horses?"

Mack laughed and replied, "They're all fine Booger. How are you?"

With a look of exasperation and a heavy sigh he said, "Well, they tell me I'm gonna make it, but it was close for a while. I heard I came up here in a helicopter. That true?"

"Yeah, they flew you here from the trailhead."

"Damn it, I don't remember a thing. I wish I woulda known that. I always wanted to fly in one. Probably my only chance and I missed it. Damn snake!"

"Aw, you might get another chance someday, and maybe you'll even be conscious for the ride." He laughed a little, as he looked around at all the paraphernalia surrounding his friend. The heart monitor, pulse monitor and oxygen saturation monitor all showed Booger was a long way from being critical. There was an IV bag of normal saline along with two other bags of medicine piggy backed to it hanging beside him, dripping needed drug-infused fluid into his veins.

Sam stepped forward, laying her hand on his unaffected leg, not the one encased in a half a mile of gauze. "Mack told me you popped that snake like a bullwhip. I guess you showed him what for. What did the doctors say about the bite?"

Booger laughed a low chuckle without smiling and said, "Yeah my daddy taught me that trick. The last thing that went through that snake's mind was his ass. He was a big ole sucker, that's why I wasn't too concerned. I guess he figured I was gonna kill him, so he wanted to kill me first. I killed him though and I'm still here.

"The doc said I was lucky I got here when I did. Said it was going to be a long hard road but maybe they can save my leg. He didn't make no promises though. It looks awful, all swole up and such. They had to cut the skin to keep it from busting open. I reckon I'll be all right.

"I got things to do. I'm gonna get out of this place as quick as I can." Wanting to change the subject to something different than his difficult situation he asked Mack, "So, did you find those hikers? Were they fishin' like we figured?"

Mack didn't want to go into it, but he was asked so he replied, "I found the girl, Booger. The boy had been killed. Some raggedy ass dope cook had her. He had a camp back up the hill off that trail we were on."

A surprised look changed to a more serious expression on Booger's face. "You rescued her, didn't you?"

"Yeah, I got her, Booger."

"From the way your head looks, it took a little doing."

"Well, I got caught. The guy thumped me on the head, and then he had me tied up for the night."

"Dang it boy, how'd you get loose?"

"Somebody shot him, then I got loose."

Booger squinted his eyes and stroked his bear. His eyes were fixed on Mack. He looked around then said in a low voice, "Was it that fella who lives up there on the other side of the lake? I ran across him when I was up there one day scouting around. My horse pitched me off on some rocks, and he helped me out a little bit. The war messed him up, but he seems like a nice guy. I take him a load of canned goods and some necessaries every so often. He don't like to come to town. You know about him?"

"When I was up there lookin' around, I ran across him up that creek. His waders had filled with water and he was drownin' under that waterfall. I roped him and pulled him out. We talked a while and yeah, he seems like a nice guy. He said he keeps watch over that area. I guess it's his way of dealing with his troubles."

"Did he know about that dude cookin' the drugs up there?"

"He didn't mention it, but he did say he'd seen a lot of traffic stoppin' just short of the lake, probably at that trail leading to the cook's camp."

Booger thought about it for a minute then said, "So, who shot the guy and helped you get away?"

"It was a girl that was in camp with him, as far as I could tell. She shot him with my gun, untied me and then got on my horse and rode away. When I got to the trailhead, the horse was in the trailer."

"Hmm. Lucky for you she hated him enough to kill him right then, probably did us all a favor."

Mack saw no need to go into the whole background story. That story would be better told on the porch at the X Bar ranch over cold libations. "Yeah I was pretty lucky. She did so us all a favor. He was sure no loss." Now Mack wanted to change the subject. "So, what about your horses. Do you have anybody to take care of the place while you're laid up?"

"Yeah, I got plenty of friends to help out. I'll make some phone calls this afternoon. I guess ya'll are gonna be headin' back pretty soon. It seems I'm no longer a suitable host." He chuckled a sorrowful laugh.

"Yeah, we gotta be getting back to Texas. We gotta get back to work. If you don't need us, we'll probably head out in the morning. If you need us to help, we can probably stretch it another couple of days."

"Naw, Mack, you've helped me quite a bit. Saving my life ought to do it." He laughed at his low-key gratitude. "I guess if you're gonna go back, you might as well take those saddles with you. Income from cowboyin' and runnin' hunts is gonna be shot all to hell with this bum leg and all. I can't afford to pay you now."

"Why don't you just keep those saddles? They fit those horses perfect. When I took them off there was an even sweat on their back and no hot spots. I'd say everything worked good, and they seemed to ride really well. You don't worry about payin'. You just take care of yourself and come back stronger. Don't mess around and lose that leg, pard. I don't wanna be makin' a stirrup to fit a peg leg."

His spirit was lifted a bit and with sincere gratitude he said, "Dang, pard, you know you don't have to do that but I sure appreciate it. We'll settle up when I get better. Thanks." He extended his hand and Mack shook his calloused paw, making sure not to disturb the IV catheter protruding from it.

"Don't mention it, my friend. You just take good care of yourself. We're gonna let you get some rest now. I want to go check on the hiker. Her name's Sandy, by the way. Ya'll may run across each other here in the hospital. We'll come by and check on you tomorrow on our way out. You need anythin' from the ranch?"

"No, I guess not. Everything I'd want from there they won't let me have. There's a bottle of fine whiskey in the cupboard if ya'll are of a mind to partake. I'm sure they'd frown on that in here. Thanks for all you've done, and Sam it was sure good to meet you. I wish we coulda had more time, under better circumstances. Ya'll are gonna to have to come back when I get out of here."

Sam took his hand in hers and said, "Booger, it's a pleasure to meet you. I look forward to the next time. I got a little time in on that mule of yours. You're right. He's hard headed but real smart. I think I can get him to come around, but it's gonna take some work. Next time, for sure. You take care now."

"I'll see ya'll in the morning," he said with a smile, as the pair walked out the door.

They found the main nurse's station for the floor and Mack asked the busy nurse, "Could you tell me where I can find a girl that was brought in yesterday? All I know is her first name is Sandy."

The veteran nurse eyed the cowboy with the knot on his head suspiciously. She guardedly asked, "Are you family?"

Mack knew her game and what she was thinking. She was protecting a patient. "I'm not family. My name is Mack McWhirter. I'm the guy that rescued her. Has she had any family come to visit?"

Her countenance changed at his revelation. "Oh, Mack, in that case you can find her on the next floor up. I haven't been up there, but I've heard about her. I don't know if her family is here yet. Take the elevator up one floor and ask at the nurse's station. I'll let them know you're on your way up." She stopped talking to Mack and she looked at Sam. Mack turned to walk away, while the girls held eye contact. The nurse silently communicated to Sam, *Girl, you have on helluva man there.* Sam cracked a slight knowing smile.

The elevator doors opened to reveal the nurse's station. Behind the counter stood two smiling nurses. One said, "You must be the hero." Mack got embarrassed and blushed a little, and Sam punched him in the shoulder and said, "Hero." The nurses giggled.

The second nurse said, "Sandy is in room 213 but the sheriff's with her right now interviewing her. He asked for privacy."

Disappointed at the timing, Mack said, "Oh, well could you tell me how she's doing? Has she had any family come to see her?"

"Her family is on the way from California. Physically, she's stabilized and doing well considering what she's been through. Emotionally, she is still fragile. She's communicating more but there's a long way to go."

"Has she been told about her boyfriend yet? I didn't tell her anything about him when she asked."

The nurse frowned and lowered her voice, "No, we haven't broached that subject yet. She keeps asking though. It will have to come out soon, but we're waiting till she is stronger. That was a horrible thing that happened."

"It certainly was. Uh, I won't hang around for the sheriff to get finished but would you do me a favor and give me a call if anything changes? I'll try to come back by tomorrow before I head home." He wrote his phone number on a piece of paper, handed it to the nurse and said, "Thank you."

"I sure will. I'll pass it along to the next shift, too." As he turned to get back on the elevator she said, "And Mack? You did a brave thing up there."

He stepped into the elevator and before the doors closed he smiled and shrugged. "Anyone would've done the same." The doors closed.

In the close confines of the elevator Sam put her arm around his broad shoulders and with pride in her voice said, "I don't think just anyone would've done the same. You did a brave thing."

The doors opened as Mack put his arm around her waist, pulling her in close. "Enough of this hero crap, let's go get something to eat." They stepped off the elevator, walked through the lobby and out into the dry darkness of the New Mexico night. "And after that, I'm sure looking forward to laying in a soft bed." He turned and kissed her on her temple then said, "With you."

21

BLACK TRUCKS AND ODD OCCURRENCES

Mack had just enough time to realize how comfortable the bed was and how good it felt to have Sam beside him before the soft linen and bare skin had a reverse effect. It should've fired his engine up but exhaustion won and he fell asleep.

Sam watched him as he slept. She knew how lucky she was to be here with him and made a promise to herself that she'd no longer let the burden of responsibility keep them apart.

In the morning she woke before him and picked up where she'd been when she fell asleep, watching him. She stroked his chest, and he began to smile. He lay there with his eyes closed, feeling her hand as it caressed his chest. Finally, he opened his eyes to look at the raven-haired angel in the bed with him. He noticed the room was filled with sunlight and said, "Man, oh man, I guess I was a little tired."

She laughed and said, "You were asleep as soon as your head hit the pillow. I don't see how you made it all day, anyway. This bed sure is nice, isn't it?"

He rolled over on top of her, pinning her in the luxurious softness. He pulled her arms up over her head and kissed her. "The best thing about it is you're in it." He kissed her again, longer this time and said, "I'm gonna get a shower — a hot one this time — then let's see about some breakfast."

"Well, okay if that's what you want to do."

He hopped out of bed to get in the shower, and she followed him into the bathroom. He turned and looked at her quizzically and she said with a mischievous grin, "I'll see if I can't make this shower just a little hotter for you." He smiled and pulled the curtain back.

The two clean and happy lovers dried each other off and got dressed, taking their sweet time about it. They left the room to go downstairs to the café for a big plate of *huevos rancheros* and fresh tortillas. Mack told Sam he thought the best thing about Mexican food in this desert state was they sure knew how to dress up a breakfast.

They dallied over breakfast and coffee for a while, just hanging out together. It was beginning to feel like a mini vacation for them and they welcomed it. It was a time full of happiness that he was still alive and relief that their friend was going to be okay. They didn't talk about it, but it was in the back of both of their minds. Nothing like a near death experience to make life all the sweeter. Priorities were falling in place for both of them.

With breakfast finished and all the coffee gone, they decided to check out of the room and get on with the day. The clerk at the desk, when she saw his name on the form, gave Mack a concerned look. Mack noticed and asked, "Is everything okay? Did that credit card run all right?"

"No, that's all okay. It's just that I recognized your name here. Last night two guys came in asking what room you were in. We never give out that information, but I wouldn't have anyway. They sort of had a gangbanger look about them. They looked pretty suspicious. When I told them we don't give out information, they kept trying to find out anyway. Finally, they gave up and left. Do you know them?"

Mack was concerned. Sam grabbed his arm, hearing this made her a little antsy. "No, I don't know many people up here. Did you see what they were driving?"

"I think it was a black truck," she said with a look of helpful concern on her face. "One of those tall four wheel drive ones. The parking lot was pretty quiet that late at night and that's the only one I saw moving."

"Thanks for the heads up. I'll keep an eye out," he said as they walked out to his truck. As a precaution, Mack did a close inspection of the exterior and underneath before they got in.

Sam slid into the seat and said, "That makes me sort of nervous, Mack. I wonder if it has anything to do with what happened up on the mountain."

"I have no idea. Only one person up here knows me. I wonder what sort of cow pile I've kicked. I guess I might tell the sheriff about that. Maybe he knows something from investigating the scene. It could be gang related, I guess. They're always into drugs."

He pulled his truck out onto the highway headed south, and added, "I guess that'll be our first stop. I'll go give my statement and then we can go button up Booger's place and hit the road for home. Sounds like we need to be gettin' out of here."

"Yeah, the sooner the better," Sam said as she kept a vigilant eye on her surroundings.

The ride back to Cimarron was filled with theories about what the late night visit could've meant. The mystery of how they knew he was at that hotel was a whole different question, adding import to the situation. The familiarity was discomforting for both of them. Nothing was reasonably solved by the time they arrived at the sheriff's office.

Mack parked the truck and Sam nervously asked, "You want me to wait here or come with you?" She had very little experience with the seamier side of life or with law enforcement, and the mystery of it all was making her a bit skittish.

"I don't know how long this will take. You can come with me if you want. Not much to see or do out here, anyway." He didn't want to bring it up that he didn't want her to be by herself.

She jumped at the invitation, and they walked up the police department's gravel walkway and past the sheriff's car through the front door.

The matronly receptionist coldly said, "May I help you?"

Mack decided to attack her with sweetness and said, "Yes, ma'am. How are you today? I think I was supposed to come by and see the sheriff to give a statement. I was involved in that search for the hikers. I found the girl. I think he wanted an official statement, since both of us were pretty busy the other day."

She looked over her glasses and asked, "Is your name McWhirter?"

"Yes, ma'am." He smiled as he said it, but nice did not seem to be working.

"I've heard about you. Have a seat. I'll see if he is in." She got up and went through one of the three doors in the foyer.

They sat and Mack wondered why she'd had to see if he was in. He wouldn't be hard to miss in this cramped three-room office building. Why didn't she just say, "I'll see if he wants to talk to you?" She didn't seem to be one to mince words.

The gatekeeper stepped back into the foyer and held the door open as she indifferently said, "The sheriff will see you now."

When Mack and Sam stepped into the sheriff's office, he was seated behind a desk covered with papers and folders. He didn't stand to greet them, he simply looked up at Sam and said, "Ma'am, this will be an official statement being made here today pertaining to a murder investigation. If you like, you can have a seat in the foyer."

Mack extended his hand to the sheriff, just to catch him off guard. He halfway rose out of his seat to uncomfortably shake Mack's hand. "How are you today, sheriff? There won't be anything come out in this conversation that I haven't already told her about. I don't mind if she's in here."

The sheriff stared blankly at Mack. Tilting his head slightly he said, "Captain McWhirter, I have procedures to follow. Ma'am, would you mind?"

The tone was set for the unpleasant interview. Mack looked at her and nodded his head, and Sam returned to the foyer. He understood there were procedures for an official deposition, since he'd been through many. The sheriff didn't have to be an ass about it. This one would be a clash of personalities, as far as Mack was concerned.

"Do you prefer to be addressed by rank or just your name? I thought it might be by rank, since you took it upon yourself to demand thousands of dollars worth of our resources, Captain."

"Well, sheriff, right now I'm not on duty, I'm just a saddle maker up here visiting a friend. When I asked for that helicopter and ambulance, I was in paramedic mode and decided that was best for the patient. Wouldn't you want the best care possible for one of your volunteer searchers and the victim?"

"Yes, I would, Mr. McWhirter. It was just rather presumptuous of you to order those resources. That decision is usually up to our personnel. But that's neither here nor there at this point."

"I agree," said Mack, still wanting the last word in this verbal chess game. "But I was the only one there and there wasn't much time to wait. What sort of questions do you have for me today?"

"I've been to the crime scene. I'd like to get your version of what happened. Just so you know, I'm recording this deposition concerning your involvement with the events leading up to and following the murder in the Vallle Vidal valley. Please state your name."

"Peyton McWhirter."

"Please give me your version of the events during the search for two lost hikers through and up to up the time the victim was recovered and you returned to the trailhead."

"Okay. Mr. Privett and I were searching for the lost hikers on the trial to the mountain lake. We were searching for clues or trail signs up the—"

"Excuse me a minute. Could you state for the record why you deviated from the official search grid and went freelancing away from the search area?"

Mack could tell the game was on. The Sheriff was trying to direct the official record to lean in his favor. This was not Mack's first time to play administrative chess. "Mr. Privet and I saw evidence at the hikers' camp to indicate they went fishing. There was an official proceeding underway and we decided not to interrupt. With us being on horseback, we knew we had enough time to search the lake area and make it back to search our assigned grid before the people on foot were finished."

"However, that was not the case, now, was it?"

"We did encounter some difficulties, yes." Mack decided to give his deposition like an auctioneer selling a farm tractor. "Mr. Privett dismounted his horse to look at a clue on the trail and in the process was snake bit. He encouraged me to continue searching alone while he went back down the mountain to seek medical treatment.

"I continued on and found a piece of a fishing rod on the trail. It was in a pile of brush that concealed another trail. I decided to investigate this trail and in the process encountered the body of the deceased male hiker. He had been hacked to death with a large blade. The female hiker was still unaccounted for, so I continued up the trail."

"You say you found the male hiker. What was his condition?"

"He was dead. May I continue?" Mack knew the tactic of muddying up the story with minute details, so he held fast to the facts.

The sheriff, knowing how things would sound on the recording, just nodded and stared with eyes like cold steel.

"I continued up the trail till I found a camp. As I observed the camp, I saw the female hiker in question tied up under a lean-to on the edge of the camp. While attempting the rescue of the female, I was assaulted and knocked unconscious. When I came-to, I was tied up and found I was now captive myself.

"I had no contact with my captor until the next morning, when he came out of the cabin and said he was going to kill us. He had a machete. He raised the machete and I rolled over on the female to protect her. I heard two gunshots. Before I could roll back over to see what happened, I could feel someone behind me untying my hands. When my hands were free, I rolled over to see an individual with long black hair walking away and the man with the machete dead on the ground.

"I yelled at the person, but they didn't acknowledge me. They mounted my horse and rode away. I untied the female, and we got into the Jeep and came down the mountain. I didn't know if there was anyone else in the area, and I decided it was best to hurry and get the girl to medical treatment. She'd been assaulted and was suffering from dehydration.

"As we made our way back down the trail, I encountered Mr. Privett. He was in shock and suffering from exposure. I put him in the Jeep and brought him down with us. I called 911, requesting medical assistance. It arrived and that's when you and I made our first contact."

Mack shot through the facts so fast, he left the sheriff in his verbal dust, struggling to keep up. He couldn't get a word in to interrupt. As Mack finished and blankly stared at him, he realized the whole statement happened faster than the sheriff had anticipated.

Usually the person the sheriff was questioning had to play catch up, but this adversary had turned the tables. "Did you notice anything unusual about the surroundings at the camp?"

"There was a tent next to the cabin that was a methamphetamine lab."

Mack knew he'd scored a hit by the slight twitch of the sheriff's left eye and his slight look of concern. He went official when he asked, "By what authority can you make that determination? Did you analyze what was in the tent?"

"In my career in the fire service I've provided fire protection for the police in disassembling many meth labs, the smell is always the same. I recognized it. The man that said he was going to kill me was exhibiting behavior consistent with being under the influence of methamphetamine. What did you think when you went up there?"

"The samples have been sent off to the lab for analysis, I make no assumptions." The sheriff stood, and as he did he casually switched off the tape recorder. "Would you like a cup of coffee?" This slight change of consideration caused Mack to wonder.

"A cup of coffee would be nice. My girlfriend might want one, too. I take mine black, she likes a little cream if you have it."

The sheriff stepped out to get the coffee, and while he was gone Mack looked all over the room for a camera. There usually was one in an interrogation room, even though this was just an office. Not seeing one, he figured modern law enforcement techniques hadn't made it here yet. The sheriff seemed upset at having to pay for medical service, so the budget must be pretty tight.

The sheriff returned with the coffee and had a seat. He neglected to start the recorder as he continued, "So, when you left the camp, what did you take with you?"

"I retrieved my wallet and cell phone from the cabin."

"That is all? You took nothing else from the scene?"

"Well, I took four bottles of water and a granola bar from the cabin. I didn't think the dead guy would mind. The girl needed fluids. I took that and the Jeep."

"The person that shot him, did you get a good look at her?"

"No, just their backside. I didn't say it was a female. All I saw was long black hair."

"Mmm-hmm. Did you see if that person carried anything away from the scene?"

"I was pretty fuzzy-headed and am struggling to remember what I do remember."

"I'm just making sure the crime scene I investigated was as intact as it should be. Sometimes, things tend to walk off. I'm just making sure."

"Well, that's all I took. What was mine and what I needed. I hope you can piece it all together."

"Yes, it's quite the puzzle. I spoke to the hiker last night, but she was no help. What you've told me will help me make a determination. If you think of anything else, I'd like to hear about it."

"You'll be the first to know. Are we through here? I've told you all I know."

"Yeah, we're finished. Thank you for coming in."

As Mack stood to leave he looked at the tape recorder, and thought, *That knucklehead forgot to turn the recorder back on. What's up with that?* He walked out into the foyer, hurriedly took Sam's hand and left the building.

"How did it go?"

"Aw, it was just a basic interview. I've done enough of them to play the game. Short and to the point — just the facts and get it over quick. I don't think he's done it very often. I think I was a step ahead of him the whole way. It was sort of weird though. Let's get outta here. Whadaya say?"

"You bet. Let's go. So, we're just going to lock up Booger's place and head on back?"

"Yeah, he said he had some friends he could count on to take care of the place. Let's make sure the horses have plenty of food and water, then hit the road back to Texas. I'm through with this place."

In the truck on the way back to the ranch Sam asked, "What kind of questions did he ask?"

"Just the normal stuff. Where were you? What happened? What do you remember? What did you do? That sort of stuff."

Mack thought for a minute replaying it all in his head. The concern of missing evidence and the recorder being turned off was strange. He got a look of surprise on his face and slapped the steering wheel.

Sam said, "What?"

"That sheriff was all concerned with whether I took anything from the scene. I told him all I took was my stuff and some water, but I just remembered I *did* take something. I forgot all about it."

"What was it? Do we need to go back?"

"No, we're not going back there at all if I can help it. When I was scoping out the camp, I saw a trail camera in a tree. It must've been an alarm or something to the cabin, that's how that guy knew I was there. Before I left, I grabbed the camera. When we got down to the trailhead, I put it in one of the saddlebags. How could I forget all about that?"

"Did you look at what was on it?"

"No. I never had time. Let's look at it when we get back to the ranch."

"That might be *very* interesting." Her comment was cut short as she yelled and pointed out the shiny black four-wheel drive truck, lifted higher than it should be. "There it is! There's that truck she was tellin' us about!"

Mack watched with concerned silence as it passed. The dark tinted windows made it difficult to see the driver, but when he looked in his rear view mirror he could see on the symbol of Santa Muerta on the back window — the patron saint of Mexican bad guys and the drug cartels. He knew about that from working with the cops on drug raids. He'd seen little alters set up around a statue of a skeleton in a colored robe holding a scythe inside drug houses. There'd be candles burning and offerings of money and alcohol surrounding it. The offerings were for safe passage as they made their drug deals or other illegal endeavors. These were bad people, made worse by the presumption of protection. He wondered what these bad boys were doing out this way. Booger said there'd been some strange things going on.

Mack pulled his truck up to the gate at Booger's ranch, and Sam automatically got out to unlock the gate and open it. She stood and turned with a shocked look on her face, motioning for him to come look. He stood beside her, looking at the lock. It'd been cut. "Something sure is wrong here," Mack said. "I bet those gang-banging bastards in the black Chevy cut the lock to get to Booger's ranch. This ain't good."

He pulled the truck through and Sam closed the gate and then got back in the truck. "On second thought, why don't you drive? I'm going to get out at that last bend and look at the situation before we drive into something."

He pulled his pistol out of the holster mounted on the seat and they switched places. At the last bend in the road, he got out and climbed up on the hill overlooking the house as Sam waited for the signal to drive on.

Mack topped the hill and what he saw below filled him with anger and a desire for revenge. Both doors on Booger's old truck were flung open and all the stuff that had been inside was now blowing around on the ground. Between the house and the barn lay all the dogs, each dead in a pool of blood.

The front door of the house swung open freely in the dusty breeze. The new saddles had been thrown from the porch rail and lay in the red dirt. Evidently the intruders had come and gone. There was no movement to be seen. He waved Sam on, still watching with his gun ready, just in case.

Sam saw the carnage and could only sit in the truck and cry for the dead animals. Mack walked down from the hill in full protective mode and hurried to the truck. "I'm going to check the house," he said to his grief-sickened girlfriend. "You stay in the truck, and leave it running."

He cautiously walked up the steps to the porch and into the house. What little Booger had was carelessly strewn about the rooms. All drawers and closets were open, and the place had been ransacked. The old Winchester 94 was still leaning against the wall by the door and the silver trophy buckles were still in the shadow box on the wall. This wasn't a burglary. Somebody was looking for something in particular.

He went back out on the porch and set the rockers upright. He had a seat and motioned for Sam to join him. She'd composed herself so she came and sat beside him. "What the hell happened here, Mack?"

"Somebody was looking for somethin' they thought Booger had. The inside of the house is completely tore up. I sure don't know what it could be. He never let on about anythin'. Stuff of value is still here."

The couple sat on the porch in silence for a while until Sam asked, "Didn't you say you had that trail camera here?"

"Oh, yeah, I keep forgetting about that thing. I put it in the saddlebag of that saddle right there. I wonder if they got it."

Mack walked down off the porch to the saddle on the ground. He squeezed the saddlebag and found the camera was still there. He undid the buckle on the flap, took it out and went back to sit beside Sam.

He opened the access panel then fumbled with the little buttons trying to get the pictures to come up on the little screen. Finally, he hit the right button and looked at the screen. His face went from electronic confusion to wide-eyed shock and anger. He gritted his teeth and hissed, "This is what they were looking for, right here."

He turned to show the little pictures to Sam, but his ringing phone interrupted him. He handed the camera to her then answered his phone. "Mack McWhirter."

The female voice on the other end of the line was full of sorrow and regret. "Mack, this is Wanda Sanchez. I'm the nurse you spoke to at the hospital yesterday."

"Hi, Wanda. Yes, I remember you. How are you today?"

She sniffled and said, "I'm not worth a damn, Mack."

"What's wrong?" Mack asked with a foreboding feeling.

"Mack, Sandy died last night."

22
A PHOTO OP

Mack and Sam looked at each other in speechless shock, each for different reasons.

Mack spoke first, clearing his tightening throat and blinking his misty eyes. He haltingly told Sam, "Sandy died last night."

"Oh, that poor girl. What happened?"

"The nurse couldn't tell me much, just that she had a breathing difficulty, lost consciousness and never recovered from it."

"That's just horrible. I'm so sorry." She set the trail camera down, moving out of her chair to hold Mack tightly so he'd know she was with him in this sad time. It was a hard loss for him. He'd fought hard for that girl. Captivity and battle creates a bond between people, like a blacksmith forge welds iron.

Many minutes passed before she could feel his tight embrace of dependence relax, signaling he was back in fight mode and leaving his emotions behind. She moved back to her chair, letting the silence take its course.

It was his move but she wanted him to make it soon. She'd discovered things while he was on the phone.

After a while of staring of into the distant New Mexico countryside, he shook it off and put this bad feeling in the box in his mind where he put all his anguished thoughts. He was looking at his boots

176

when he said, "I saw my pictures on that trail camera. What else was on there?"

She handed him the camera and said, "Take a look for yourself." He held it and mashed the replay button. The pictures went backwards in sequential order. There were three of him as he walked up and then laid down watching and one picture of the snake-armed bastard dragging the struggling Sandy by her hair. That was almost more than Mack could tolerate in his emotional state. A few pictures of the snake-armed meth cook walking by on the trail, carrying what looked like jugs of supplies, and some young Mexican boys wearing taco creased hats walked by carrying boxes. There were some photos of deer and other animals that had happened by, and then the first picture, the one mistakenly taken when the camera was set up. Sam flinched like she was hit with electricity when he jumped out of his chair, throwing the trail camera into the chair beside him.

"Damn it!" he screamed as he stomped around on the porch and into the house. She let him go. He stomped through the house full-blown mad as he went to the icebox to get a beer. He walked into the kitchen, slamming the door behind him. He didn't really want privacy. He just wanted to slam a door out of anger. He opened the icebox, roughly grabbing a bottle of beer and twisting the top off.

The kitchen door had rebounded back open and he stomped the floor back into the living room. Standing in the middle of the room, he anxiously and aimlessly spun around. Then, he saw it. The note was stabbed onto Booger's bedroom door, held there by a cheap switchblade knife. Scrawled in pencil the note read,

WE WANT THAT CAMERA. BRING IT BACK.

The gravity of the situation got his attention; he now knew what the game was. His mood spun from anger to tactical analysis. Mack realized at that point he was in a game of life and death poker. He held a good hand that could win the game, but it was the same hand that Wild Bill Hickok held — the dead man's hand. Getting out of this wouldn't be easy.

Mack went back out to the porch where Sam was waiting for him to calm down. He was calmer and in command mode, just like fighting a fire. He had a plan. "We have to get you out of here. It's fixin' to get nasty. Whether we want it or not." He showed her the note.

She read it and her hand started to shake with fear. "Give it back, this isn't our fight. You just give it back and we'll leave. We don't have a dog in this fight, Mack."

His hard and calloused hands held her shaking ones still as he looked her in the eye. "I'm not gonna sugar coat it with you, Sam. It's just not that easy. If they get the camera back, I still have knowledge of it. They won't let me leave. That camera is the trump card right now. As long as I have it I'm a little better off. It's gonna be a fight. I don't want you around for it."

"Who are they? I don't wanna leave you here by yourself. Maybe I can help you."

"I would bet a paycheck it's everybody whose face is on that camera. At least I know who the players are. I just don't know why. That first picture is the one that worries me the most. It will just be easier to take care of things if you're not here. I'd worry about you so much I wouldn't have my mind on my business. Please, you have to go." His pleading eyes accentuated his request.

Her eyes welled up with uncommon tear. She knew there was no room for negotiation. She buried her face in his shoulder and whimpered, "Okay, I'll go. But you promise me you'll come back to me." She raised her tear stained face from his shoulder, and with her wet eyes lighting up with fire she said, "You promise me, Mack."

He smiled. "Oh, I'm comin' back. You can damn sure count on that. We've been apart too long. I'll be there for you."

She quietly stared at him, considering what he'd just said. *He's right. We've been apart and it was mostly my fault. I never thought it would happen to me but I let work and responsibility overcome my personal time, like a cloud can overtake the sun. My time with the man I love is the most important thing. He's secure enough to let me go and I didn't realize I'd gone so far away from him.* She swore to herself right there, *When he comes back, I'm gonna stay close by him.*

Resigned to the fact she asked, "So, where am I going and how are we going to do this?"

"You'll go to Amarillo. Driving by yourself would be too risky, so I think you should take the bus. The bus station in Amarillo is downtown and there's a fire station near there. I know some guys there. I'll call them and they'll hide you till I can get there."

"Are we leaving right now?"

"Right now. Quicker is better. I imagine they're watching us. That would be the right way to act anyway. We'll go to Cimarron and run around town some. You can sneak out of the truck and onto the bus when it gets there. I'll wait till the bus leaves with you on it."

She laughed a little at his plan. It seemed like something off of TV show. "Then what?"

He laughed at the corny plan too and said, "It should work. We aren't dealing with the brightest crayons in the box here. You get to Amarillo before they know you're gone and I come out here to circle the wagons. They want that camera, so they'll have to come get it. When they do, hell will rain down on them."

Sam had complete confidence in Mack's abilities. "Well, let's get on with it. Waiting is worse than leaving. Come on, before I change my mind."

Anxious for the fight and wanting to keep Sam safe he said, "Okay then, let's get going."

Sam sat close to Mack on their ride into town. Both were hyper-vigilant, watching their surroundings constantly. Knowing they were most likely being observed from the shadows they moved slowly and with flair so they were easy to spot.

The first stop, before the bus got there, was the western store. Sam got a big cowboy hat with an old west crease to it and a new pearl snap shirt. She wore it when they went to the ice cream parlor for a double dip cone. The lady at the dry goods store complimented her on her hat as they perused what the store had to offer.

Mack made a good deal on a long black wig, including the Styrofoam display head it was being displayed on. From the window of the store, they saw the Greyhound bus pass on its way to station. They casually left the store, got back in the truck and drove around to the back of the bus station.

Mack parked under a tree, behind some bushes, and Sam changed her shirt and put her hair up in a bun under an old fire department cap. After confirming nobody was watching, Mack kissed Sam and said, "I'll see you in Amarillo."

"Damn right you will," she said and scampered in the back door of the bus station.

Mack set up the wig head wearing the cowboy hat on the back of the seat next to him, and put his arm around his new "girlfriend" so he could support the head and move it around. He drove back in front of the bus station and parked a distance away, but close enough to see the girl in the brown shirt and blue ball cap board the bus.

The bus pulled out onto the highway and Mack said quietly, "Vaya con Dios my love."

He headed out of town back toward the ranch when he saw the black Chevy truck stopped at a convenience store. He slowed down to get a good look as two men whose faces he recognized from the trail camera came out of the store. They saw him as he passed and started gesturing and laughing. Mack turned his new girlfriend's head toward them and in a high pitched girly voice he said, "Come on you little bastards, let's play Poncho Villa."

23

It Almost Worked

S am sat in the foul smelling velour comfort of the Greyhound bus as it left Cimarron and the ensuing battle. She had little emotional comfort as she rolled along watching the monochromatic landscape of New Mexico fly by. She was confident the plan had worked. She was headed toward safety in Amarillo and Mack was headed to a showdown.

She sat in the middle of the bus, by a window. There were only eight or ten other travelers onboard, and they all kept to themselves. It didn't matter though, because she was in no mood for conversation. Concern for Mack flooded her mind.

Even with her smooth evacuation out of Cimarron she was safe but still afraid for her man. He had plenty of fight in him and wasn't one to walk away from confrontation. She really didn't know what he was fighting for, but she did know he wanted a definitive end to the story. *Maybe he's fighting for the girl who died, he carries things like. Or maybe he thought Booger Red was in danger. Whatever it is, I can't relax until he's safe in my arms again.*

She always tried not to ride public buses. She didn't like them and the fact that they stopped at every little town along the route just made her feel like she was traveling at the speed of dark. Case in point, they just got going at a good pace when they stopped at the first stop, at least there weren't many towns between Cimarron and Amarillo.

The bus slowed then hissed to a stop at the bus station in Springer. One person got off and two Mexican men got on. One stood in the door by the driver and the other walked down the aisle looking for a seat. He stopped at Sam's seat and looked at her with a greasy grin. She didn't smile when she looked up at him thinking. *There's no way I'm sitting with this guy.*

He bent over and quietly said to her, "You're supposed to come with us." Before she could tell him to go to hell, she heard a metallic click in his right hand. She looked down to see a switchblade knife in his hand. She was trapped. He sneered, "We have your boyfriend, and we'll take you to him. Come quietly, señorita."

He stepped aside and let her step into the aisle. He put the blade close against her back, just for emphasis, as they walked up the aisle. The other thug jointed them as they stepped off the bus.

She said nothing as the punks led her to their shiny black Chevy truck with the *Santa Muerta* sticker on the back window. They pushed her inside and slid in on either side of her, then forced a blindfold over her fearful eyes. She didn't know what to do. She knew she should be scared but she was too mad. In her anger she broke her silence. "How did you bastards know I was on that bus?" *I thought the plan worked pretty well.*

The driver chuckled and said, "Oh, señorita, we know everything that goes on in Cimarron. We have people everywhere. It was a good try, though. That big hat looked good on you." He brushed her hair with his hand, and she returned the touch with an elbow to his throat. It was a blind shot but it connected effectively.

As he clutched his throat, gagging and gasping for air, the other one thought it was hilarious. He slapped his knee and laughed loudly. "Oh, José, she's a tough one. You look out for her. She gonna kick your ass." Still laughing he continued, "Remember, El Jefé said not to hurt her, no marks. Remember? Ha-ha-ha! When you can talk again you, might apologize to the señroita and maybe she won't hurt you no more!"

With fire in his grimacing, watery eyes he squeaked to his partner, "Tie her arms, Pepé, you son of a goat. I'll get my chance later." Still holding his dented throat, José started the truck and headed back to Cimarron.

Pepé had his hands full in the close confines of the truck as he tried to get a rope around Samantha and keep her blindfolded. Finally, she was tied and things settled down.

Sam concentrated on what she couldn't see. She counted the turns and which direction they went, noting about how long between each one. She listened but outside sounds were drowned out by the ranchero music pulsating from the radio. She committed to memory the two cattle guards they passed over before they came to a stop. If they went over the rumble of cattle guards then they must be off the main road away from everything.

The truck stopped and they made her get out. She wanted to run, but being blindfolded and bound made that out of the question.

She was led up some steps, onto a wooden porch and through a door out of the sunlight. The two Mexican captors chattered in Spanish, probably about her. She knew she was in a building and thought she heard a low voice, maybe Anglo, say, "In there. Untie her."

She was led through another doorway where they took her blindfold off. Her eyes were already accustomed to the dark, so she could see she was in a small room with boarded up windows and a dirty mattress on the floor.

When the rope came off her upper body, she saw something else — an opportunity. She kicked Pepé square the nuts, and when he bent over in pain she caught his nose with a powerful upper cut. He was hurt and blinded, staggering around the room.

José tried to grab her in the darkness but she turned it on him and got him in a headlock, trying to tear off his ear. She rammed his head into the door facing, sending him to his knees. He was barely conscious.

Pepé was lucky enough to find a corner in his blind staggers and tried to protect himself from the banshee by assuming a fetal position. Sam saw her chance and ran out of the room, right into the business end of a .357 magnum. The man holding the big gun said, "Now, hold on little lady. Where do you think you're going? You're a long way from town and any help. Why don't you just have a seat while I clean your room?"

He yelled at the two failed thugs, "Ya'll get your chili-eating asses out here. Now! You ain't good for nothin.'"

José came staggering out, trying to hold his ripped ear on his swelling head, and Pepé was still holding his crotch, his nose bent sideways on his face. They kept their distance from Sam as they came back into the room. The man with the gun said, "Your room's ready, if you would be so kind as to step in."

Subdued but not beaten, she walked back into the room. The door slammed behind her and she could hear the lock clicking into place. She was stuck like a dog in a crate, and it was dark. Her mind began spinning options. There had to be a way out.

On the other side of the door she could hear the boss berating the Mexican thugs. "You stupid little sons-a-bitches, you couldn't put a chicken in a coop. I don't know why I keep you around. You better be grateful your uncle's such a powerful guy. Damn it! I'm surrounded by dumbasses everywhere I turn.

"Where's her phone? You did get that, didn't you? Give it to me." It was quiet for a moment, then he said, "Here, call this number.

Tell him we have the girl. Tell him to meet you in the morning at nine o'clock at the lake. Tell him not to talk to the sheriff and to come alone, and to bring that trail camera. We'll trade it for the girl. Can you do that? Make damn sure you do and don't screw this up. I don't care who your uncle is. I'll shoot you in the head right here if you mess it up!

There were heavy footsteps stomping around the room, then she heard one of the thugs on the phone. "Listen closely to me… No, but we have her. … Shut up and listen to me. You bring the camera to the lake in the morning at nine o'clock and we'll bring her. We'll trade it for her. Don't talk to the sheriff and come alone."

"What did he say?"

"He say he be there. Boy, that guy sure is mad. He say he gonna whip my ass and everythin.'"

"Well that girl in there sure did, it probably wouldn't be much of a problem for him to do it too. I'm gonna go to town to take care of some things. You two knuckleheads stay here and watch her. Don't open that door for anything, you hear me? Don't open it till I get back."

"Sî, Jefé."

She heard a car start then drive off. Her guards in the other room rattled on in Spanish for a while, then it was silent. She figured they'd fallen asleep. She inspected the room like a tiger in a new cage. As far as she could tell, there was no way out of the room. The windows were boarded up tight from the outside and there were no loose floorboards to pry up. She was a prisoner without options. She lay down on the floor, the mattress was just too repulsive, and pondered her situation.

As is common for people in dire straits, she began to think about her life — her accomplishments and regrets. The only two regrets that came to mind were that she'd let her business overshadow her relationship with Mack. If they could get out of this mess she vowed to no longer have that regret. The other sorrow in her life was that she hadn't listened to her grandfather when he tried to teach her the old ways. Her efforts to rectify this loss had led her to Johnny Running Bull.

She lay captive on the floor and day dreamed about that day in Fort Worth.

She'd begun to regret not paying attention to her native roots on the reservation. Her grandfather was deep in tribal tradition but, as it often goes, his son cast it to the side. She remembered when her grandfather was very old, her father had forced him to move out of his tipi and into their little house on the reservation. Her father said an old man would die living in a tent. She'd always thought it was the other way around.

She was right, he didn't last too long living in the house. Before he died, he told her a lot of things about the old ways, some she remembered and some not. Now that she was curious, she wanted to learn more. There weren't many Natives living around Stephenville and the ones who did knew nothing of the old ways.

There was a pow-wow at the Cowtown Coliseum in the Fort Worth Stockyards, and Sam took Mack to see it. The drum hadn't started yet when they walked in. The announcer was naming off the names of Native veterans, then made various announcements about the pow-wow. It was supposed to start at noon but it was almost one o'clock. Sam remembered something about "Indian time" from her reservation days.

They found a good seat on the front row and soon the drum started. She was surprised by her reaction when the singers started. The drum seemed to mirror her heartbeat. She closed her eyes and the music took her back to her childhood on the Redbud Reservation. She could see herself as a young girl with braided hair, riding bareback across the rolling grass hills of the reservation. Her body started moving involuntarily to the music as it consumed her consciousness.

Mack had touched her on the leg and asked, "Are you okay?"

"I am better than okay," she'd said, as she opened her eyes to see the dancers spinning and jumping in all their feathered regalia. The colors of the feathers, fur and intricate beadwork were a blur. "It is all so beautiful." The beating of the drum and the bells on the dancers' legs along with the singing took Sam to a happy place in her mind.

The pace changed when it was the women's turn to dance. They moved slowly around in a circle around the drum. As Sam intently studied their fine regalia, she didn't notice the old man with tight braided hair coming down the aisle with the help of a cane.

He surprised her when he tapped her on the shoulder and asked, "You look like a pretty girl, do you mind if I sit here?"

"I don't mind at all. Please, have a seat."

"My name is Johnny Running Bull. Who are you?"

"My name's Samantha Nawaji, and this is my boyfriend, Mack McWhirter."

The old man nodded acknowledgement to Mack and directed his attention back to the dancers. After a while he said, "Stands firm."

"Pardon me?" said Sam.

"Your name, it means stands firm in Sioux. Did you know that? You must be a tough old gal." Johnny looked her up and down. "You better be, a woman that looks as good as you. What do you do?"

Mack interjected, "She sure is a tough one." He chuckled and the old man ignored him or couldn't hear him. Most likely the former. Mack found his place in the conversation and went back to watching the dancers.

"I didn't know that and thank you, I am. I train horses for a living."

The old man thought a minute before he asked, "Are you of the Sioux nation?"

"Yes, sir. I was born and raised on the Rosebud Reservation. I left when I was a teenager. Never been back."

The old man nodded a few times as he listened to the music and watched the dancers. In a few moments he said, "That's a shame. We need good-looking women on the rez to keep the young men there. They leave too fast. I left, but that's another story." After a pause he asked, "Do you talk to them?"

She didn't know who he was speaking of and she asked, "Who? The boys on the rez?"

Now the old man was confused. He gave her a funny look. "No, the horses. Why would you talk to the guys up there? You have this big old white boy here to talk to. I wondered if you could speak to the horses and if you listen to them. I've known people that can do that. What did you say your name was?" He now focused his attention on Sam.

"Nawaji is my last name, and yes, I think I can talk to the horses. Most people don't know what that's about so I don't say much about it."

Old Johnny stared at her for a while. "Nawaji. I knew a man by that name a long time ago. He's dead now. He could talk to the horses. He knew a lot. I'm a medicine man and I know a lot of things. He was almost as smart as me, but with horses he was smarter. I wish I could remember his first name but that was a long time ago." He kept looking at Sam, as if searching for answers.

Sam got that flutter in her gut, the kind you get when you just know a big fish is going to bite your hook or you know the right numbers will come up at the exact instant the dice leave your hand.

Old Johnny seemed old enough to have run with her grandfather. She said, "My grandfather's name was Thomas, Thomas Nawaji. Does that ring a bell?"

He pondered the name a minute. His face lit up and he got more wrinkles on his brow as he said something in his native language and dropped his cane to give her a big hug. He almost fell to the floor, and would have if she hadn't hugged him back and held him up.

"You are Thomas Nawaji's granddaughter! I just thought you were a good-looking woman to talk to but you're Thomas Nawaji's granddaughter. I am so happy to meet you, child! I've never seen you at pow-wows before. Where have you been?"

Mack picked up the old man's cane and gave it to him, while Sam held her embrace. She was so happy at her good fortune in meeting someone who knew her grandfather. *Perhaps he's someone who can school me in the old ways,* she'd thought.

She released Johnny, and was giddy and talking fast as she said, "I came here to talk to Native people. I didn't listen to my grandfather and I left the rez too soon. I want to get reconnected to my people. This is my first pow-wow since I was a child. I want to get back in touch with the Native ways. I'm so happy to meet you and know you knew my grandfather! What brings you down here? Did you come just for this pow-wow? That's a long way."

Johnny Running Bull swelled with pride that he'd found a good-looking Native girl who wanted to learn the old ways from him. He'd tried to pass on his knowledge before he died, but no one was interested, except the new age crystal-waving white people who thought it was cool. He had no time for them.

He'd known his time was short ever since he'd been moved here against his will by his son. Fort Worth, Texas sure wasn't South Dakota and it would kill him. He said in seriousness, "Child, we've been brought together by the powers today. I can see it now. My son moved me here for a reason, and I now know it wasn't his idea. I was sent here to meet you, the granddaughter of Thomas Nawaji. I live here now with my son and his family. Do you live here?"

Sam was ecstatic when she said, "I live in Stephenville, about an hour away. I think we were brought together, too. It's not so far that we can't visit. I've been looking for you. Can you teach me the old ways, Johnny?"

The tired old man now had a spark in his eyes and a new reason to live. It's funny how things can happen in the blink of an eye. "Child, I can and will. There's so much to learn. It's the last thing for me to do before I die. Thank God teaching you will take a while."

It had taken a few years, and Johnny Running Bull's heart finally gave out about a year ago but not before he'd shown her the things she wanted to learn. She'd even gone with his family to South Dakota to bury him on Indian soil. It was a homecoming for her.

These thoughts gave her comfort as she lay there in her present predicament. She quietly sang a song he'd taught her in the Sioux language. It was a song of power. She sang herself to sleep and dreamed of her childhood.

Hunger and thirst woke her. She knew there was no chance of help from her captors, so she tried to meditate to raise herself above her needs. The door suddenly swinging open and a flashlight brighter than the sun hitting her in the face broke her concentration. She was blinded while the two wannabe gangsters ran in, each taking an arm and roughly slapping her wrists in handcuffs.

They stood her up and walked her out of the dark room and into the blast of sunlight. In a paradox of relief, the blindfold was placed back over her eyes. She stumbled down the steps to the dirt and she heard the voice of the man with the gun say, "Put her in the car."

Once again she was hyper-vigilant to her surroundings. They slammed the door of the car, and she could hear a radio talk show turned way down low playing on the radio. *Either we're way outside of town or that radio has really bad reception. I'm mostly hearing static.*

24
COME AND GET ME

"Shut up and listen to me. You bring the camera to the lake in the morning at nine o'clock and we'll bring her. We'll do the trade there. Don't talk to the sheriff and you come alone."

Mack's rage filled eyes stared at the silent phone. Those words were like gasoline dribbling onto the fire that was building inside him. Right before he threw the phone off the porch, he remembered that it was his only source of contact with the kidnappers. He stifled the impulse, put the phone in his pocket and sat down while his temper smoldered.

He sat seething on the porch and went into battle mode. He realized that mad is not a good decision-making frame of mind, so he concentrated on formulating a plan to calm down. He evaluated his strategy and tactics from every angle then put together a rough plan of action. He mumbled to himself, "Time to play Pancho Villa, boys. This just might work."

He didn't want to but he knew he had to spend the night at Booger's ranch. It was tactically more defensible than any place in town, and there were fewer witnesses. He searched through the ransacked house for anything he might be able to use. He found an ancient single shot twelve-gauge shotgun and a box of shells in a closet. He'd never shoulder this gun to shoot it, from the looks of it, but it would come in handy. He also found a box of leg traps, a dozen of which still worked, in the barn. There was also a spool of smooth wire that could be useful.

He stood on the porch with Booger's good Steiner binoculars and surveyed the area, he didn't not want anyone to see what he was about to do, especially the bad guys if they were watching. The barren landscape surrounding him told he was alone.

He took the shotgun and the wire and walked down the road to the house. It passed between two red sandstone hills. At that point, on the house side of the hills, he laid the loaded shotgun. He piled rocks on the buckshot-loaded gun, securing it in a position just about car door high. He then ran the wire across the road, fastened it to the trigger and pulled back the hammer. No vehicle would get past this point.

Back at the house, he positioned the traps in a perimeter, one behind every piece of anything that could be used for cover. They were all cocked and ready to catch varmints. Since the house would be the primary place anyone would look for him, he decided to sleep in the barn. He only had about an hour of sunlight left, so he went to set up a sniper hide in the barn. He'd sleep there.

He found a choice place for the hide. It was slightly elevated and commanded a full field of view from the main road to the house. Satisfied with that, he went back to the house to get Booger's old Winchester 94, a box of ammo and the last of the elk roast. *Man I'm gettin' tired of this stuff. I'm never gonna eat elk again. Maybe the two last beers will help me choke it down.* He took the rifle and the meal back to the barn to settle in for the night.

Long after sundown, the calm New Mexico night lulled him into sporadic dozing. He fought to stay awake so he wouldn't be surprised but the calm was too much. He drifted off, dreaming of

Sandy, the poor dead hiker. They were on a hike together in a beautiful meadow, and she was asking him why her boyfriend had to die. Then she asked why she had to die. In the dream, Mack s had no answers to her questions.

He was about to speak to her when — *BOOM!* A shotgun blast blew the dream apart, and he awoke mad about Sandy's death and wondering where he was. He cleared his sleepy mind and got his bearings, realizing the shotgun had been triggered.

He listened and watched for any activity out toward his trap before he went to investigate. It was quiet, so he got down and carefully worked his way around through the rocks to the hill by the trap. He climbed the back side of the hill, and off to his left he could see the shotgun laying on the ground. Its recoil had blown it out of the rock pile.

He looked over the crest of the hill expecting to see a disabled automobile but there was nothing there. *Maybe somebody on foot was sneaking up the road to the house.*

He stealthily lay on top of the hill with his rifle ready. He listened for any moaning or signs that someone was hit. Silence. He couldn't see anything in the dark between the hills, so he switched on his flashlight and hoped giving away his position wouldn't be the end of him.

He shined the beam of the flashlight to the area of the trip wire. The light ran along the wire revealing a splash of blood on the ground. *Got him!* The light continued along the wire to illuminate the shattered body of a coyote up against the rocks. With the perceived threat abated, he stood and under his breath said, "Damn it! Got the wrong coyote."

Walking back to the barn, he looked at his watch. 3:30 a.m. He settled back into his nest in the barn, trying to get some fleeting sleep till the sun came up to start this day of reckoning.

The sun broke through the biting cold of the night, warming the new day. The light of the morning roused Mack from his sleep, and he stood and stretched out the muscle kinks earned by sleeping on feed sacks. He stumbled down to the house to rustle up a cup of coffee and quickly re-evaluate his plan for the day. He had to be at the lake in Valle Vidal well before nine o'clock.

As he sat on the porch drinking his coffee, he wondered how Sam felt waking up as a captive this morning. His building anger strengthened his resolve to rectify the injustice. *Those Mexican gangbangers will pay a high price today. Accounts will be paid in full and problems will be solved this morning, one way or the other.*

He wasn't coming back to Booger's place, so he locked up the house and made sure the horses and mule had water. He grabbed the camera, the rifle and a bag of canned goods, and then climbed into his truck to head toward the showdown at the Valle Vidal.

His mind was a whirl of thoughts as he drove. He had to get in place at the lake and trade Sam for the camera. He had no use for the camera or the crime and politics of Colfax County. He hoped to get her back and leave. He knew in his heart the whole thing could and most likely would go south. If it did, his only concern was keeping Sam safe, whatever the cost.

He knew why the Mexican drug boys wanted the camera with all those faces on it — that was some heavy evidence. They were probably just the worker bees and were probably nothing too important to the bigger operation. But they had Sam, which made them his highest priority.

He turned his truck onto the road to the Valle Vidal. At the trailhead, the gravel road led up to the lake. The crime scene tape was still in the trees at the old Jeep trail leading to that camp from hell. He went on to the lake, parked his truck and just sat there.

Before he got out, he looked all around the green lakeshore and as far as he could see into the dense woods. He was glad nobody else was in the area. That meant nobody to get in the way.

He got out of his truck with the sack of canned goods and trekked off into the woods to Turtle's camp. Half an hour of busting brush took him to the well-concealed campsite. It was just as he'd seen it the other day. Turtle wasn't there, but Mack knew he was watching from a vantage point somewhere close. If he waited long enough, the old sniper would materialize out of nowhere to have a visit, but Mack did not have the time for that right now.

He scribbled a note on a piece of paper and left it under a rock by the campfire so Turtle would see it easily. He left the canned goods by his food stash and he walked back down through the brush to the lake.

Once back at the truck, he took out the old Winchester, assured it was loaded and cocked, and then leaned it within reach behind a pine tree. The Ruger .45 long colt was tucked in his belt at the small of his back, ready to settle any ensuing arguments. His untucked shirt concealed the decision-maker.

He looked at his watch; it was 8:30. He anxiously sat on the tailgate of the pick up with the trail camera beside him and waited. He dearly hoped this would be short and simple, but figured it was probably a game of life and death.

At 8:50, he saw a car making its way up the valley. *Oh great*, he thought, *what a great day for somebody to decide to come fishing. I'm going to have to try to get rid of them.* As the car got close he saw it was the sheriff's car. *That's worse than fishermen, he is gonna screw up this whole deal. Those punks won't bring her here if he's around.*

Mack slid off the tailgate and checked his phone for any sort of a signal in case they tried to contact him in this confused mess. He walked to the open driver's side door and hit his horn a short blast and returned to his seat.

The sheriff stopped his car about forty feet from Mack's truck and got out. He stood alone beside his car and said, "I figured I'd find you up here McWhirter."

Annoyed at his presence and wondering why he'd say that, Mack asked, "Yeah, sheriff, it's a nice place. Thought I might do a little fishing. What brings you up here?"

"I'm just up here takin' care of some loose ends on my investigation. What's that there beside you?" He played dumb, hoping Mack hadn't figured out how to review the pictures.

Mack played along. Looking down at the camera then back at the sheriff, he said, "It's a trail camera. Thought I might put it up in the woods to see if any elk come through this way. Might just come hunting sometime."

"Mmm-hmm. You mind if I take a look at it?" he said, not moving any closer.

Protective of his ace in the hole, Mack said, "There's nothing on it to look at yet."

The sheriff gave him a long stare and laid all the cards on the table. "Aw, I bet there is." He turned to open the back door of his squad car, saying, "How about if you let me look at that, I'll let you look at this?" He pulled Sam out of the car, blindfolded and handcuffed.

He took the blindfold from her eyes, and she squinted in the mountain sunlight and screamed, "Mack!"

The breath of life left Mack's body at the sight, but when he inhaled he inflated with rage. He hated a bad man but he hated a bad cop worse. One that held his girlfriend hostage he hated with more hate than a freight train could carry. He held it in check though and he replied," Sounds fair to me. I don't need it. Take those cuffs off her."

He stood holding the camera in his left hand. His right hand was twitching to reach behind him and settle everything right there. Mack had his eyes fixed in a hard glare, holding out the camera while he walked toward the sheriff.

The bad cop removed the handcuffs, throwing them into the back seat of the squad car. Sam was crying as he pushed her toward Mack and grabbed the camera from Mack's hand. Sam frantically reached out to hug Mack's neck but he intercepted her and with his left arm brushed her around behind him, shielding her. His right hand was ready if need be.

In a voice as cold as winter glass he said, "Looks like a good deal to me, we both got what we wanted. I'm going back to Texas and forgetting all about New Mexico." He turned to guide Sam, at arms length, back to his truck.

The unmistakable sound of gun steel sliding on leather caused Mack to falter his pace. He whispered to Sam, "My gun is in my belt," as he turned to face the sheriff. The fat man in the khaki brown uniform with the shiny round badge stood there, smiling holding his gun at his side. *The old Navajo man had said he saw seen a snake wearing the concho,* Mack thought.

"Not so fast there, McWhirter. I didn't say you could go. Little lady, would you reach behind him and with two fingers pull that pistol out of his belt in the back? I expect that's what that bulge is. Real easy now. Toss it over here." He angled his gun up a little as he spoke.

Sam had stopped crying and did as she was asked. She tried to move to his side but Mack instinctively kept her behind him. The sheriff picked up the Ruger, admiring it before lifting his belly and sticking it in his belt. "I told you I was up here takin' care of some loose ends. Well, this about finishes it. I got the camera and without you two around, everythin' will be fine. All I got to do is find a new cook. Oh, that reminds me, you being a fireman and all, you ought to know just how bad a police officer hates being lied to. You do know that, don't you?"

Mack was silent as he stared a hole in the pompous cop.

"That bullshit you told me 'bout somebody with long black hair shootin' my cook? Hell, boy, both you and I know it was that little meth head Star. Probably did it with this gun right here." He patted Mack's old Ruger stuck in his belt. He shook his head and said, "Too bad about her, though."

Mack squared up like he was going to fight but the waving gun held him in place. "What did you do to her, you son-of-a-bitch?"

With feigned surprise, the Sheriff said, "I didn't do nothin' to her. I could've arrested her but she was dead. She got on the losing end of a bad drug deal with José and Pepé at the bus station. Such a pity.

"Then you kept on lying about stealin' evidence from the crime scene. You just don't know when to stop. If you'd stopped lyin' to me and told the truth, well then maybe we wouldn't be havin' this conversation. You could've been the big fireman hero for savin' that girl, rest her soul. Isn't that what you firemen do? Play dominos and be heroes?" He laughed at his slight.

Mack asked, "So, did you kill Sandy too, just to tidy up?"

"I wouldn't say I killed her, no. I just gave her a snack during our interview. Who knew she had such a fatal peanut allergy. The hospital should've known. There was a note right there on her bed."

He smiled as he raised his gun to aim. "You hit the nail right on the head, McWhirter. I am tidying up. Nice and organized just like my little business here. No loose ends."

He put his thumb on the hammer of the weapon aimed at his defiant target. Mack smiled an odd smile as he stood, shoulders squared off, staring his assailant in the eye as he faced eternity with Sam cowering behind him.

He stared into the evil eye that was behind the gun sight of the 357. There was a loud meat slap sound followed by the report of a large caliber rifle and a piercing shriek from Sam. The revolver in the sheriff's hand pivoted on his trigger finger as it fell to the ground. The evil sneer changed to a quizzical look at Mack.

Mack could see a hole just off center in the sheriff's badge that was in the middle of a spreading crimson stain on the crisp khaki tan uniform. The soiled lawman looked incredulously at the badge he defiled and then followed his gun to the ground. The dirt beneath him slowly became the same color as the stain of blood under the badge.

25

ANGEL ON HIGH

The instant the 30-caliber hole appeared in the badge, everything switched into slow motion. There was the surprising sound of the bullet impact, followed by the boom of the shot. Silence. *Whoom!* The echo of the gun shot came back up the valley. When it happens quickly there's silence in death. The Sheriff spoke not a word as sinful life left his body and he fell.

Sam stood in jaw-dropped shock, holding onto Mack. He was mildly surprised, like if a book was slammed in a library, but bore no repulsion nor regret for the dead body of the dirty cop that lay in front of them. He was glad the threat had been revealed and dealt with. His only concern was what to do next.

When Sam got her voice back, she shrieked again in horror, her hands hiding her face from the upsetting scene that lay before her. She cried, "Mack, what just happened?"

He held her close, turning her away and gently moving her toward his truck and away from the carnage. "Babe, it looks like we have friends in high places." He looked toward the trees on the other side of the lake, raising his hand with a victorious thumbs-up sign. A flash of sun on a small mirror acknowledged the gesture.

He helped Sam up into his truck, where she could cry off her shock. "Now you just stay here. Pretty soon we're going to be covered up with cops. Don't get out of the truck unless one of them tells you to. Okay? We're going to be all right. We'll leave as soon as they let us."

She plaintively looked at Mack with tear-reddened eyes. " Aren't we in a helluva lot of trouble? There's a dead cop laying there."

"No, sugar, not in any trouble anymore. We didn't shoot that man and he was going to shoot us. We're going to be okay. You stay right here."

"Okay," she said through her tears of shock, happiness and relief.

Mack went to the sheriff's car to kick over the can of worms that was going to be squirming around them shortly. He took the microphone on the mobile radio, keyed the mike and said, "Unit calling base."

"Base, go ahead."

"I'm with the sheriff's car at the lake up in the Valle Vidal. The sheriff has been shot and presumed to be dead. You probably should send some deputies out here."

The now frantic voice from dispatch said, *"Unit calling repeat. Who are you?"*

"I said the sheriff has been shot. My name is McWhirter. Send someone out here quick."

Still flustered and frantic, the dispatcher replied, *"Received. Units are being dispatched right now. You need to stay at that location. Is the shooter still in the area?"*

Mack replied, "I'll be here when they get here. Location of shooter is unknown at this time. Out." He knew where the shooter was; he was silently running like a buck deer just below the ridgeline up in the hills, heading toward the pickup point at the trailhead.

Mack closed the door to the patrol car and walked back to his truck. On the way past the pine tree, he grabbed the Winchester, dropped the hammer to make it safe then slid it into his back seat. *Appearance is everything. No need to add questions to what's coming.*

He climbed in beside Samantha, and quietly held and comforted her while they waited.

In a few minutes, he could hear the sirens reverberating up the valley. The deputies were the first to arrive. They slid their cars to a stop and jumped out with guns drawn. One of the enthusiastic crime fighters didn't get his car all the way into park and it rolled off toward the trees, he never noticed as it hit a big pine tree. He was busy securing the perimeter.

The crew of deputies was running around yelling like a bunch of guinea hens with a snake in the yard. Mack inadvertently brought the flurry of activity to a stop when he stepped out of his truck. One of them saw him and raised his pistol, screaming, "Freeze!" The other two raised their pistols but didn't know at what, they were spinning around searching for a likely target.

Trying to calm the frenzied pack, Mack held his open hands out at shoulder level calmly saying, "Hold on, boys. I'm the guy that called. The shooter is gone, I think. Ya'll put those pistols up. Okay? We don't want anybody else gettin' shot today.

The alpha male of the trio approached Mack, still holding him at gunpoint. He yelled, "Down on your knees. Hands behind your head. Do you have any weapons?"

Mack did as he was told in this volatile situation, hoping none of these deputies were in on the sheriff's game. "No, I don't have any weapons. The sheriff has my gun tucked in the front of his belt."

The deputy frisked Mack. Satisfied he presented no threat, he said, "Stand up. Who are you? Tell me what happened here."

"My name is Peyton McWhirter. The sheriff took my weapon and was getting ready to shoot me and my girlfriend in cold blood when he was shot. It sounded like the shot came from across the lake."

The deputy loudly asked, "Well, where's your girlfriend now? I don't see her here."

"She's over there in my truck. I told her to stay there till ya'll moved her."

Flustered that he'd missed a person in his scene size up, he yelled at another deputy standing there staring at the dead sheriff, "Jones, get over to that truck and check out that girl!"

Jones broke his trance and scampered over to the truck to talk to Sam.

Mack could hear more sirens coming up the valley. He figured it must be the highway patrol. They tended to be the higher level of authority in situations like this, where a cop had been shot.

As the alpha deputy continued to fire questions at Mack in no sort of order, a Chevy Tahoe with the New Mexico Highway Patrol insignia pulled up. An important looking officer jumped out of the passenger side of the vehicle and walked with a purpose toward Mack and his interrogator. He glanced at the dead sheriff as he walked by, but never faltered.

He got to the deputy and forcefully inquired, "Who's in charge here, deputy?"

"That would be me, sir. I'm second in command under the sheriff."

The higher-ranking officer looked down at the dead sheriff and said, "Well, I guess you just got promoted. Can you tell me why your two knuckleheads are rummaging around my crime scene?" He pointed at the other two deputies meandering around the dead sheriff and his car. They were picking up stuff and then dropping it, with no purpose in their actions.

The alpha deputy yelled at the other two, "Ya'll get your asses over here!" then puffed up and said, "With all due respect, this is *my* crime scene. I was the first one here and it's my jurisdiction. I'm glad you showed up to help, but understand this is *my* crime scene."

More Highway patrol cars were coming up the hill as the two officers started their jurisdictional pissing match.

The Highway Patrolman had to have been a Marine Drill Sergeant before he put on the badge. He pulled his shoulders back, puffed out his chest, spun his volume knob to about eight and got in the face of the small town deputy that was trying to be somebody. His eyes were wide and his back straight as he screamed at the shrinking small town officer, "*Your* crime scene? Evidently you're confused, deputy — and I use that term loosely!

"When I pulled up here, you lost all crime scene privileges. All you did was mess up *my* crime scene. Do you hear me? This is *my* crime scene now, boy. You understand that? You have no authority here. *I'm* the authority! But I'll tell you what, I'm going to let you keep a little bit. You see that rock pile about five hundred yards down the road?" He shot his finger toward the pile and the deputy nodded, as he bent backwards trying to get away from the tirade.

"You take your two crime scene-destroying Bozo buddies and you go down there. That's my perimeter. You don't let anybody past that point unless they have a Highway Patrol badge or a letter from the governor! Do you understand? *Nobody!* Get your asses down there and secure my perimeter. *Now!*"

The deposed alpha deputy squeaked out a "Yes, sir," and quickstepped to gather the other two, since they now had an assignment. He loudly berated them as the three climbed into one car to go guard the road.

The officer in charge switched his demeanor like changing a shirt. He turned to Mack and asked, "Now, who are you, sir?"

The abrupt change caught Mack off guard. He'd been preparing for an ass chewing too. "My name's Peyton McWhirter, but they call me Mack. I was here with my girlfriend when it happened."

"Where's she?"

"Over by that truck in the shade."

"Well then, why don't we go over there and you can tell me what happened. By the way, my name is Sergeant Mont."

The two men shook hands as they walked toward Sam. The big officer had her full attention after witnessing him take command of the scene. They got over to her and Mack said, "Sam this is Sergeant Mott."

She extended her quivering hand and shook his hand saying, "Samantha Nawaji, pleased to meet you."

"Pleased to meet you, ma'am. Now, if ya'll could start at the beginning and tell me just what you saw here."

While the other proficient law officers processed the crime scene in a methodical manner, Mack went into the long story about what all led up to the sheriff laying dead in the New Mexico sun. He also related the story of his kidnapping, why it happened, how he was almost killed, and who'd saved his life.

It was important now for everyone to know about Phoebe, so he also told her story and included the sheriff's admission that he'd had her killed. While he was on that subject, he also mentioned that the Sheriff had admitted killing Sandy, the hiker, as well. Including information about how the Mexicans had kidnapped her off the bus in Springer and that she'd recognized the sheriff's voice while she was blindfolded.

Mack told the officer about the game camera with the incriminating pictures on it, and that he thought he was dealing with the Mexicans when he came to trade it for Sam. He finished up with how surprised he'd been when the sheriff showed up instead, and about how a shot from the woods had saved his life.

Officer Mont patiently listened to the whole story without interrupting. When Sam and Mack were finished he asked, "So, why didn't you contact the sheriff when you found out she'd been kidnapped?"

"Because his picture is the first one on that trail camera, the next one is him with the meth cook. He was dirty and couldn't be trusted. I thought I was dealing with the Mexicans and I figured I could handle them. Plus I'd planned to be gone before I had to deal with him. Everything happened too fast for me to call anybody else."

"You said you could deal with the Mexicans. Did that include having a sniper in the trees when you made the trade? Just a little insurance, maybe?" He cast a suspicious eye at Mack.

"I was armed. A sniper would've been handy to have if I knew any, but the only guy I know up here is laid up in the hospital with a snake bite. The only reason I came to New Mexico was to bring him some saddles I'd made. I haven't been up here in fifteen years. I don't know where that shot came from, but I'm damn sure glad it came."

"Yeah, you're a pretty lucky fella, I guess." He still wasn't convinced and had more questions to clarify some points. A helicopter coming over the mountain, and then circling for a place to land interrupted him. He looked up and said, "Looks like the big boss is here. I'll go give him a briefing and I'll be back to finish up. I have a few more questions for ya'll."

Apprehensively Sam asked Mack, "What's going on, Mack? Are we in trouble?" Sam's only previous contact with law enforcement had been getting a traffic ticket. She was in unfamiliar territory.

"No, I don't think so. He just has certain questions to ask and wants to get to the truth of the matter. It is mighty coincidental that the sheriff was holding us at gunpoint, and then he gets shot from out of nowhere. After all, a cop was killed here. They're just not convinced yet that he was a *bad* cop. They get touchy when it is one of their own."

"Where *did* that shot come from, Mack? Did you know someone was up there?"

"I'll answer that later, just be calm," he said as he kept a close eye on what was going on around the scene. Sergeant Mont and the big boss stood talking off to the side. Every once in a while, they'd both look over at Mack and Sam, and then keep on talking.

At one point, the officer retrieved the trail camera from beside the dead sheriff and they both replayed its pictures. They conversed a while longer, and then Sergeant Mont walked off to supervise the crime scene investigation. The big boss stood alone for a while and headed over to talk to Mack and Sam.

As he approached, they could see he was a big man of about six foot three. His chiseled face and lean frame told he'd seen and done many things in his career in law enforcement. The white hair peaking from beneath his hat was evidence he'd been around a while.

His genuine smile revealed teeth yellowed by too many years of coffee and cigarettes. He extended his hand saying, "Hello, I am Commander Dirickson. Samantha and Mack? I'm glad to meet you, but I'm sorry it's under such dire circumstances."

They both shook his sun-wrinkled hand.

He didn't ignore Sam, but he addressed Mack when he got right to the point, "Mack, I've been briefed on your statement to Sergeant Mont and we have a problem here. I'm not going to gift-wrap it all pretty, that's not my way. I'll just tell you flat out that you're both in a lot of trouble."

26
MAKE A BREAK
FOR THE BORDER

S am shuddered and her eyes filled with tears as she considered being charged with murder. Mack stared intently at the Commander as he waited for the next shoe to drop.

The Commander stood tall and firm as he reassured her, "Relax, Samantha, you're not under arrest or charged with any crime. If I could have a few minutes alone with Mack, then he can fill you in on the particulars." He put his hand on Mack's shoulder and said, "Let's walk down here by the lake, away from all this."

"We're going to be all right, aren't we Commander?" Sam asked as she headed toward the truck to have a seat and sort things out.

"Ma'am, we're going to try very hard to make things all right," he said as he guided Mack down toward the lake.

As they walked, the Commander asked, "So, what do you do for a living, Mack?"

"I'm a Captain with the Stephenville Fire Department. Been there eighteen years."

"I'd heard you were a paramedic, too. We were monitoring the rescue as soon as they put a Medivac copter on it. That's big stuff up here."

Mack started wondering if this was going to be some buddy-up sort of covert question and answer interrogation. It seemed like the Commander was asking questions he already knew the answers to. Interrogations were always tricky.

He eased Mack's anxiety but not his caution about talking when he said, "What we're going to talk about is strictly off the record. This is just cop to firefighter, okay? If these things I'm going to tell you ever come out, then I'll call you a liar and have you arrested. Understand? But I think this is information you need to have."

Mack was taken aback at the import of the impending conversation but said, "We never spoke, sir."

"Exactly. I'm glad we understand each other. Being a fire officer, I'm sure you're familiar with these sorts of conversations. Sergeant Mont wants to arrest you. Your story of an unknown shooter is a little farfetched, I must admit. But we've been advised by the Parks Service that there's a crazy hermit living up there on that mountain. If he's up there, we'll find him with the infrared camera on the helicopter. He's probably up there right now, watching us from under some bush.

"The main point of this whole situation is that a cop was killed. Evidence from that camera shows he was a dirty cop. We've known there was a meth operation going on in this part of the state for a while, but we couldn't pinpoint the source. I established a secret taskforce of my most trusted officers and undercover people to find it.

"Evidently that Sheriff was successful at derailing our efforts. Our intel from the streets tells us it's cartel related and involves some big money. In your statement, you referenced a black Chevy pickup with the Santa Muerta emblem on it. The only people who really know about that emblem and its significance are the bad guys and us — guys like you and me.

"That got my attention, it's the symbol for the cartel boys. I don't know why, but they all drive shiny black Chevys, too. We thought we had all of them accounted for in Albuquerque and Santa Fe, but to have one show up this far out is a new development. I told you all that so you'd know, you've kicked the top off of a cartel anthill.

"They'll probably hold you accountable for killing their cook. When they catch wind of that dead sheriff, which I'm sure they'll know about before we leave here, they'll pin that on you, too. He was probably bought and paid for, so they'll want revenge for the loss of their investment. I could arrest you and put you in protective custody but I couldn't insure your safety. Big money makes men do crazy things. Even my men."

The big picture was coming into sharp focus for Mack as he listened. "So, Commander, what you're tellin' me is my life's in danger."

"Mack, yours and anybody else with even the briefest contact with you. For instance, the girl you called Phoebe and the rescued hiker. They're both victims."

Mack thought about what the officer said, letting the gravity of his situation sink in. He not only had himself to think about but more importantly, he had Sam. He didn't want her anywhere near danger. "So what can we do? I have to get out of here and get back to Texas. Can you give us an escort out of the state?"

The officer shook his head while staring at the ground, "I'm afraid I can't offer that. I don't have the resources and even if I did, I wouldn't trust them. If the cartel got to this sheriff, who's to say they didn't get to one or more of my patrol officers, too? Money and death threats can really sway a man from his morals. If I gave you an escort, I might just be setting you up for an ambush. The only people I trust are those closest to me, and I am constantly reassuring myself about them."

Mack sorrowfully shook his head saying, "It seems we're in a tight spot."

"I'm sorry to say you are, son. I'm being truthful with you and I regret I can't fix it for you. I'll tell you what I can do though. If word hasn't gotten out yet, they'll still think the sheriff handled the situation. Before they can mobilize and hunt you down, you and your girlfriend can make a break for it to Texas. I'll put out a bulletin to all units on the road not stop your vehicle under any circumstance. If a highway patrol unit attempts to stop you, don't stop. If you can get any sort of identification of the unit, then let me know after you're safe in Texas."

The Commander placed his hand on Mack's shoulder to guide him back up the hill. As the two warriors from different battles walked, the Commander said, "My advice to you is to leave here now. Go gas up your truck if you need to, then stomp that gas pedal all the way back to Texas."

Mack turned his head to look at his new friend and said, "I sure appreciate the help. Just one more thing, though. Can I have my gun back? I've had that old Ruger a long time, and I'd hate to lose it."

The big man in charge looked up at the crime scene then said, "It looks like they're winding it down now." Knowing the full value of a weapon in this circumstance he said, "I don't see any problem with that."

The two men got up to Mack's truck, and Mack peeled off to get ready to get Sam out of harm's way. The Commander went over to the pile of brown paper bags holding evidence and pulled a bag off of the top. Any objections from the other officers were silenced with one stern look from the stone-faced Commander. He walked back over to Mack and Sam, ripped the bag open and handed Mack the revolver through the open window, saying "*Vaya con Dios*, my friend."

"Thank you, Commander, and thanks for the help."

Sam also chimed in, "Thank you."

He smiled and replied, "Thanks for helping with our coyote problem up here."

They drove past the crime scene tape and on down the rough road. Mack smiled and waved at the banished, sour-faced deputies as he drove past them.

Elated at not being arrested but concerned with being in trouble Sam asked, "So, if we're not under arrest, what sort of trouble are we in, Mack?"

He just wasn't sure how to phrase the answer to that question. *How do I tell the woman I love that there are a few people who want us dead?* He pondered it a minute deciding on brutal honesty and warped humor. "Well, babe, I got good news and I got bad news. Which do you want first?" When she stared at him with a scowl, he considered humor was not the way to go.

She cautiously said, "Uh, give me the good news."

"We're going to get back to Texas a lot quicker than we thought. We have a green light to go as fast as we want."

Preparing for the ominous answer she said, "And the bad news?"

He looked her in the eye with raised eyebrows and replied, "There are some people that want to kill us."

Surprise and fear cloaked her face. Her only response was, "Oh, Mack."

Mack slowed the truck and pulled to the side of the road as he explained, "The Mexicans probably think the sheriff has killed us already, so they're going to be pretty relaxed. As long as nobody knows we're alive, we ought to be in Texas in under an hour. The

Commander radioed all his units on the highway. They won't stop us, so we're going to get out of here as fast as this old truck will take us."

Sam startled and screamed at the banging and scuffling in the bed of the truck. There were two slaps on the roof of the truck and Mack began picking up speed. She quickly turned to see what had happened and was shocked to see a man in full camo with face paint grinning through the back window. She screamed, "Mack, there's a man in the back of the truck!"

Mack was grinning too. "Yeah, that's Turtle. Ya'll will meet when we stop."

Still shocked and not knowing what was happening she asked, "Turtle? What kind of name is that? Who *is* he?"

Still grinning, he angled his head toward her and said, "Aw, he's just a friend from the mountain. Remember when I said I had friends in high places?"

Turtle lay in the bed of the truck with his head comfortably on his duffle bag and his rifle securely in the black Pelican case beside him. He was a little tuckered out from his long run through the mountain forest. He figured he'd catch a nap during the short ride to the Springer airport.

Mack was solving the mystery for her while he drove fast, telling her everything Commander Dirickson had told him. He paused in his explanation when he noticed a black truck coming toward them. The sun was to his back and it cut through the dark window tint of the black Chevy.

Sam screamed, "It's them!" as soon as she saw it was José and Pepé. They saw it was Mack facing them, and José stomped on the brakes, smoking the tires to make a U-turn. Mack tapped the brakes to bump Turtle's head on the truck bed and wake him up.

Sam kept an eye on the black Chevy as it smoked its screaming tires, trying to catch up to them. She came eye to eye with Turtle as he poked his head up to see what was going on.

Mack pumped his fist with his thumb extended back behind them. Turtle turned to look and disappeared again.

The black truck was making good time, and gaining on them. It was about a hundred yards behind and slowly closing the gap when Sam saw something long and straight come out of the passenger side window. She screamed, "He's got a gun!"

Turtle's head appeared at the back of the truck bed, it was low and close over his rifle. As the pursuing passenger got in position to fire at Mack's fleeing truck, Turtle touched off a round and a boom resounded through the cab of the truck. The bullet found its mark in the engine block of the Chevy, and the truck was immediately enveloped in a cloud of steam and smoke.

Mack never let off the gas and Turtle laid back down. At this point, Sam was wound tighter than a nine-day clock.

The airport where Turtle's friend kept his helicopter was just south of town, which meant he had to run the canyoned gauntlet of the buildings in town and he couldn't do it very quickly.

Mack figured the Mexican thugs had already alerted their gangbanging buddies to the fact that the rumors of his demise had been greatly exaggerated — the cat was out of the bag. He didn't know what the road had in store for him but he knew he didn't want to include Sam. He had to find a safer avenue for her.

He didn't know where the bad guys were but evidently there weren't any in Springer. He passed through downtown without incident, even though he was nervous as a fox at a hound convention.

He did a slide turn into the Springer Municipal Airport and came to a stop in front of Hanger #7, just like Turtle'd told him to. Turtle bailed out of the bed of the truck, carrying his duffle bag and gun case. He came around to the window to thank Mack for extricating him from his hot zone on the mountain. Before he could say anything, Mack said, "Turtle, I got one more favor to ask. Can you take Sam on that bird and ya'll land at Dalhart? I'll be right there to pick her up. I'm worried that it's liable to be a little hot between here and there. I want to keep her safe."

Sam heard this and got indignant. "What the hell're you talking about, Mack? I'm going with you! I am *not* leaving you again." She glared at him with fire in one eye and love in the other.

He held her shoulders with a stern but loving look on his face and said, "Hon, you're going with Turtle. I don't want to leave you either but this is best for both of us. I don't want to have to worry about you. Probably nothing will happen from here on, but I can't promise that. You ride that helicopter to Dalhart, and then sit down and have a Dr. Pepper. When you finish, I'll be there and we can go home. Now, we ain't got much time; we gotta get going."

The helicopter was spooling up for take off as the two embraced in the cab of the truck. Turtle still stood at the window of the truck, feeling even more uncomfortable than he had been while being bounced around in the back of the truck on the ride over here.

Sam buried her face in Mack's shoulder and said, "You better make it to Dalhart. We've come too far for me to lose you now. You hear me? You *better* be there." She released her grip on him, kissed him and slid out of the truck.

Mack turned to Turtle and said, "I appreciate this, brother. See you in Dalhart."

Turtle smiled as he shook Mack's hand. "No problem, bud. Thanks for gettin' me out of there, and I mean that in a lot of ways. I'll deliver her safely. You watch your ass out there. I'll see you in Dalhart." He turned toward the waiting helicopter, took Sam's arm and guided her to their ride. Mack could tell Turtle was in his element helping people, no matter how violent that help might be. He watched as they boarded and the bird took to the sky.

Knowing his friends were safely on their way, Mack headed back out to the highway. He slid a ZZ Top CD in the player, cranked up the volume and yelled, "Let's play Pancho Villa!"

27

BEING THE RABBIT

Mack cautiously drove back through Springer. His senses were on high alert and his vision was clear. He hoped there'd be no more confrontation but he wasn't counting on it. He guardedly navigated his way to the other side of town and open country.

When he saw the rolling grasslands spread out before him and the town was a memory, he nailed the gas pedal to the floor. Thankfully there wasn't much traffic on the road this evening. Driving at 130 mph, he had to have his attention fixed at least a quarter mile ahead. He snapped the air passing a highway patrolman sitting on the side of the road, and caught a glimpse of the officer waving as he passed. Mack felt secure that the plan was in place coming together.

The road was flat and straight, allowing him to easily fly on it. He replayed the events of the past few days, and the good karma he'd experienced had him believing he'd been a part of a true miracle. Twice he'd helped people and twice those people had saved his life. He was still in awe at the realization. He had deep regret for the overwhelming sorrow two families would face at the news of the murder of their daughters, though. He was glad the beast responsible had died a violent death, just as he thought he was at the pinnacle of his evil deeds.

The wheel of considerations spun in his mind, as it slowed it stopped on the only point of consideration that was relevant in his life right now — Samantha. He remembered asking her, "*Why don't you come with me, it'll be fun.*" *Yeah, fun.* He wanted her back in his life. All he wanted was to distract her from her preoccupation with her business. All he wanted was for her to be back with him.

He chuckled to himself as he thought, *Nothing like a near death experience to make or break a relationship.* He felt like their life together would be more solid now, after all of these shared experiences. Not necessarily something he would want to do again to get closer together. Maybe a couple's retreat to the Bahamas next time would be a better plan.

Daydreaming of the past and the clear road around him distracted him from the task at hand —getting to Dalhart as fast as he could. His speed had dropped down to eighty miles an hour. He didn't notice the black dot on the horizon of the roadway behind him, nor did he notice it was rapidly growing larger.

The cracking explosion of his outside mirror snapped his attention back to the present. He naturally looked in that mirror to see what was behind him, but there was only a jagged frame flapping in the wind. He stomped on the gas and looked in his rearview mirror. A black Chevrolet truck was about seventy-five yards behind him, and gaining fast.

There was a man leaning out of the passenger side window firing a rifle. He could see puffs of smoke as he fired. The wind and road noise drowned out the reports. He took his pistol out of the seat holster, but at over 100 mph, shooting out of his window wasn't really an option.

He thought about stopping the truck to fight it out and finish it, like an old Indian fighter out here on the plains, hiding behind his pony. The math wasn't right for that — he had six bullets and the box of ammo was somewhere under the back seat. They had a lot more bullets.

He weaved the truck from side to side, which was more difficult to do and maintain control with his speedometer pegged out. He was glad for two things, the guy behind him was a poor shot — he had only connected once out of countless rounds fired, and there would most likely be a Texas Highway patrol car at the state line. There always was.

He looked at his watch, anxious that the state line was fifteen or twenty minutes away at this speed. All he could do was drive and run away. He hated running away. Two lucky bullets struck the tailgate of his truck with a piercing metallic pop and Mack decided he didn't mind running so much.

His total concentration was on the road ahead of him, maintaining control of his weaving truck and keeping distance between him and that rifle. Out of habit, he looked out his left side to where the mirror used to be. With his slight glance to the side, he noticed a helicopter coming his way off to the north. It was descending rapidly. It was only one hundred feet off the ground when it passed through the space between Mack's truck and the truck chasing him.

The rifle continued to fire, and the tailgate loudly popped three more times. The helicopter took up a position in the sky, flying along side the fatal parade like it was observing the whole proceeding.

Mack's eyes went from windshield to rearview mirror like a metronome. He couldn't afford to look at the helicopter off to his right.

There were some small hills up ahead. He looked in his rear view to gauge the distance he had between him and the rifle, though it mattered little since his truck was doing all it could do. In the mirror, he saw the windshield of the black truck suddenly turn white with the glisten of shattered glass and the truck began to veer off the road.

He glanced at his speedometer to see they were still doing well over 100 mph. The black truck ran off the road, through a barbed wire fence, over a small mesquite tree and up a small hill. In his mirror, he saw the truck take to the air with an impressive hang time, and then disappear into a ravine. A big cloud of red dust and smoke confirmed a major impact.

Mack let off the throttle. He glanced out his window at the helicopter flying beside him. There was Turtle, fastened in a harness, sitting in a door of the bird with his feet on the skids. He held his rifle and was grinning ear to ear. Mack had a spasm of happiness to see Sam's smiling face in a window. Turtle pointed to the east and they increased altitude and air speed to the airport.

Up and over a little rise in the road lay the Texas state line. Mack was never so glad to see the "Welcome to Texas" sign in his life. A Texas state trooper was parked behind the sign. He was standing outside his car with a rifle slung on his shoulder, waving Mack over.

Mack pulled over and parked in front of the trooper's car. He peeled his white knuckled hands off the steering wheel and got out, gladly stepping onto Texas soil. "I've never been so glad to see you in my life," he said as the trooper approached.

The young trooper smiled and said, "I heard you were headed this way. I was supposed to keep an eye out for you. They said there was a black Chevy chasing you. Are they still behind you? I'm not going to let them over the line if they are."

Mack grinned as the two men shook hands. "I doubt it. Last time I saw them, they'd wrecked out about ten miles back."

"Good! I hope it killed them. One of the New Mexico patrol boys tried to stop them outside of Springer and they shot his windshield out and sent him to the hospital."

"Oh, dang. I hope he's okay."

"I think he is. They said it was only glass cuts and he wrecked his car, so that's always an ambulance ride. I wish I could stay to hear your story," he said as he glanced at Mack's bullet riddled tailgate "They just called me to work a wreck over on the other side of Texline. Welcome back to Texas. Stay safe, bud." The trooper returned to his car and sped off.

Mack got back in his truck to head to the airport. He was ready to collect his prize and take her home. He was more relaxed now. He was in his home state and the whole ordeal was finished. He drove on toward the city of Dalhart. He had to find the airport. He wasn't sure where it was but it couldn't be too hard to find in such a small town.

The only thing he could see on the flat landscape were some big standing tanks up ahead, then the buildings of the town further down the road. He'd heard someone say once that west Texas was so flat you could see tomorrow from where you stood, and if you turned around you could see yesterday. He never wanted to see yesterday again.

As he drove closer to the tanks up ahead on his right he saw a large scraped off area beside them. As he got closer, he saw the unexpected but welcome sight of the helicopter.

Mack slid his truck to a stop on the dirt pad. At the sound of crunching gravel, Sam came running out from the shade on the back side of the aircraft. She leapt into his arms, wrapping her legs around his waist.

She hugged him viciously as he held her off the ground. "We made it! We made it! I'm so glad to see you. We made it!" They kissed passionately as he lowered her to the ground. Neither wanted to let go of the other, but Turtle came walking up, still grinning.

In the short time Mack had known him, he'd never seen his Turtle's face crack into a smile this big. "You gotta admit, that was a hell of a shot," Turtle said. "I don't like to brag, but that was a *hell* of a shot. Both of 'em."

The pilot came walking up and Turtle introduced them, "Mack, I'd like you to meet Jerry Hopkins. He flew the Medivac copter with my unit over there. It sure comes in handy to know friends with skills."

Mack knew all to well how it paid to have friends with skills. "Glad to meet you, Jerry. I sure do appreciate all you did. I'm not sure I could've got out of that tight spot without air support. I appreciate you gettin' Sam out of there safe and sound, too. If there's ever anything I can do for you, just holler."

The accomplished pilot laughed as he released Mack's pumping handshake. "Aw, it wasn't much, just flying. You looked like you could use the help. I had a great time, it was like the old days."

"Between you and Turtle here there's been some super hero stuff going on. You can't tell me anything less. Ya'll saved my ass."

Turtle spoke up and said, "Mack, I'm sorry, but we have to get goin' and get this bird back in the hangar before dark. We're gonna have to take off."

"No problem. Nice to meet you, Jerry, and thanks again. Turtle, thank you for everything. Give me a call. You got my number." Mack thought for a split second and added an invitation back to normalcy of a previous life, "Let's go fishing."

Turtle shook Mack's hand then embraced him. "You're welcome, brother, and thank you for everything. Thanks for gettin' me off that mountain and back into life. Helpin' you gave me a reason to get back on that horse you talked about. We might just have to do some fishin'. It'll be a while, but I can show you where the fish are."

Turtle and Jerry climbed back into the beautiful grey machine, wound it up and lifted into the sky. They headed toward Amarillo as Turtle's face grinned at them from the window.

Mack and Sam stood there holding hands, watching as it disappeared. Sam looked over at Mack and said, "Let's go sit on the porch."

He smiled at the thought. "Let's do it. It'll take some time to get there, though."

She looked at him with want in her eyes and said, "For you, I have all the time in the world."

28

LAZARUS' DAUGHTER

Samantha awoke with a start from her posttraumatic nap. The rapid-fire sequence of life threatening and life saving events had taken its toll. Being in the safe confines of Mack's truck with his reassuring hand rubbing her neck had put her out like a light. She hazily looked around trying to get her bearings. "Where are we now?"

"We just passed through Quanah. I think Stephenville moved while we were gone. This drive is taking forever."

"Dang, when will we hit the next town? I gotta find a bathroom."

"Well, if it's an emergency, I can pull over. Lots of brush out there," he said with a chuckle. He knew she wasn't above it if need be.

He could tell she was considering it but she said, "I'm just not feeling *that* western right now, something indoors suits me better at the moment."

"The next town is Chillicothe, and I wouldn't swear they even have a gas station with plumbing. Vernon is after that, and it's some ways off. I think there's a rest stop up here pretty close, I'll pull in there. I could stand to stretch my legs, too."

The rest stop came into view, and Mack pulled the truck into the Texas Highway Department temple of tourism and personal comfort. Sam hopped out of the truck, quick-stepping to the rest room.

She was glad there were no cars in the parking lot and no people inside. She had no time to wait in a line.

She quickly picked a stall with an open door. She thought she was alone in the restroom but next to her she heard a whimper and a muffled cry. Looking under the divider, she could see two legs but the pants weren't bunched around the ankles. When she heard another quiet sob, she cautiously asked, "Are you okay?"

The girl on the other side sniffled and replied, "Yeah, I'm all right."

Still curious and sensing a problem, Sam asked, "Why are you crying? Are you sick or did you get left? I didn't see any other cars in the parking lot. Do you need help?"

The slight concern from another human being in this makeshift roadside confessional opened the teary floodgates for the traveler. Between the sobs, the girl managed to say, "I guess I'm not okay. I've been trying to get to Fort Worth for two days, and my ride went off and left me here a few hours ago. Now I'm stuck and I don't know what I'm going to do."

Sam heard the paper roll spin and the girl blew her nose. The voice from the other side of the divider tried to compose herself, then cautiously asked, "Would you happen to be driving toward Fort Worth?"

Sam stood and flushed, signaling she wanted to talk face to face. She stepped out of the stall and went to the sink to wash her hands. The other stall door opened, she turned to see a ragged vagabond of a girl step out. The girl had tear-swollen eyes, shaggy blonde hair, and her clothes were layered and dirty. She carried only a small backpack for luggage. She looked pitiful. Sam had a soft spot for those exiled from society. "Wash those tears off your face, get yourself together and meet me outside. We'll talk."

Sam stepped out of the restroom and walked over to the vending machine are. She could see Mack walking around his truck, inspecting the bullet holes and all the damage from running the gauntlet. She got a Dr. Pepper and a candy bar from the machine, just as the girl sheepishly came out. Sam handed her the refreshments and smiled.

"Thank you," the girl said quietly, as she gratefully took the gift. In her heart she meant thank you for listening.

Surely Mack won't have a problem giving this girl a ride. Hopefully he's not soured on helping strangers in distress yet. He's hasn't had a good track record for the past week but he seems to be on a roll. This girl doesn't seem to have a relationship to drug runners, killers or dirty cops. She just needs help. "We can give you a ride to Fort Worth. No problem. Come on, let's hit the road," Sam said as she turned to walk toward the truck.

"Thank you, I sure appreciate it," The grateful girl murmured.

Mack was walking up the sidewalk to find Sam as the two girls came toward the parking lot. As they walked, Sam said, "My name's Sam. What's yours?"

The girl turned her head toward the parking lot as she said, "My name's— *MACK!*" She ran toward him with outstretched arms.

It took him a shocked moment to comprehend what was happening. The girl he'd given up for dead was here at the wind blown west Texas rest stop, running toward him. "Phoebe?" She made a springboard flying monkey move, latching onto him with a full body embrace, burying her face in his shoulder. "Oh, Mack, I'm so glad to see you."

Sam was surprised and confused. *Phoebe? This is the girl that saved Mack's life?* She stood by, waiting for Phoebe to relax her grip. She could empathize with her happiness, finding Mack out here was akin to floating in the shark-infested ocean and finding a boat with a Captain just floating by.

Mack peeled her off of him and set her on the ground. She was grinning ear to ear. He was still in shock. "What? ... But when— Where? ... How in the—? ... Dang, it's good to see you!"

"I found her in the restroom," Sam explained. "I didn't know who she was. She just needed a ride."

Mack grinned at Sam as he put his arm around her shoulders. "I sure am glad we stopped here and you found her. Phoebe, this is Sam. I guess ya'll have met. Let's get in the truck and get on out of here." Mack turned toward the truck holding both girls by the shoulders as he went.

Once in the truck and headed east, Mack asked, "So, Phoebe, I heard you were dead. You better start at the beginning and tell me how you ain't." He studied her in the rear view mirror. She didn't look good. She was more pallid and drawn than he remembered. She looked worse now than when she'd been doped up. She had some nervous ticks going on and was sweatin' like a pig. *Must be drug related. Probably being off the drugs is worse than on.*

Phoebe was elated to be back with Mack, and anxiously revealed her story. "After I got down off the mountain and back to the horse trailer, there were some hikers there that had got tired and given up. I left your horse at the trailer and rode back to town with them. I think I told you I was going home and that *was* where I was headed. I was going to use the last of my money for a bus ticket to Fort Worth. My ride took me to the bus station."

"So I guess you missed the bus or something?"

"Yeah, or something. While I was waiting for the bus, two guys in a black truck grabbed me and kidnapped me. They said they had orders. They took me way out of town and were telling me how they were going to have some fun with me before they kill me. I was scared and crying, but those bastards just thought it was funny. They thought they were pretty tough around a scared girl.

"I wasn't gonna let it be easy though. While we were driving, I went crazy on one of them. I hit him in the throat with my elbow and scratched him up pretty good. I might've bit his ear almost off. He was bleedin' a lot. I made sure he wasn't going to be able to use his balls, too.

"The driver stopped the truck, jerked me out and threw me on the ground. The other one got out and he had a big knife. The guy who had me on the ground ripped my shirt off, but when he did he got scared and jumped off of me like he had seen a rattlesnake or something. They both were scared and jabbering in Spanish and pointing at me."

The story scared Sam, but Mack's curiosity was building. "What happened to make him stop?"

"I traveled for a while with a Mexican gang chick, she said she was a *chola*. It must mean badass, because she was. She gave me a medallion. She said *Santa Muerta* would protect me. I just wore it because I thought it was pretty.

"Well it scared the crap out of that guy that was fixin' to rape me. He apologized for hurtin' me and said he couldn't kill me but I had to leave New Mexico. He threw the guy I beat up in the back of the truck, because he was still pretty mad, then drove me to Springer and told me to leave.

"They left me there, but they stole all my money. I think it was the guy I hurt that stole everything. Anyway, I've been hitchin' rides tryin' to get back to Fort Worth. I told you I was going home and I meant it.

"My last ride ditched me at the rest stop. I guess I was gettin' weird and freaked him out. I'm havin' a bad time, Mack. I'm off the meth, but it's hurtin'. I'm gonna need some help quick. I need to get home."

Mack listened intently. *She might be telling the truth about being off the stuff. She certainly looks like she's detoxing.* He'd heard that getting off the stuff was incredibly hard but it could be done. "So how long has it been since you had any?"

"I haven't had a hit since I came off the mountain. I was pretty strung out up there, so it lasted a while. I'm sure hurtin' now. I'm going to do it. I had what they call a moment of clarity up there. Sort of weird, since I was so high."

"What happened up there to change things for you?"

She thought carefully before she spoke, and tears filled her eyes. "You're the only good thing to come along in my life in a very long time. You cared. I told you all the things I haven't thought about in ages, and you didn't judge me. When we were up there and that bastard was fixin' to kill you, it was just like that time in the arena when I ran away. I could see clearly. He was evil and evil was gonna take away all the good I had.

"When I shot him, I killed all the evil I'd been holdin' onto since I ran away. That part of my life is dead now and I'm headed toward the good. I can't do that with drugs. That's over for me, but I know I'm gonna need help. I'm not that strong by myself."

The cab of the truck was silent as the trio rolled on down Highway 287 toward Fort Worth and a new life for Phoebe. The silence let her words sink into their minds and hearts.

Mack's thoughts were on what he could do to help. He looked over at Sam as she stared straight ahead, quiet tears rolling down her cheeks. "Phoebe, I think you've got more strength than you give yourself credit for. I think you can do it. Do you have a plan? Do you think your parents will help?"

"I've thought about them. I don't think I can count on them for nothin'. I was embarrassin' enough for them when I ran off. I think havin' to explain a junky daughter to their friends would be more than they could take. I guess I'll try to find a county health program or somethin'. Surely there's somethin' like that in Fort Worth. Rehab clinics are expensive, so I know I can't do that."

Mack pondered the point a minute and said, "I can ask our medical director at the Fire Department. He might have some ideas. Surely there's a way to get it done."

"That would be great. Like I said, I'm gonna do it, I just don't know how yet."

Sam sat there quietly. Phoebe was Mack's friend so she let them do their friend thing. When she'd taken it all in and cried a little, she thought she understood who Phoebe was and more importantly who she could be. "I'll tell you what we're gonna do."

Mack turned and looked at her, surprised that she was taking the conversational bull by the horns. *What's cooking in that beautiful brain of yours?*

"There's a place out in the country between Stephenville and Dublin called Serenity. I overheard Tinsley Bryant talkin' about it. He's headed there after that video shoot. It's one of those hidden rehab places for celebrities. It seems he has a bit of a coke problem. He said they have a really high success rate, and that's why he's goin' there. That's where you're goin', too, Phoebe."

Mack tried to concentrate on keeping the truck on the road as he stared at Sam with surprise and love in his eyes. He knew by the tone of her voice it was going to happen, regardless of any outside influence. He also knew her feelings about money — what was the use of having it if you couldn't do something good with it. When he came to the Highway 281 exit in Wichita Falls, he took it south to Stephenville. He knew Fort Worth wasn't going to happen.

Phoebe couldn't believe what Sam said. "Well, yeah, I'll just march my happy ass right up there and say 'sign me up.'" she said with street smart sarcasm, "Can I pay this out for the next hundred years? I don't think my parents are gonna be interested in footin' that bill. They want sure returns on their investments and I'm pretty sure they don't have much faith in me."

Sam turned in the seat and looked the skeptical girl in her sunken eyes. "Your parents don't have to be involved or even know about it. Nobody does. We have faith in you and we'll take care of it. It's not a problem. All you have to do is get it done. You saved Mack's life and now I want to save yours."

The gravity of the offer, if it was an offer rather than a statement, hit Phoebe square in her hardened heart. "You'd do that for me? You must be angels sent from heaven."

FROM THE AUTHOR

I would like to thank everyone who has taken the time to read my books. The encouragement I receive is the wind in my sails. I work very diligently to make my stories accurate and interesting. The positive responses I receive make all the work worth it. When I read a review from someone I don't know it is very humbling to know they enjoyed the book. This helps me to know I am on the right track.

I would also like to invite everyone to follow me on Facebook (**www.facebook.com/phil.dunn.589**) I've been posting about the research activities I do for my writing. Facebook is like life (I can't believe I wrote that down), it helps to have friends and I need many of them to get the word out about this fledgling author.

- Limited edition hardcover books are available on my website, **www.phillipdunn.net.** These will be autographed with a personal inscription.

- If you would like to get to know the author as well as you know Mack, I've started a blog of my observations of life and short stories. Find it at:

www.phillipdunnauthor.wordpress.com

COMING IN SPRING OF 2017

Skeleton Crew

Mack benevolently takes a group of wounded warriors fishing down in deep south Texas, close to Mexico. It'll be fun.

What's the worst that could happen?

www.ingramcontent.com/pod-product-compliance
Lightning Source LLC
Chambersburg PA
CBHW020506120726
47904CB00003B/721